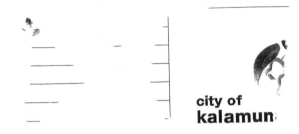

city of
kalamun

The Governess Game

Also by Tessa Dare

Girl Meets Duke
THE DUCHESS DEAL

Castles Ever After
ROMANCING THE DUKE
SAY YES TO THE MARQUESS
WHEN A SCOT TIES THE KNOT
DO YOU WANT TO START A SCANDAL

Spindle Cove
A NIGHT TO SURRENDER
ONCE UPON A WINTER'S EVE (novella)
A WEEK TO BE WICKED
A LADY BY MIDNIGHT
BEAUTY AND THE BLACKSMITH (novella)
ANY DUCHESS WILL DO
LORD DASHWOOD MISSED OUT (novella)

Stud Club Trilogy
ONE DANCE WITH A DUKE
TWICE TEMPTED BY A ROGUE
THREE NIGHTS WITH A SCOUNDREL

The Wanton Dairymaid Trilogy
GODDESS OF THE HUNT
SURRENDER OF A SIREN
A LADY OF PERSUASION

THE SCANDALOUS, DISSOLUTE,
NO-GOOD MR. WRIGHT (novella)

Tessa Dare

The Governess Game

GIRL MEETS DUKE

AVONBOOKS

An Imprint of HarperCollinsPublishers

THE GOVERNESS GAME. Copyright © 2018 by Eve Ortega. All rights reserved. Printed in the United States of America. No part of this book may be used or reproduced in any manner whatsoever without written permission except in the case of brief quotations embodied in critical articles and reviews. For information, address HarperCollins Publishers, 195 Broadway, New York, NY 10007.

First Avon Books mass market printing: September 2018
First Avon Books special mass market printing: September 2018
First Avon Books hardcover printing: August 2018

Print Edition ISBN: 978-0-06-285167-3
Digital Edition ISBN: 978-0-06-267213-1

Avon, Avon & logo, and Avon Books & logo are registered trademarks of HarperCollins Publishers in the United States of America and other countries.

HarperCollins is a registered trademark of HarperCollins Publishers in the United States of America and other countries.

FIRST EDITION

18 19 20 21 22 LSC 10 9 8 7 6 5 4 3 2 1

For my children, the Darelings,
because apparently I have a trend with this
series—dedicating books to people I hope will
never read them. My daughter served as a
brilliant consultant on Rosamund and Daisy's
characters, and my ever-clever son taught me that
some kids learn best in unconventional ways.
Darelings, I love you both. I promise that
out of all my books, this is the one and
only page I'll ever force you to read.

(Bonus: I've now embarrassed you
in front of thousands of strangers.
Mom achievement unlocked!)

Acknowledgments

To Bren, Tessa, Elle, Steve, Ruth, Kelly, Rose, Mr. Dare, and the Darelings:

There's no way I could have finished this book without each and every one of you. Thank you, from the bottom of my sleep-deprived, over-caffeinated, eternally grateful heart.

Prologue

lexandra Mountbatten had common sense. That's what her friends believed.

The truth was, Alex had no sense at all—at least, not when it came to charming gentlemen with roguish green eyes. If she possessed any wisp of rationality, she wouldn't have made such a fool of herself with the Bookshop Rake.

Even now, more than half a year later, she could revisit the embarrassing scene and watch it unfolding, as though she were attending a play.

The setting: Hatchard's bookshop.

The date: a Wednesday afternoon in November.

The personages: Alexandra, of course. Her three closest friends: Nicola Teague, Lady Penelope Campion, and Emma Pembrooke, the Duchess of Ashbury. And, making his first appearance in a starring role (trumpet fanfare, please)—the Bookshop Rake.

The scene proceeded thusly:

Alexandra had been juggling a tower of Nicola's books in one arm and reading her own book with her free hand. A copy of Messier's *Catalogue of Star Clusters and Nebulae*, which she'd plucked like a pearl from the used-book section. She'd been searching for a secondhand copy for ages. She couldn't afford to buy it new.

One moment, she'd been blissfully paging through descriptions of astronomical nebulae, and the next . . .

Bang. A collision of cosmic proportions.

The cause remained unclear. Perhaps she'd taken a step in reverse, or maybe he'd turned without looking. It didn't matter. Whosoever's elbow jostled the other's arm, the laws of physics demanded an equal and opposite reaction. From there, the rest was gravity. All her books fell to the floor, and when she looked up from the heap—there he was.

Ruffled brown hair, fashionable attire, cologne that smelled like bottled sin—and a smile no doubt honed from boyhood as a means to make women forgive him anything.

With affable charm, he'd gathered up the books. She'd been no help at all.

He'd inquired after her name; she'd stammered.

He'd asked her to recommend a book—a gift, he said, for two young girls. In response, she'd stammered yet more.

He'd drawn close enough for her to breathe in his woodsy, earthy, oh-so-manly cologne. She'd nearly fainted into the antiquities section.

But then he'd looked at her with warm green eyes—truly *looked* at her—the way people rarely did, because it meant allowing the other person to truly *look* at them, too. Equal and opposite reactions.

He made her feel like the only woman in the bookshop. Perhaps the only woman in the world. Or the universe.

The moment seemed to last forever, and yet it was over much too soon.

Then he'd made her a dashing bow, bid her *adieu*, and strolled away with Messier's *Catalogue of Star Clusters and Nebulae*, leaving Alexandra holding an insipid book of stories for "obedient girls."

End of scene.

Or at least, it should have been the end.

Alex resolved to scrub the encounter from her mental slate, but Penny—the incurable romantic among them—wouldn't allow it. Since he hadn't given his name, Penny anointed him with increasingly ridiculous titles. First he was merely the Bookshop Rake, but as the weeks wore on, he made a rapid ascent up the rungs of the peerage. Sir Read. Lord Literature. The Duke of Hatchard's.

Stop, Alex told her again and again. *That was ages ago, and I haven't thought of him since. He certainly hasn't thought of me. It was nothing.*

Except that it wasn't quite nothing. Some idiotic corner of her memory embellished the encounter with rainbows and sparkles until it resembled . . . something. Something too mortifying to ever admit aloud, even to Penny, Emma, and Nicola. In truth, Alex avoided admitting it to herself.

From that day forward, whenever she visited Hatchard's—or the Temple of Muses, or even the Minerva Library—she looked for him. Imagining that they might collide once again, and he would confess, over afternoon tea that lingered into dinner, that he'd been haunting the bookshops, too—hoping to meet with her. Because, naturally, in those two minutes of painful one-sided conversation, he'd divined that an incoherent, clumsy, working-class girl small enough to fit into the average kitchen cupboard was everything he'd always yearned to find.

You're exactly what I've been searching for.

Now that I've found you, I'll never let you go.

Alexandra, I need you.

Common sense, feh.

Alex worked for her living, setting clocks in the homes of wealthy customers, and she didn't have time for dreams. She set *goals*, and she worked to achieve them. Feet on the ground, shoulders squared, and head on straight.

She would not—absolutely not—be carried away with romantic fantasies.

Sadly, her imagination ignored this memorandum. In her daydreams, the afternoon tea led to walks in the park, deep conversations, kisses under the stars, and even—Alexandra's dignity wilted just thinking of it—a wedding.

Truly. A wedding.

Do you take this man, Anonymous Bookshop Rake with Horrid Taste in Children's Literature, to be your wedded husband?

Absurd.

After months of attempting to quash this madness, Alex gave up. At least the fantasies—foolish as they might be—were hers to keep secret. No one else need ever know. In all likelihood, she would never meet with the Bookshop Rake again.

Until, of course, the morning that she did.

Chapter One

The morning began in the same way as most of Chase's mornings lately. With a tragic demise.

"She's dead."

He turned onto his side. As he blinked, Rosamund's face came into focus. "What was it this time?"

"Typhus."

"Charming."

Using the sofa's upholstered arm for leverage, he pushed to a sitting position. As he did so, his brain sloshed with regret. He rubbed his temples, ruing his behavior the night before. And his licentiousness in the very early morning. While he was at it, he decided he might as well regret his entire misspent youth, too. Clear a bit of his afternoon schedule.

"It can wait until later." Once his head ceased ringing and he'd washed off the cloying scent of French perfume.

"It must be now, Daisy says, or else the contagion could spread. She's preparing the body."

Chase groaned. He decided it wasn't worth arguing. Might as well have it done with.

As they began climbing the four flights of stairs to the nursery, he interrogated his ten-year-old ward. "Can't you do something about this?"

"Can't you?"

"She's *your* little sister."

"You're her guardian."

He grimaced, rubbing his throbbing temple. "Discipline isn't one of my particular talents."

"Obedience isn't one of ours," Rosamund replied.

"I've noticed. Don't think I didn't see you pocket that shilling from the side table." They reached the top of the stairs and turned down the corridor. "Listen, this has to stop. Quality boarding schools don't offer enrollment to petty thieves or serial murderesses."

"It wasn't murder. It was typhus."

"Oh, to be sure it was."

"And we don't want to go to boarding school."

"Rosamund, it's time you learned a harsh lesson." He opened the nursery door. "We don't always get what we want in life."

Didn't Chase know it. He didn't *want* to be guardian to a pair of orphaned girls. He didn't *want* to be next in line for the Belvoir dukedom. And he most assuredly did not *want* to be attending his fourth funeral in as many days. Yet here he was.

Daisy turned to them. A veil of dark netting covered her straw-colored curls. "Please show respect for the dead."

She waved Chase forward. He dutifully crossed to her side, bending down so that she could pin a black armband around his shirtsleeve.

"I'm sorry for your loss," he said. *So very sorry. You don't know how sorry.*

He took his place at the head of the bed, looking down at the deceased. She was ghostly pale and swaddled in a white shroud. Buttons covered her eyes. Thank God. It was damned unnerving when the eyes looked up at him with that glassy, empty stare.

Daisy reached for his hand and bowed her head. After leading them in a recitation of the Lord's Prayer, she poked Chase in the ribs. "Mr. Reynaud, kindly say a few words."

Chase looked to the heavens. God help him.

"Almighty Father," he began in a dispirited tone, "we commit to your keeping the soul of Millicent. Ashes to ashes. Sawdust to sawdust. She was a doll of few words and yet fewer autonomous movements, yet she will be remembered for the ever-present— some might say permanently painted—smile on her face. By the grace of our Redeemer, we know she will be resurrected, perhaps as soon as luncheon." He added under his breath, "Unfortunately."

"Amen," Daisy intoned. With solemnity, she lowered the doll into the wooden toy chest, then closed the lid.

Rosamund broke the oppressive silence. "Let's go down to the kitchen, Daisy. We'll have buttered rolls and jam for our breakfast."

"You'll breakfast here," he corrected. "In the nursery. Your governess will—"

"Our governess?" Daisy gave him a sweet, innocent look. "But we don't have a governess at the moment."

He groaned. "Don't tell me the new one quit. I only hired her yesterday."

Rosamund said proudly, "We were rid of her in seventeen and a quarter hours. A new record."

Unbelievable.

Chase strode to the world map on the wall and plucked a tack from the border. *"There."* He stabbed an unsuspecting country at random, then pointed at it with authority. "I am sending you to boarding school *there*. Enjoy"—he squinted at the map—"Malta."

Fuming, Chase quit the room and made the journey back down the four flights of stairs, and then down a half flight more and through the kitchen—all the way to his private retreat. Upon entering, he shut and locked the door before exhaling a lungful of annoyance.

For a gentleman of leisure, he was damned exhausted. He needed a bath, a shave, a change of clothing, and a headache powder. Barrow would arrive in an hour with sheaves of papers to look over and bank drafts to sign. The club had a bacchanalian revel this evening. And now he must hire yet another governess.

Before he could face any of it, he needed a drink.

As he made his way to the bar, he navigated a card table draped with a dustcloth and a stack of paintings propped against the wall, waiting to be hung. The apartment was a work in progress. He had a well-furnished bedchamber upstairs, of course, but for now he needed a space as far away from the nursery as architecturally possible. The arrangement was for the girls' benefit as much as his own. He would rather not know what mischief his wards wrought at the top of the house, and they must never learn of the devilry he practiced at the bottom of it.

He uncorked a bottle of wine and filled a large glass. A bit early in the day for burgundy, but what of it. He was, after all, in mourning. Might as well lift a glass to Millicent's memory.

He'd downed half the glass in one swallow when he heard a light knock at the door. Not the door to and from the kitchen, but the door that opened onto the side street.

Chase cursed into his burgundy. That would be Colette, he supposed. They'd had their fun the other night, but apparently neither his well-established reputation nor the parting bouquet he'd sent had communicated the message. He would be forced to have "the talk" with her in person.

It's not you, darling. It's me. I'm an irredeemable, broken man. You deserve better.

All of it was true, as hackneyed as it sounded. When it came to relationships, sensual or otherwise, Chase had one rule.

No attachments.

Words to live by, words to make love by. Words to send wards to boarding school by. When he made promises, he only caused pain.

"Come in," he called, not bothering to turn around. "It's unlocked."

A cool draft swept across his neck as the door opened, then shut again. Like the whisper of fingertips.

He took another glass and filled it. "Back for more, are you? Insatiable minx. I knew it was no accident you left your stocking here the other"—he turned, holding the wineglasses in his hands and fixing a roguish half smile on his face—"night."

Interesting. The woman who'd entered was not Colette.

She was very much not Colette.

A small, dark-haired young woman stood before him. She clutched a weathered brown satchel in her hands, and her eyes held abject horror. He could actually watch the blood draining from her face and settling at the base of her throat as a hot, fierce blush.

"Good morning," he said amiably.

In reply, she made an audible swallow.

"Here." Chase extended his left hand, offering her a glass of wine. "Have this. You look as though you could use it."

HIM.

It was him. She would know him anywhere. Those features were etched in her memory. He was indelibly handsome. Roguish green eyes, mussed dark hair, and that lopsided smile so seductive, it could steal a woman's virtue from across a crowded room.

Alexandra found herself standing toe-to-toe (she was too small-statured to manage face-to-face) with the Bookshop Rake, in the flesh.

So. Much. Flesh.

Sleeves rolled to the elbow, open shirt, no cravat . . . Alexandra dropped her gaze to keep from staring. Good Lord. Bare feet.

"I . . . I . . . Forgive me, I thought this was the servants' entrance. I'll leave straightaway." She ducked her head to hide her face, praying he wouldn't recognize her. If she left now, and quickly, this encounter might be survivable.

"You weren't mistaken. It was the servants' entrance until a few weeks ago. I'm adapting the space for my own purposes. A sort of gentleman's retreat."

She swept her gaze about the room. His "purposes" were easy enough to discern. Well-stocked bar. Plush chaise longue. Plum-colored velvet drapes. A rug fashioned from the hide of some shaggy beast. On the wall, a rack of antlers.

And there it was, the aforementioned forgotten stocking. Draped over one of the stag's forked prongs like a white banner of surrender.

She'd wandered into some sort of pleasure dungeon.

Embarrassment seared her from the inside out. A sheen of sweat broke out on her brow. "I'm clearly intruding. I'll return another time." She tightened her grip on her satchel and attempted to sidle around him.

But he wouldn't be sidled so easily. He was too quick, too tall. Too muscled and male. He slid sideways, blocking her path to the door. "Believe me, I am delighted to see you."

I'd be delighted if you didn't see me at all.

Alex shielded her face with one hand and slanted her gaze to a painting propped against the wall. It featured a woman bare to her skin, save for a strategically positioned fan. "I left a card last week. I meant to speak with your housekeeper about offering my services."

"Yes, of course."

"Then perhaps you could direct me to her."

"I conduct all the interviews myself. Saves time, I find."

She looked up in surprise. It was beyond unusual for the gentleman of the house to interview his own employees—let alone an employee whose sole duty would be to adjust the clocks to Greenwich time once a week.

"Forgive me. I've run ahead of myself." He inclined his head in a perfunctory bow. "Chase Reynaud."

Chase Reynaud.

Mr. Charles Reynaud.

Mrs. Alexandra Reynaud.

For the love of God. Stop.

He set aside the glasses of wine and wiped his hands on his trousers. "We can discuss your immediate employment. Make yourself comfortable."

Alex would rather make herself invisible. She moved toward the windows lining one side of the room, partly wishing to disappear behind the draperies. But also because she was drawn by the glimmer of brass.

Could it be . . . ?

Yes. Pushing aside a fold of aubergine velvet, she found confirmation of her hopes.

A telescope.

Since childhood, Alexandra had been fascinated by the night sky. Life aboard a merchant frigate didn't offer many ways to amuse oneself after sundown. She'd borrowed her father's spyglass so often, he'd finally given in and bought her one of her own. Here in London, she made do with a collapsible pocket telescope she'd purchased for sixteen shillings at a lens grinder's shop. A hobbyist's instrument.

But this . . . ?

This was, without question, the most astonishing object she'd ever touched.

Without thinking, she bent to have a look through the eyepiece. She found the instrument to be directed at an attic window of the house across the way. The servant quarters of a pretty young housemaid or two, no doubt.

Alex swung it away from its sordid direction, pointing it toward the gardens in the center of the square. Heavens, she could make out individual blades of yellow-green grass pushing through the soil.

Behind her, glassware clinked. She startled, jumping back from the telescope, knocking it on its swiveling mechanism, and sending it into a nearby vase, which she had to lunge to catch before it hit the floor. What a display of professional skill. *Why yes, I'm here to offer my services handling intricate, expensive machinery.*

"Forgive me. I didn't catch your name, Miss . . . ?"

Her tongue was a sailor's knot. "Mountbatten," she managed. "Alexandra Mountbatten."

Then he tilted his head and looked at her. Truly *looked* at her, with that same deep, searching gaze he'd given her in the bookshop.

Her heartbeat paused in anticipation.

Alexandra didn't expect a confession of unrequited love, of course. At most, a simple *Haven't we met somewhere?* Perhaps even *Oh, yes. Hatchard's, was it?*

"Miss Mountbatten. Pleased to make your acquaintance."

Oh. He had no memory of meeting her at all.

A stroke of luck, she told herself. If he did recall her, she would have lingered in his memory as a clumsy, stammering, bookish ninny, not an object of admiration. This was a boon, truly. Now she could cease wasting time thinking of him.

It would be completely irrational to feel disappointed. Much less hurt.

However, her powers of reason flew out her ear whenever this man was involved. She *did* feel wounded, just a little. Inside her, the sharp proof of her foolishness twisted and scraped at her pride.

He cleared the tea table of a candlestick with guttered tapers and two emptied brandy glasses. He whisked the forgotten stocking from the antler prong and—after casting about in vain for an appropriate place to store it—wadded it into a ball and stuffed it behind a pillow.

"I truly should go," she said. "I seem to have interrupted something, and I—"

"You're not interrupting anything. Nothing of consequence, at any rate." He patted the back of an armchair. "Sit down."

She numbly took the offered seat. He dropped onto the chaise across from her. From the way he sank into the cushioning, Alexandra suspected the upholstery had strained and bounced beneath many a torrid encounter.

In one last farcical swipe at decency, he ran a hand through his disheveled brown hair. "I've two that need looking after."

Clocks.

Yes. Concentrate on the clocks. Those ticking things with dials and gears and numbers. They were how she made her living, and she'd been knocking on the door of every servants' entrance in Mayfair to find more clients. She wasn't here to gawk at the sprinkling of hair on his chest, or ponder the meaning of his black arm-band, or flog herself over silly fantasies that he would sweep her into his arms, confess his months of suffering for love of her, and vow to abandon his sinful ways now that she'd given him reason to live.

She slammed the lid on her imagination, buckled the strap, af-fixed a padlock, and then pushed it off a cliff.

This was just another business call.

He went on, "I can't tell you much of their history. They'd been passed around by several different relations before they landed with me last autumn."

Family heirlooms, then. "They must be precious."

"Oh, yes," he replied dryly. "Precious indeed. To be honest, I've no idea what to do with the two of them. They came along with the title."

"The title?" she echoed.

"Belvoir." When she did not respond, he added, "As in, the duke of it."

A wild burst of laughter escaped her.

A *duke*? Oh, how Penny would gloat over having guessed that.

"Believe me," he said, "I find it absurd, as well. Actually, I'm merely heir to a duke, for now. Since my uncle is infirm, I've been handed the legal responsibilities. All the duties of a dukedom, none of the perks." He waved aimlessly in her direction. "Well, then. Teach me a lesson."

"I . . . I beg your pardon?"

"I could inquire as to your education and experience, but that seems a waste of time. We may as well have a demonstration."

A *demonstration*? Did he want to know how clockworks oper-ated? Perhaps he meant the chronometer. She could explain why it kept the right time when clocks could lose several minutes a day.

"What sort of lesson did you have in mind?"

He shrugged. "Whatever you think I might need to learn."

Alex couldn't hold it in any longer. She buried her face in her hands and moaned into them.

He leaned toward her at once. "Are you ill? I do hope it's not typhus."

"It's disappointment. I expected something different. I should have known better."

He lifted an eyebrow. "What precisely were you expecting?"

"You don't want to know." *And I don't want to tell you.*

"Oh, but I do."

"No, you don't. You really, truly don't."

"Come now. That kind of protestation only makes a man more intrigued. Just have out with it."

"A gentleman," she blurted out. "I expected you'd be a gentleman."

"You weren't wrong. I *am* a gentleman. Eventually, I'm going to be a peer."

"I didn't mean it that way. I thought you'd be the respectable, considerate, honorable kind of gentleman."

"Ah," he said. "Yes, that was a mistaken assumption on your part."

"Obviously. Just look at you."

As she spoke, her gaze drifted downward, toward his broad shoulders. Then toward the rumpled linen of his shirt. Then toward the intriguing wedge of masculine chest exposed by his open collar. The skin there was smooth and taut, and the muscular contours were defined, and . . .

And she was openly staring now.

"Look at this place. Wineglasses scattered on the table. Perfume still lingering in the air. What kind of gentleman conducts an employment interview in this . . ." She indicated their surroundings, at a loss for the word. ". . . cave of carnality?"

"Cave of Carnality," he echoed with amusement. "Oh, I like that. I've a mind to engrave that on a plaque."

"So you understand my mistake now." The words kept pouring out of her, rash and unconsidered, and she couldn't put them back in the bottle. She couldn't even find a cork. "When I opened the door, I was fool enough to expect someone else. A man who'd never allow a lady to wander London with only one stocking and call it 'nothing of consequence.' Stockings are of consequence, Mr. Reynaud. So are the women who wear them." She made a defeated wave at his black armband. "All of this whilst you're in mourning."

"Now that, I can explain."

"Please don't. This lesson is cruel enough already." She shook her head. "Then there's the telescope."

"Hold a moment." He sat forward. "What has a telescope to do with anything?"

"That"—she pointed with an outstretched arm—"is a genuine Dollond. A forty-six-inch achromatic with a triple object-glass of three-and-three-quarters-inch aperture. Polished wood barrel, brass draw tubes. Capable of magnifying land objects sixty times over, and celestial objects to one hundred and eighty times. It's an instrument most could only dream of owning, and you're letting it gather dust. It's . . . Well, it's heartbreaking."

Heartbreaking, indeed.

In the end, Alex had only herself to blame. All the clues were there. His dreadful taste in books. His charming grin that made promises no man could intend to keep. And those eyes . . . They held some kind of potent, brain-addling sorcery, and he went about jostling young women in bookshops without the decency to keep them hidden beneath a wide-brimmed hat.

Her only consolation was that he'd forget this conversation the moment she left, just as he'd forgotten her before.

"Thank you, Mr. Reynaud. You've given *me* a much-needed lesson today." She released a heavy sigh and tipped her gaze to the wall. "Antlers. Really?"

After a prolonged silence, he whistled softly through his teeth.

She rose to her feet, reaching for her satchel. "I'll show myself out."

"Oh, no, you won't." He stood. "Miss Mountbatten, that was capital."

"What?"

"Absolutely brilliant. I would very much like to engage your services."

Perhaps she had this all wrong. Maybe he was not the Bookshop Rake after all, but the Bookshop Madman.

Then he went and did the most incomprehensible thing yet. He looked into her eyes, smiled just enough to reveal a lethal dimple, and spoke the words she'd stupidly dreamed of hearing him say.

"You," he said, "are everything I've been searching for. And I'm not letting you get away."

Oh.

Oh, *Lord*.

"Come, then. My wards will be delighted to meet their new governess."

Chapter Two

*G*overness?

Alexandra was speechless.

"I'll show you upstairs." In a display of masculine presumption, Mr. Reynaud took the satchel from her grip. As he relieved her of its weight, his hand grazed hers. The fleeting brush of warmth pushed her brain off balance. He turned and walked to the back of the room. "This way."

She shook life into her frozen arms and followed. How could she do otherwise? He'd taken her satchel—and with it her chronometer, plus her ledger of clients and appointments. Her livelihood was literally in his hands.

"Mr. Reynaud, I—"

"They're called Rosamund and Daisy. Aged ten and seven, respectively. Sisters."

"Mr. Reynaud, please. Can we—"

He led her through a kitchen and up the stairs. They emerged into a first-floor corridor. She followed him down a passageway with walls covered in striped emerald silk. From the springy plush beneath her boots, she would have guessed the corridor to be carpeted in clouds. Her work took her into many a fine London house, but she never ceased marveling at the luxury.

He led the way up the main staircase, taking the risers two at a time.

"They carry the last name Fairfax, but it's likely an adopted name. They're natural children. Some distant relation sired a few by-blows and left their guardianship to the estate."

As they climbed flight after flight of stairs, Alexandra could scarcely keep pace with him, much less change the topic of conversation.

"I'm sending them to school at Michaelmas term." He added wearily, "Assuming I can bribe a respectable school into taking them."

At last, they reached the top of the house. Alex darted forward to grab his sleeve. "Mr. Reynaud, please. There's been some sort of misunderstanding. A grave misunderstanding."

"Not at all. We understand one another perfectly. I'm a paltry excuse for a gentleman, as you say. I'm also no fool. That scolding you delivered downstairs was brilliant. The girls need a firm hand. Discipline. I'm the last soul on earth to teach them proper behavior. But you, Miss Mountbatten? You are just the one for the job." He gestured at the rooms that opened off the passageway. "You'll have a bedchamber to yourself, of course. The nursery is this way."

"Wait—"

"Here we are." He flung open the door.

Alexandra's mind refused to make sense of the scene. Two flaxen-haired girls stood on either side of a bed. A beautiful bed. A grand four-poster with a lacy lavender canopy, gold-painted posts, and matching bed hangings tied back with pink cord. The bed would have been any young girl's dream. Beneath it, however, was a nightmare. The white bed linens were streaked and spattered with crimson.

"You're too late." The younger of the two turned to face them, her expression eerily solemn. "She's dead."

"Curse it all." Mr. Reynaud heaved a sigh. "Not again."

CHASE COULDN'T BELIEVE it.

Twice in one morning. Insupportable.

He put down Miss Mountbatten's satchel, stalked to the bed, and swiped a finger along the soiled linens. Red currant jelly, by the looks of it.

"It was the bloody flux," Rosamund said.

Of course it was. Chase set his jaw. "From now on, there will be no jelly. None, do you hear? No conserves, no jam, no preserves of any kind."

"No jelly?" Daisy asked mournfully. "Whyever not?"

"Because I am not eulogizing another leprosy victim covered in sores that weep marmalade! That's why not. Oh, and no mushy peas, either. Millicent's bout of dyspepsia last week ruined the drawing room carpet."

"But—"

"No arguments." He leveled a finger at his morbid little wards. "Or I'm going to lock the both of you in this room and feed you nothing but dry crusts."

"How very gothic," Rosamund replied.

"I'm afraid I must be going now." The faintly voiced interruption came from Miss Mountbatten, who'd remained near the doorway.

And who, shortly thereafter, made a stealthy reach for her satchel and vanished through said doorway.

Damn it.

He strode to the map and jabbed a tack into the first empty expanse he saw. "Start packing your things."

"There aren't any boarding schools in the Lapland," Rosamund said.

"I'll put up the money to start one," he said on his way to the door. "I hope you like herring."

Then he ran after his newest—and please, God, not latest to quit—governess.

"Wait." He took the stairs three at a time, vaulting over the banister so as to catch her on the next landing. "Miss Mountbatten, wait." With a flailing swipe, he caught her by the arm.

They stood wedged in the stairwell. She was short, and he was tall. The crown of her head met him mid-sternum. Conversation was comically impossible. He released her arm and took two steps downward so he might look her in the eye.

Her gaze nearly knocked him down the stairs. For a woman of small stature, she made a prodigious impact. A delicate snub of a nose, olive skin, and a glossy knot of midnight-black hair. And fathomless dark eyes that pulled on something deep in his chest. He needed a moment to collect himself.

"Millicent is Daisy's doll. She kills the thing at least once a day, but—" Curse it, he'd left red smudges on her sleeve, and God only knew what substance she presumed it to be. "No, it's not what you think. It's only red currant jelly." He held up his stained index finger. "Here, taste for yourself."

She blinked at him. "Did you just invite me to lick your finger?"

He wiped his hand on a fold of his shirt. God, he was making a hash of this. If she worried for her virtue, that wouldn't aid his case. Any sensible young woman would hesitate to accept employment in the house of a scandalous rake—even if the rake's wards were perfect angels. Chase's wards were incorrigible, morbid hellions.

In fact, the post offered few advantages, save one.

"I'll pay you handsomely," he said. "An astronomical sum."

"There's been a mistake. I came to offer my services as a timekeeper. I'm not a governess. I've no training, no experience. And governesses are gently bred women, aren't they? I don't meet that qualification, either."

"I don't care if you're gently bred, roughly bred, or a loaf of brown bread with butter. You're educated, you understand propriety, and you're . . . breathing."

"I'm certain you'll find someone else to fill the post."

"The post has been filled. And vacated. And filled and vacated several times over. Sometimes multiple times in one day."

You're not doing your offer any favors, Reynaud.

"But you're not like the rest of those candidates," he hastened to say. "You're different."

She *was* different.

Here was a woman who'd just schooled him within an inch of his dignity. She thought him a crude, unintelligent layabout. A paltry excuse for nobility and a waste of good tailoring. Miss Mountbatten—quite wisely—wanted nothing to do with him.

And Chase was positively desperate to keep her near.

The desire rising in him wasn't physical. Well, it wasn't *entirely* physical. She was pretty, and he appreciated a forthright woman who knew what she was about. But mingled with the attraction was something more. A wish to impress her, to be worthy of her approval.

She made him want to be better. And wasn't that an ideal quality in a governess? He *had* to keep this woman in his employ.

"It's only for the summer," he said. "A year's wages, for a few months of work."

"I'm sorry." She sidestepped him and continued down the stairs.

"Two years' wages. Three."

"Mr. Reynaud . . ."

Chase caught her at the door. "It comes down to this. Those girls need you."

He waited until she looked at him, and then he reached into his arsenal of persuasion.

A hard swallow, indicating a manful struggle with emotion.

An intense, searching gaze.

The husky whisper of a confession.

"Miss Mountbatten." Hell, why not go for it all? "Alexandra. *I* need you."

There. That line worked on every woman.

It didn't work on her.

"No, you don't." A flash of irony crossed her face. "Don't worry. You'll forget me soon enough."

And then she did what Chase yearned to do, often. She flung open the door, fled the house, and didn't once look back.

Chapter Three

*T*wo hours later, Alexandra found herself standing on a Billingsgate dock.

Terrified.

The June morning was soaked with sunshine, but she'd left Mr. Reynaud's house in a mental fog. Her distraction was such that she'd made two wrong turnings on her well-trod path to London Bridge, and now she had missed the noon coach to Greenwich.

The rational solution was to take a wherry down the Thames. However, the mere sight of the boat sent an irrational shiver rippling down her spine.

I can't. I just can't.

But what were her alternatives?

If she risked waiting for a later coach, the bridge would be madness, crushed with carts going nowhere. She'd never make it home before dark.

She could call off the journey entirely. However, calibrating the chronometer once a fortnight was her signature promise to customers. They paid for precise Greenwich time, and she delivered it, without fail.

Just do it, she told herself. *It's time to move past this, you ninny. You were raised on a ship, after all. A merchant frigate was your cradle.*

Yes. But it had nearly been her coffin, too.

Nevertheless, here she stood ten years later. Alive. She could survive a brief jaunt down the Thames to Greenwich.

She could do this.

As the boatman loaded bundles and helped passengers into the wherry, she hung back, waiting until the last possible moment.

"Are you coming, miss, or ain't ye?"

"I'm coming." Alex accepted his hand and boarded the boat, wedging herself on a plank between two older women and settling her satchel on her lap.

When the boatman cast off the ropes mooring the wherry to the dock, she decided to set her mind on something else. Now that she knew better than to fantasize about Chase Reynaud, a good portion of her brain was suddenly available for other pursuits. Naming all the constellations bordering Ursa Major, perhaps.

Drat. Too easy. She rattled through the list in moments—*Draco, Camelopardalis, Lynx, Leo Minor, Leo, Coma Berenices, Canes Venatici, Boötes*—and there her concentration fractured. Once the first oar hit water, she couldn't piece a single thought together.

She balled her hands in fists and dug her nails into her palms, attempting to distract herself by means of pain. That didn't work, either. She felt nothing but the lift and roll of water beneath the craft. That terrifying sensation of coming unmoored. Drifting untethered.

No. She couldn't do this after all.

Alex pushed to her feet, making her way to the edge of the boat. They hadn't yet pushed off. Still just a foot from the dock. "Wait," she told the boatman. "I've just recalled something. I need to disembark."

"Too late, miss. You can cross again when the boat comes back." He moved to push off with the oar.

"Please." She was begging now, her voice cracking. "It's urgent. I must get off the boat. I . . ."

"Sit down, woman," he barked, bracing his oar to push off.

Alex was frantic, wild. She scrambled atop the rail of the boat, wavering on her toes. The other passengers cried out in alarm as the boat tipped to one side. The boatman gripped the hem of her frock, attempting to yank her down into the boat. His grasping only increased her desperation.

She quickly judged the distance between the wherry and the dock. She could make it, she thought, but only if she jumped.

And jumped *now*.

She made the leap.

Her judgment wasn't faulty. If not for her boot slipping on the wherry's edge, she would have made the jump cleanly. Instead, she plunged into the water with a splash, gasping as she went and catching a foul, wretched mouthful of the Thames.

When she surfaced, a man on the dock caught her under the arm, pulling her up and helping her scramble out of the river.

On the dock at last, she sputtered and choked with relief.

That's when she noticed it had gone missing. Her satchel. The chronometer. When she'd tumbled into the river, it had fallen from her grip and sunk into the depths.

Her livelihood, gone.

A sob wrenched from her body, like a droplet wrung from damp cloth.

One more thing the water had taken from her. It was the insatiable monster in her life. Jonah's whale. Devouring everything she loved, but spitting her back out, again and again, more lost and lonely than ever.

And once more, there was nothing to do but pick herself up and start over.

"WELL? WHAT DO you think?" Chase spread his arms and turned slowly, putting on a display of his unfinished apartment. "I'm remaking it into a manly retreat."

Barrow stared at the shambles of what had formerly been the housekeeper's quarters. "Where are Mrs. Greeley's things?"

"I've moved her to a bedchamber on the second floor. Far superior accommodations."

"Dare I ask the reason behind this renovation?"

Chase went to pour them two tumblers of brandy. "Until Rosamund and Daisy go off to school, I need somewhere to escape."

"A grown man escaping from two little girls. Now that's rather pathetic, isn't it?"

"Come now. I don't know what to do with children. There's no point in troubling to learn. I'm not going to sire any of the grimy things. Even if I wished to marry, there's no use searching for a wife. You've laid claim to the best woman in England."

"This is true."

John Barrow Sr. had been Chase's father's solicitor, and from the time Chase and John Jr. had been boys, it was understood they would continue the family tradition. Also understood, but never spoken of, was the reason why. They were half brothers. Chase's father had impregnated a local gentleman's daughter, and his loyal solicitor had taken it upon himself to marry her and raise the child as his own.

So Chase and John had grown up together, sharing both tutors and paddlings. Squabbling over horses and girls. Despite the disparity in their social ranks, they'd maintained a close friendship through school and beyond. A damned lucky thing, on Chase's part. Now, with a dukedom at stake, he needed a trusted friend to help manage the estate.

"How is my godson?" Chase asked. "Speaking of grimy things."

"Charles is living up to his namesake, unfortunately."

"Ah. Charming every woman in sight."

"Lying about while everyone else does the work."

"I'll have you know," Chase said indignantly, "I have been hard at work during your absence. Witness the renovation in progress around you. I built that bar myself, thank you very much. It only needs a few coats of lacquer. And if that's not sufficient for you—in the past week alone I've gone through a decade of bank ledgers, given seven orgasms, and interviewed five governesses. And no, none of the governesses were recipients of the orgasms, although a few of them looked as though they could use one."

"Five candidates, and you didn't find one to hire?"

"I hired each and every one of them. None of them lasted more than two days. In fact, the latest didn't even make it past the nursery door. A pity, too. I had hopes for her. She was different."

Normally, Chase was the one coaxing women to leave. He wished he'd been able to make Alexandra Mountbatten stay.

Barrow peered at him. "That was odd."

"What was odd?"

"You sighed."

"That's not odd at all. Not lately."

"Well, it was the tone of the sigh. Not weary or annoyed. It was . . . wistful."

Chase gave him a sidelong look. "I have never been wistful a day in my life. I am entirely devoid of wist." He tugged on his waistcoat. "Now if you'll excuse me, I have an engagement this evening. The women of London can't pleasure themselves, you know. I mean, they *can* pleasure themselves. But on occasion they generously let me have a go at it."

"Who is she this time?"

"Do you really care?"

"I don't know. Do you?" Barrow gave him a look that cut like a switch. "Someday you'll have to put a stop to this."

Chase bristled. "You are a solicitor. Not a judge. Spare me the moralizing. I make women no promises I don't intend to keep."

In truth, he made no promises at all. His lovers knew precisely what he had on offer—pleasure—and what he didn't have to give—anything more. No emotional attachment, no romance, no love.

No marriage.

As war, illness, and his own unforgivable failures would have it, in the space of three years, Chase had gone from fourth in line for his uncle's title to the presumptive heir. It was a development few could have imagined, and one that nobody, Chase included, had desired. But once his uncle let go the thin cord connecting him to life, Chase would become the Duke of Belvoir, fully responsible for lands, investments, tenants.

There was only one traditional responsibility he wouldn't take on.

He wouldn't be fathering an heir.

The Belvoir title should have been Anthony's by rights, and Chase refused to usurp his cousin's birthright. His line was the crooked, rotting branch of the family tree, and he meant to saw it off. Cleanly and completely. It was the least he could do to atone.

And since there would be no marriage or children in his future, didn't he deserve a bit of stolen pleasure in the present? A touch of closeness, now and then. Whispered words in his ear, the heat of skin against skin. The scent and taste and softness of a woman as she surrendered her pleasure to him.

A few scattered, blessed hours of forgetting everything else.

"Which of these would look better hanging above the bar?" Chase held up two paintings. "The fan dancer, or the bathing nymphs? The nymphs have those delightful bare bottoms, but that saucy look in the fan dancer's eyes is undeniably captivating."

Barrow ignored the question. "So if you haven't found—or kept—a governess, who's minding the girls?"

"One of the maids. Hattie, I think."

No sooner had he said this than screams and a thunder of footsteps came barreling down the stairs.

Hattie appeared in the doorway, her hair askew and her apron slashed to tatters. "Mr. Reynaud, I regret to say that I cannot continue in your employ."

He cut her off. "Say no more. You'll have severance wages and a letter of character waiting in the morning."

The maid fled, babbling with gratitude.

Once he heard the door close, Chase sank into a chair and buried his face in his hands. There went his plans for the evening.

"Now *that*," Barrow said, "was a despairing sigh."

The front doorbell rang. "I'd better answer that myself." Chase rose to his feet. "I'm not certain I have any servants remaining to do it."

He opened the door, and there she was: Miss Alexandra Mountbatten. Soaked to the skin, her dark hair dripping.

He tried not to look downward, and when he did so anyway, he told himself it was out of concern for her well-being. He *was* concerned for her well-being. Especially if one defined "well-being" to mean "breasts."

So he noticed her nipples. What of it? He spent a ridiculous portion of his waking hours thinking of nipples. Hers just happened to be the nearest, and the most chilled. Hard as jewels beneath her bodice. Red as rubies, maybe. Or pink topaz, pale amethyst . . . ? No. Given her dark coloring, they were most likely a rich, polished amber.

The chattering of teeth pulled his attention back upward. God, he was every bit the repulsive cad she'd called him, and more.

She caught her bluish bottom lip beneath her teeth. "Is the post still available?"

He didn't hesitate. "Name your price."

"Ten pounds a week. Another hundred once they've gone off to school."

"Five pounds a week," he countered. "And two hundred once they've gone off to school."

"One more thing." From beneath a dripping umbrella of eyelashes, her eyes met his. "I want the use of your telescope. The one down in your . . ."

He crossed his arms and leaned against the door. "Cave of Carnality?"

"Yes."

Chase supposed he *had* offered her an astronomical sum. Besides, he wasn't making use of it. "Very well."

She sniffled. "I'll report first thing tomorrow."

He caught her arm as she turned to leave. "Good God. At least come in and get warm first."

I'll warm you.

He chased the errant thought away, like he would an eager puppy. She was in his employ now, and there would be no such ideas. Even he had that much decency.

"Thank you, no. I'll need to pack my things."

She walked away, leaving a trail of sloshy bootprints. Chase looked about the entrance hall for an umbrella and found none.

Of course there wouldn't be a greatcoat, either, not in the middle of June.

With a curse, he bolted through the door empty-handed and dashed after her. "Miss Mountbatten."

She stopped and turned on her heel. "Yes?"

"You're not leaving dressed like that." He shrugged out of his tailored topcoat, shaking it down his arms.

"I can't accept your coat."

"You can, and you will." He swung the coat around her shoulders and tucked it tight. She was so petite, the garment's hem nearly reached her boots. The sight was equal parts comic and piteous.

"But—"

He jerked on the coat's lapels, drawing them together. "Yes, yes. I know you're bossy. As a governess, it's to your credit. But I'm your employer, as of two minutes ago. For as much as I'm paying you, I expect you to do as I say." As he worked the buttons through their holes, he went on. "Given the alacrity with which you fled my offer of employment this morning, it's obvious something dire occurred to make you change your mind. If I were any sort of decent fellow, I would ask about that dire situation and sort it out. Seeing as I am a selfish blackguard, however, I intend to take full advantage of your lowered circumstances."

There, now. He had her buttoned, and he stood back to look at her. She looked like a sausage roll.

A soggy sausage roll.

A soggy, *confused* sausage roll with slick ebony hair that would feel like satin ribbons between his fingertips.

Right. He dragged himself back to the point.

"I need a governess. Not just any governess, Miss Mountbatten. I need *you*. Which is why I will not have you walking home in the rain and catching the grippe."

"But it isn't—"

"I insist. Most insistently."

She blinked at him. "Very well."

Finally, she heeded his demands. She walked down the pavement and turned the corner, disappearing from view.

As he returned to the house, Chase took note of an unexpected sensation. Or rather, the lack of an expected sensation. Miss Mountbatten had appeared at his front door soaked to the skin, and he hadn't yet felt a single raindrop.

He tipped his head to the sky. Strange. Nothing overhead but the periwinkle and orange streaks of twilight.

It wasn't raining.

In fact, now that he thought of it, it hadn't rained all day.

Chapter Four

At home, Alexandra unwrapped herself from Mr. Reynaud's coat and hung it on a peg. She'd likely ruined the thing. The garment had smelled deliciously of mint and sandalwood when he'd wrapped it about her shoulders. Now it reeked of the Thames.

After bathing and changing into a clean shift and dressing gown, she followed the scent of baking biscuits down to the kitchen. Thank heaven for Nicola and freshly baked biscuits.

She sat down at the table and laid her head on folded arms. "Hullo, Nic."

Nicola whisked a tray of biscuits from the oven. A sweet, lemony steam permeated the kitchen. "Goodness, has the day gone already?"

"It has, I'm afraid." And what a day it had been. Alex lifted her head. "Do you remember the Bookshop Rake?"

"The Bookshop Rake?" Nicola frowned. "It's not a poem or limerick, is it? I'm useless at those."

"No, it's a man. We met with him in Hatchard's last autumn. I was carrying a stack of your books in one arm, and reading one of my own with my free hand. He and I collided. I was startled, dropped everything. He helped me gather up the books."

Nicola piled the biscuits onto a plate and carried it to the table, setting it between them.

"Tall," Alex prompted. "Brown hair, green eyes, fine attire. Handsome. Flirtatious. We all decided he must be a terrible rake."

And we didn't guess the half of it. "Penny teased me for *months.* Surely you must remember."

Nicola lowered herself into a chair, thoughtful. "Maybe I do recall. Was I buying natural history books?"

"Cookery and Roman architecture."

"Oh. Hm." Biscuit in one hand and book in the other, Nicola was already absorbed in other thoughts.

Alexandra reached for a biscuit and took a resigned bite. That was Nicola for you. She jettisoned useless information like ballast. She needed the brain space to cram in more facts and theories, Alex supposed. And to come up with her ideas.

When Nicola was concentrating, she set aside everything else. She would neglect the passing of hours and days, if not for the odor of burnt cakes coming from the kitchen, or the clamor of the twenty-three—

Cuckoo! Cuckoo!

The twenty-three clocks.

So it began. The chiming, ringing, chirping, and bonging from timepieces that stood, hung, sat—even danced—in every corner of the house.

Alexandra couldn't complain about the noise. Nicola's clocks were the only reason she could afford to live in a place like Bloom Square. In exchange for a room in her friend's inherited Mayfair house, Alex bartered her timekeeping services. The din was loud enough when they all struck the hour in unison . . . but if they fell out of synchrony, the noise went on for ages.

After the last chime sounded, Alex spoke to whatever fraction of her friend's divided attention she could command. "He offered me a post. The Bookshop Rake."

"The Bookshop Rake?" Lady Penelope Campion burst through the kitchen door, flushed and breathless, holding a flour sack in one hand and clutching a bundle to her chest with the other. "Did I hear mention of the Bookshop Rake?"

With a soft moan, Alex laid her head on the table again.

"Oh, Alexandra." Penny dropped the sack, sat down beside her, and clutched her arm. "You've found each other at last. I knew you would."

"It wasn't like that. Not in the slightest."

"Tell me everything. Was he just as handsome as he was in Hatchard's?"

"Please, Penny. I beg you. Hear me out before you start dreaming up names for the children."

"Oh!" Penny snapped her fingers. "I nearly forgot the reason for my visit. It's Bixby's cart. He was chasing after the goslings, and he popped the axle out of place." At the sound of his name, the rat terrier poked his head out from the blanket. Penny clucked and fussed over him. "What a little scoundrel you are. If you had all four legs, I shouldn't know what to do with you."

Nicola reached for the sack and withdrew the contraption inside—a tiny cart she'd rigged up to serve in place of Bixby's hind legs. She turned it over, inspecting the axle. "Won't take but a moment."

"There, now. Alex, you were saying . . . ?"

"She was saying he offered her work." Nicola retrieved her little caddy of hand tools and sorted through the wrenches and pliers. "That's all."

"Of course he offered her work," Penny said. "As a pretext. That way he can see her once a week. He's taken with her."

Alex placed both hands on the table. "If you're going to make up your own tale, I can retire to bed."

"No, no." Penny fed Bixby a biscuit. "We're listening."

Alexandra poured herself a cup of tea and began at the beginning. By the time she reached the end of her tale, the plate of biscuits had been devoured to crumbs and Bixby was racing circles around the table with the aid of his cart.

"He ran after you and gave you his coat." Penny sighed. "So romantic."

"Romantic?" Nicola made a face. "Did you miss the bit where he keeps two little girls locked in the attic and feeds them nothing but dry crusts?"

"Not at all," Penny returned. "It's one more reason to accept. Just think of how much those orphaned girls need her."

Alex rubbed her temples. How she missed Emma. She adored all three of her friends, but Emma was the most understanding among them. A former seamstress, she'd once worked for her living, too. At the moment, however, both Emma and her heavily pregnant belly were happily ensconced in the country.

Nicola tsked. "Alex, I can't believe you accepted the post."

"I couldn't say no. He offered me an astronomical sum. I will make more in two months than I could hope to make in two years of clock setting. Besides, after what happened at the dock, I didn't have a choice."

"Of course you had a choice. You might have asked your friends for help," Penny said. "We are always here if you need us."

"We could have scraped together the money to replace your chronometer." Nicola looked up from her tinkering. "And you know you are welcome to stay with me as long as you wish."

"That's lovely of you both. But what if you loaned me money I couldn't repay?" She turned to Nicola. "What if you decide to marry, and your husband doesn't want a spinster in the house?"

Nicola chuckled. "Me, married. Now that is a laugh."

"No, it isn't," Penny protested. "It's entirely likely that a dashing gentleman will fall in love with you and propose."

"But would I want to accept? That's the question."

Alexandra was grateful the conversation had veered to Nicola. The risk she was taking was so enormous, she couldn't contemplate it. No more than a snowflake could contemplate summer. If she failed in this post, she could lose any chance of supporting herself thereafter. And as much as she adored her friends, Alex craved a place of her own.

A home.

Even a tiny cottage in the country would do nicely, so long as it was hers. She longed to feel real earth beneath her feet and let her toes burrow into the soil like roots. No more drifting on tides.

However, her plan required money. A large amount of money.

She scoured the papers for notices of cottages to let and made careful note of the rents. She'd drawn up a budget, then calculated the lump sum she'd need to have saved in the bank in order to live on the interest.

Four hundred pounds.

In three years, she'd managed to save fifty-seven.

Now she had the chance to walk away with two hundred and fifty pounds by Michaelmas. For that sum, she would shovel the Shepherd Market middens during the height of summer. Naked.

"I have to go upstairs and pack my things. I've promised to report tomorrow morning."

"Be careful of him, Alex," Nicola said. "If he is truly a rake, as you say."

"Believe me, there's nothing to fear. He isn't interested in me. He didn't even remember meeting me. Apparently I was quite forgettable."

"Stop." Penny stole Alex's hand. "I will hear none of that. You are not forgettable."

Dear, sweet Penny, with her heart for lost and broken creatures. No doubt she recalled the name and personality of every last mouse in the cupboard. But most people weren't Penny, and this wasn't the first time Alexandra had raised her hopes, only to be disappointed.

"It doesn't matter whether he recalled me or not. I'll be looking after his wards. I will scarcely see him."

"Oh, you will see him," Penny said. "Especially if you go wandering about the house at night. Try the library first."

"Lock yourself in your room," Nicola countered. "I'll make you a deadbolt."

"Stop, the both of you. I'm accepting a well-paid situation for the summer. Until yesterday, I was setting clocks; tomorrow, I begin as a governess. It's not romantic. It's not dangerous. It's work."

"You don't have to be sensible *all* the time," Penny said.

Easy enough to say, for a lady with a house of her own and a thousand pounds a year. Penny and Nicola didn't have to be sensible all the time, perhaps, but Alexandra did. She couldn't afford to be swept away.

Fortunately, there was no longer any chance of that happening. Never mind that he'd ensorcelled every other woman in London. Alex knew better. Now that she'd seen his shameless nature, Chase Reynaud had lost all appeal. She would never be tempted by him again.

Not his smile.

Not his eyes.

Most certainly not his bare chest.

Nor his voice, forearms, wit, charm, or large feet.

And not his warm, delicious-smelling coat, either.

Oh, Alex. You are doomed.

Chapter Five

$\mathcal{A}$lexandra reported for duty the following morning. This time, she knew to knock at the front door. And, to her profound relief, the housekeeper answered.

Mrs. Greeley looked her up and down. "I thought you were the girl who sets clocks."

"I was," Alexandra answered. "Apparently now I'm a governess."

"Hmph. By the end of the day, you'll be the girl who sets clocks again." She waved Alex toward the stairs. "Come, then. I'll show you to the nursery. I'll have Jane prepare you a room, and Thomas will bring up your trunks in a bit."

Alex suspected Jane and Thomas would be waiting to see if she lasted the morning before they went to the trouble.

When she entered the nursery today, she did not come upon another murder scene. Thank goodness. This time, she had the chance to take a proper look at the surroundings—and what she took in left her breathless.

The room was a fairyland. All done up in frothy white and buttery yellows and blushing pinks. Like the window of a confectionery. White wainscoting lined the bottom half of the room, and here and there painted ivy tendrils climbed the sky-blue walls. The room offered no shortage of playthings. Alex saw rocking horses, miniature tea sets, and marionettes. An upholstered window seat had been wedged under one of the eaves, and beneath it ranged a shelf overflowing with books.

Considering the freshness of the paint and the lavish quality of the furnishings, she deduced two things: First, the room had been done up expressly for these two girls. Second, no expense had been spared.

"That one there is Rosamund." The housekeeper pointed to the elder of the two girls.

Rosamund sat reading a book in the window seat. She didn't look up.

"And that's Daisy," Mrs. Greeley said.

Daisy acknowledged her at least, dropping in a slight curtsy. Her eyes, pale blue and wide as shillings, were downright unsettling. In her arms, she cradled a doll. A quite expensive one, with a head carved from wood, covered with gesso, and painted with rosy cheeks and red lips.

Alexandra crossed the room to Daisy's side. "I'm most pleased to meet you, Daisy. This must be Millicent."

Daisy took a step in retreat. "Don't draw too near. She has consumption."

"Consumption? I'm sorry to hear it. But I've no doubt you'll nurse her to a swift recovery."

The girl shook her head gravely. "She'll be dead by tomorrow morning."

"Surely she won't—"

"Oh, she will," Rosamund said dryly, speaking from the window seat. "Best to have a few words prepared."

"A few words prepared for what?"

Without moving her lips, Daisy made a few dry, hacking coughs. "Millicent needs quiet."

"Yes, of course she does. Do you know what I hear is the best remedy for consumption? Fresh air and sunshine. A stroll to the park should set her up nicely."

"No outings," Mrs. Greeley declared. "They're to focus on their lessons. Mr. Reynaud was very clear."

"Oh. Well, then. Perhaps we can soothe Millicent another way." She thought on it. "Perhaps tea with heaps of milk and sugar, and a dish of custard. What do you think, Daisy? Shall we give it a go?"

"No custard," Mrs. Greeley said.

"They're not allowed custard, either?"

"That's Daisy's fault," Rosamund explained. "She gave Millicent a nasty case of the grippe and used it for phlegm."

Daisy shushed them all, clutching the doll tightly to her chest. "Please. Allow her some peace in her final hours."

"I won't disturb your peace if you don't disturb mine," Rosamund said. "You had better not wake me with hacking and wheezing in the middle of the night."

Now that she had Rosamund's attention, Alex decided to try with her. "What are you reading?"

"A book." She turned a page.

"Is it a storybook?"

"No, it is a book of practical advice. *How to Torture Your Governess in Ten Simple Steps.*"

"She's likely writing the second volume," Mrs. Greeley muttered. "The cook will send up your luncheon at noon."

The housekeeper disappeared, leaving Alexandra alone with her two young charges. Her stomach fluttered with nerves.

Steady, she told herself. Rosamund and Daisy were only girls, after all. Girls who'd been orphaned and passed from home to home, guardian to guardian. If they greeted a newly arrived governess with mistrust, it was only natural. In fact, it was sensible. Alex had been an orphan, too. She understood. It would take time to build trust.

"We won't have any lessons today," she announced.

"No lessons?" Rosamund lifted an eyebrow from behind her book. "What are we going to do all day?"

"Well, *I* intend to acquaint myself with the schoolroom, then perhaps write a letter or read a book. How *you* spend the day is yours to decide."

"So you intend to bilk our guardian for wages while letting us do as we please," the girl said. "I approve."

"That is not my intent, but we have the whole summer for lessons. Of course, if you wished to begin today, I could—"

Rosamund put her nose back in her book.

Alex was relieved. The truth was, she had no idea where to even start. Being a governess hadn't sounded so difficult last night—she had an education, after all—but now that she was here, she felt at a loss.

While the girls were occupied, Alex had a look at her surroundings. One side of the space had been designated as a schoolroom. She found it furnished with just as much attention and thought as the nursery. Two child-sized writing desks, an adult-sized table with a wide, flat top, and a bedsheet-sized slate hanging on the wall. On the slate, in careful script, someone had chalked five words:

- *Letters*
- *Ciphers*
- *Geography*
- *Comportment*
- *Needlework*

Alex moved on to a world map affixed to the wall. The continents were peppered with tacks in a seemingly random arrangement. Malta, Finland, Timbuktu, a speck of an island in the Indian Ocean, the Sahara Desert.

Daisy appeared at her elbow. "Those are the places Mr. Reynaud says he's sending us to boarding school."

Alex considered the options. "Well, if I were you, I'd take Malta in a heartbeat. It's quite lovely. Surrounded by azure seas."

"You've been to Malta?"

"I've been all sorts of places. My father was a sea captain." Alex rearranged the tacks, pushing them into common trading ports. "Macao. Lima. Lisbon. Bombay. And I was born near here." She placed the final tack.

"Where's that?"

"Read for yourself."

Daisy flashed a glance over her shoulder, then whispered, "I can't."

"Ma-ni-la." Alex sounded out the syllables for her. "It's a port in the Philippine Islands."

Seven years old, and she couldn't yet read. Oh, dear.

"Say, Daisy. I'm wondering if we have enough pencils and bits of chalk. Would you help me count them out?"

"I—"

"Daisy," Rosamund interrupted sharply. "I think I hear Millicent coughing."

As her sister went to nurse her ailing patient, Rosamund fixed Alex with an unflinching—and unmistakable—look. *Stay away from my sister.*

Alex's spirits dipped. The challenge before her was already intimidating. She had no teaching experience, the younger of her two charges had not yet learned to read, and her employer would be completely unhelpful.

However, it was plain that the most formidable obstacle in this entire endeavor would come in the shape of a mistrustful, strong-willed, ten-year-old girl.

So. The war of wills began here.

If she didn't want to leave this house penniless, it was a war Alexandra had to win.

Chapter Six

That evening, Chase stood in the doorway of his governess's bedchamber, waging a fierce battle with temptation.

He'd stopped by her room with the most innocent of motives. He intended to see that she'd settled in, and be assured that the accommodations were to her liking.

What he was doing, however, was admiring her sweet, round little bottom.

It wasn't as though he'd intended to ogle her. He wasn't some perverse old man leering through a peephole in the closet. Her door was open, and her back was to him, and she hadn't taken note of his presence—probably because she was bent over that cursed telescope.

So there it was, presented for his view. The most delightful peach of a backside. More generously rounded than he would have guessed, given her slender figure.

At his sides, his hands instinctively cupped, estimating size and plumpness.

Chase, you despicable bastard.

He shook out his hands and cleared his throat. "Miss Mountbatten?"

Startled, she stood bolt upright and reeled to face him. "Mr. Reynaud."

"So. Do you like what you see?"

"Do I like what I . . . ?"

Her gaze wandered over him. In his evening attire, he could only imagine he made a markedly different picture than he had on their first meeting. He'd actually bathed and shaved, and gone to the trouble of buttoning his cuffs.

She stammered. "I . . . er . . . that is to say, I should imagine that—"

"The room," he said. "Does it meet with your satisfaction?"

"Oh, that," she said with relief. "Yes. Thank you. Very much. I wasn't expecting something so spacious."

"Mrs. Greeley usually gives the governesses a chamber next to the nursery, but I told her you required the one with the largest window and a clear view of the sky. I'll send up a maid to assist you in unpacking your things."

"I've already unpacked them," she replied, looking self-conscious. "There was only the one trunk."

"Oh. Yes, of course." He strolled across the room to the window, taking a look at the arrangement of the telescope and window. "There's space out here for a narrow verandah. I'll have plans drawn up for a platform and railing this week."

"That's too generous of you."

"Nothing of the sort. It's entirely self-interest. If you're satisfied with your accommodations, you're less likely to leave." He bent and squinted to peer through the telescope. "Why did you want it? I can't help but be curious."

"Well, our agreement is temporary. At the end of the summer, I will need a new occupation."

"I should think you'd go back to setting clocks."

She shook her head. "I'm planning a new business venture. Instead of selling the time, I'm going to sell comets."

"Selling comets?" He laughed a little. "Oh, I must hear this. Pray tell, how do you intend to catch them?"

"The aristocrats are positively mad for comets, but most don't have the time or interest in doing the work. I'll search the skies and chart observations, and then I'll find a patron willing to pay me for the effort."

"So you'll find the comet, and this patron claims it as his discovery? That sounds highly unjust."

"I'm not interested in it for the glory. A woman of my station has to be more practical than that."

"So you intend to be an astronomical mercenary. I'm impressed."

She smiled a little. "That makes it sound far too exciting. It's boring work. A matter of searching the sky, one dark patch at a time, looking for anything smudgy."

"Smudgy? A proper scientific term, that."

"I'll show you an example, if you like."

She joined him, crowding into the small window alcove, and bent to adjust the telescope—affording him, should he choose to take it, a view directly down the neckline of her frock. Chase pulled his gaze away, but not swiftly enough. That split-second view of two celestially perfect crescents of soft, feminine flesh was going to linger.

In need of distraction, he swept a gaze around the room—which, in its own way, was equally revealing.

This was the sum total of her possessions? The bedchamber remained empty for the most part, save for a simple dressing set on the washstand, a row of books and writing supplies on the corner table, and a few articles of clothing hanging on pegs. On the wall above the table, she'd affixed items clipped from newspapers and magazines. A map of the constellations, a card with an illustration commemorating the appearance of Halley's comet in 1759, and a few smaller notices that he had to squint to read from this distance. At the top of one, he could just make out the words "Cottage for Let."

"Here it is. Have a look, if you like." She beckoned him to look through the eyepiece.

Chase bent awkwardly, closed one eye, and peered into the brass tube. His reward was a blurry glimpse of a wholly unremarkable speck of light. "Apparently I'm a natural astronomer. I can declare with certainty"—he squinted—"*that* is a smudgy sky thing. I shall expect to imminently receive my medal from the Royal Astronomical Society."

"That's not a comet. Most of the smudges aren't. Before declaring it a new discovery, you have to rule out the other possibilities. Fortunately, others have done much of that work. There's a book by a Frenchman. Charles Messier. He catalogued a great many of the known not-a-comet smudges, so that comet-hunting observers know to ignore them." She went to retrieve a folio from the table and flipped through the pages for him to view.

"You said a book. That's not a book."

"I couldn't find a copy I could afford to purchase," she admitted. "So I borrowed it from a circulating library and copied it out by hand. After consulting Messier, one must check against lists of identified comets. If it's not among those, then you can report your smudge to the Royal Observatory for verification. Even then, nine times in ten it will have already been claimed."

"And the smudges that aren't comets. What are they?"

"Nebulae, mostly. Or star clusters."

"I'm afraid you'll have to define these things if you want me to have any idea what you're talking about. Alternatively, you can simply go on talking while I stare at your earlobe."

She blushed. "You needn't trouble yourself."

"It's no chore." He crossed his arms and leaned back against the window casing. "I'm a veritable connoisseur of earlobes, and yours is rather nice."

"I meant you needn't pretend to be interested, Mr. Reynaud. Clearly you have an engagement this evening, and I don't wish to delay you."

"I'm not pretending. I'm finding this conversation most fascinating. Even though a great deal of it is lost on me."

That wasn't precisely the truth. He was finding Alexandra Mountbatten fascinating, and nothing about her was lost on him. He wasn't all that interested in gazing at the sky himself, but he was captivated by the experience of watching *her* gazing at the sky. Her figure and earlobe weren't the half of it.

Standing this close, he could detect the faintest hint of orange-flower water about her. Not enough to qualify as a perfume. Just the suggestion that she scented her bathwater with a few sparing drops. An amount carefully poised between the indulgence of a small feminine luxury, and the economy required to make a small vial last for months.

A tiny, beaded, cross-shaped pendant was tied about her neck with a narrow satin ribbon just long enough for the coral beads to nestle at the base of her throat. Again, that balance between prettiness and practicality. The best quality ribbon she could likely afford, purchased in the smallest possible amount.

Damn, she would be a delight to spoil. If she weren't his employee, he could shower her with little gifts and luxuries. Remove all the small worries that came between her and the sky.

"Do go on," he said. "I'm listening." *And looking. And noticing.*

"Nebulae are clouds of stardust floating in space. Star clusters are just as they sound. Stars appear so close together in the sky, they're sometimes mistaken for one object. My favorite smudge, however, isn't a nebula or cluster. It's Messier's number 40. A double star. Perhaps even a binary star."

"Oh, truly." And with that, he was back to the earlobe.

She bent to peer through the eyepiece. "A binary star is created when two stars are drawn together. Once they come near enough, neither one can resist the other's pull. They're stuck together forever, destined to spend eternity revolving about each other, like . . . like dancers in a waltz, I suppose." She scribbled a note in her notebook. "The fascinating thing is, a binary star's center of gravity isn't in one star or the other. It's in the empty space between them."

He was silent for a while. "I'll be damned. You were right when you scolded me for letting this instrument go to waste."

"I'm glad you see its value now."

"Absolutely. To think, I could have been using it to seduce women all along." To her chastening look, he replied, "Come now. All that waltzing star business? It's deuced romantic."

"I would never have marked you as a romantic."

"I suppose it's all that glory-of-the-universe talk. Makes a man feel rather small and insignificant. And *that* makes a man want to grab the nearest woman and prove himself to be otherwise."

Their gazes met, and they both became keenly aware of the obvious.

She was the nearest woman.

He was not—absolutely not—going to pursue his governess. Yes, he was a rake. But for a gentleman, chasing after the house staff wasn't rakish behavior. It was repulsive.

"The girls," he blurted out, breaking the tension. "How was your first day?"

"Challenging."

"I don't doubt it."

"Can you tell me something about their interests, or their schooling? Anything at all?"

"They've had little proper schooling, but are somehow far too clever despite it. Their interests are mischief, disease, petty thievery, and plotting crimes against the house staff."

She laughed a little. "You speak as though they're hardened criminals."

"They're well on the way to it. But now you're here to take them in hand. I have every faith in you, Miss Mountbatten." He patted her shoulder gamely. "I've seen your natural talent as a disciplinarian."

She cringed. "Yes, about that . . ."

"If you're intending to apologize, don't. I richly deserved all your censure, and then some. I wish I could say you've already seen me at my worst, but that's nowhere near the case. However, I do wish to say one thing."

"Yes?"

She gave him her full attention—and she had an intimidating amount of attention to give. Only natural, he supposed. Here was a woman willing to stare into dark emptiness night after night, on the hope that someday some tiny speck might shine back. As she gazed at him, Chase found himself wishing he could reward her observation.

Only darkness here, darling. Don't waste your time.

"If my reputation worries you," he said, as much for his own benefit as hers, "it needn't. Seducing you would never even cross my mind."

She nodded. "Thank you for your assurances, Mr. Reynaud. I appreciate them very much indeed."

Chapter Seven

Seducing you would never even cross my mind.

What a perfectly timed reminder. Really, the man had a way of withering Alexandra's pride to a dried-up husk. One moment, he was listening to her babble away about comets, hanging on her words, and complimenting her earlobe, and the next, he left her with a few parting words to remind her that she was a fool.

Embroidery wasn't her favorite hobby, but Alex planned to stitch those words on a sampler and hang it above her bed:

> *Seducing you would never even cross my mind.*
> —*Mr. Charles Reynaud, 1817*

She no longer wondered at his popularity with women. Devilish charm simply radiated from him, like one of nature's essential forces. Gravity, magnetism, electricity . . . Chase Reynaud's masculine appeal.

His every lopsided grin or low, teasing word sent a frisson of excitement rushing along her skin. That alone wouldn't be a problem. But then her brain caught up all those sensations, rolled them into a ball, and set it on a shelf. As if that quivering mass of feminine reaction was something that deserved to take up space. As if it needed a name.

Well, Alexandra would label it, right this moment.

I-D-I-O-C-Y.

She heard the creak of a door down at street level, and she gave in to the temptation to peer over her windowsill. There he stood, waiting on the pavement in that immaculately tailored black topcoat. He gave his cuffs a smart tug and ran a hand through his tawny brown hair. A pair of matched bays pulled a fashionable blue-lacquered phaeton around from the mews, and the groom handed him the reins.

Off he went to spend his evening enjoying the company of others. And here Alex was left mooning over him like a fool.

She readied herself for bed and put out the candle. And then she lay awake far too long listening for the sounds of a returning phaeton, or the creak of a door. Not that it was any of her concern what time he returned home, or whether he returned at all.

She must have fallen asleep at some point, because she woke to the sensation of someone poking her in the arm.

Repeatedly.

She opened her eyes halfway. "Rosamund? Is that you?"

"She's dead."

Now Alex was awake. She sat bolt upright in bed. "Dead?"

"Millicent. The consumption took her overnight."

The doll. She meant the doll.

"You gave me a fright." Alex pressed a hand to her chest. Perhaps her heart would stop racing in a day or two.

"The funeral is prepared. We'll be waiting on you in the nursery."

Funeral?

Rosamund was gone before Alex could inquire further. She rose from bed and hastily dressed. Given her disorientation in a new room and the abrupt way she'd been roused from sleep, she didn't do a very good job of it. After two attempts, she decided she could live with misaligned buttons for the moment, and three passes of the hairbrush would have to be enough. Clenching a few hairpins in her teeth, she made her way into the corridor, winding her hair into a knot as she went.

Alex hoped the standard of attire at this funeral wasn't overly formal. She'd just jabbed the second pin into her haphazard chi-

gnon when she entered the nursery. Millicent lay in the center of
the bed, staring up blankly from the swaddling of her shroud.
The girls stood on either side. Daisy wore a scrap of black lace
netting draped over her head as a veil.

Alex struggled, mightily, not to burst out laughing. If for no
other reason than that doing so would launch the remaining hairpins in her mouth like missiles.

She completed her upsweep, composed herself, and approached
the bed. To Rosamund, she whispered, "What happens now?"

"We're waiting on—"

A male voice breezed into the room. "Such a tragedy. Deepest
sympathies. A grievous loss."

Mr. Reynaud had joined the group.

Alex slid a cautious glance in his direction. He wore the same
black coat and boots he'd been wearing the night previous. His
cuffs were undone, however, and his cravat was missing.

Probably draped over an antler prong somewhere.

He walked toward Daisy and made a deep bow of condolences before holding out his arm so that she could pin something
around it.

A black armband.

She recalled his words from a few days ago. *Millicent is Daisy's
doll. She kills the thing at least once a day.*

So this was why he'd been wearing the black armband a few
mornings past, when they'd conducted that farce of an interview
in his not-at-all-a-gentleman's retreat. He hadn't been in mourning. Not for a human being, at any rate. Perhaps she shouldn't
have judged him quite so harshly.

He bent to place a kiss on Millicent's painted forehead. "Bless
her soul. She looks just as though she's sleeping. Or awake. Or doing anything else, really."

Alex's mouth twitched at the corners, but she bowed her head
and tried to appear bereaved.

"Let us begin," Daisy said solemnly.

They formed a semicircle at the foot of the bed. Rosamund went to Daisy's right side. Mr. Reynaud assumed what was clearly his usual place at Daisy's left—which put him next to Alexandra.

She didn't want to think about where he'd been since she saw him last, but her senses gave her no choice in the matter. When she inhaled, she smelled brandy and sandalwood, and the suggestion that he'd walked through a cloud of cheroot smoke. She didn't detect any hint of a lady's perfume, however. That should not have come as a relief, but it did.

She stared at the bedpost and set her mind on tragedy.

"Mr. Reynaud, would you kindly say a few words?" Daisy asked.

"But of course." He clasped his hands together and intoned in a low, grave voice, "Almighty Father, we are gathered here today to commend to your keeping the soul of Millicent Fairfax."

Daisy nudged him with her elbow.

"Millicent Annabelle Chrysanthemum Genevieve Fairfax," he corrected.

Alexandra bit the inside of her cheek. How could the man keep a straight face through all this?

"She will be remembered for her faithful companionship. A truer friend never lived. Not once did she stray from Daisy's side—save for the few occasions when she rolled off the bed."

Oh, help. Alex was going to laugh. She knew it. Biting her tongue clean through wouldn't help.

Perhaps she could disguise a burst of laughter as a cough. After all, consumption *was* catching.

"Let Millicent's composure in the face of certain death be a model for us all. Her eyes remained fixed on heaven—and not merely because she lacked any eyelids to close."

She cast a pleading glance at him, only to catch him glancing back with devilish amusement. He *wanted* her to laugh, the terrible man. And then, just as she thought she was lost, he took her hand in his, lacing their fingers into a tight knot.

Alex no longer worried she might laugh.

Instead, her heart squeezed.

On Mr. Reynaud's other side, Daisy clasped her guardian's hand tight. Then she offered her free hand to Rosamund. The four of them had formed an unbroken chain, and Alex realized the truth. Here were three people who desperately needed each other—perhaps even loved each other—and they would all rather contract consumption than admit it.

Daisy bowed her veiled head. "Let us pray."

Alex fumbled her way through the Lord's Prayer, quietly reeling. His grip was so warm and firm. His signet ring pressed against her third and fourth fingers. The moment felt intimate. The way they stood holding hands, heads bowed in prayer, it felt less like a funeral, and more like . . .

More like a wedding.

No, no, no.

What was wrong with her? Had she learned nothing from those months of foolish imaginings? All those silly fantasies had popped like a soap bubble when it became clear he'd forgotten her completely. Chase Reynaud was not the man of her dreams. By his own declaration, he would never even think of seducing her.

She really needed to start on that sampler.

"Lead us not into temptation," Alex prayed fervently, "but deliver us from evil."

When the prayer was done, Daisy placed the deceased doll reverently in a toy-chest "grave."

Mr. Reynaud kept Alexandra's hand in his. "Well, then, Miss Mountbatten. Now that's over with, I shall leave you to your pupils." He gave her hand a light squeeze before releasing it. "Let the education begin."

Chapter Eight

The education was on hold. Before any lessons could take place, Alexandra had a ten-year-old girl to conquer.

After breakfast, the Rosamund Rebellion commenced.

Silence was her first strategy, and she'd marshaled Daisy into the campaign. Neither of them would speak a word to Alex. Indeed, once the funeral was over, neither of them even acknowledged her presence. Rosamund read her book, Daisy exhumed Millicent, and all three treated Alex as if she didn't exist.

Very well. Both sides could play at this game.

The next day, Alex didn't even try to start conversation. Instead, she brought a novel and a packet of biscuits—Nicola had sent her off with a full hamper of them—and she sat in the rocking chair to read. She laughed aloud at the funny bits—really, pigeons?—gasped at the revelations, and loudly chewed her way through a dozen biscuits. At one point, she was certain she felt Daisy gazing at her from across the room. However, she didn't dare look up to confirm it.

It became a habit. Every day, Alex brought with her a novel, and every day, a different variety of Nicola's biscuits. Lemon, almond, chocolate, toffee. And every day, as she sat eating and reading, the girls ignored her existence.

Until the morning a foul odor permeated the nursery. A sharp scent that even fresh-baked biscuits had no hope to overpower. As the day grew warmer, the ripe, pungent smell became nauseating.

The girls offered no clue as to its origin, and Alexandra would not give Rosamund the satisfaction of asking. Instead she sniffed and searched until she found the source. A bit of clammy, shrunken Stilton buried in her bottom-most desk drawer.

Well, then. It would seem the tactics were escalating. She could rise to the challenge.

Alex had exhausted her supply of biscuits. She brought in a new box of watercolors, bright as jewels in a treasure chest, placing them in easy reach.

The girls dusted her chair with soot.

Alex brought in a litter of kittens Mrs. Greeley was evicting from the cellar. No one could resist fluffy, mewling kittens. And Daisy almost didn't, until Rosamund yanked her away with a stern word.

That evening, a rotting plum mysteriously appeared in Alex's slipper—and unfortunately, her bare toes found it.

Rosamund seemed to be daring her to shout or rage, or go complaining to Mr. Reynaud. However, Alex refused to surrender. Instead, she smiled. She allowed the girls to do as they pleased. And she waited.

When they were ready to learn, they would tell her so. Until then, she would only be wasting her effort.

At last, her patience was rewarded. She found her opening.

Rosamund fell asleep on a particularly warm afternoon, dozing off with her book propped on her knees and her head tilted against the window glazing. Alex motioned Daisy closer and laid out a row of wrapped sweetmeats on the table, one by one.

"How many are there?" she whispered. "Count them out for me, and you may have them for yourself."

Daisy sent a cautious glance toward her sister.

"She's sleeping. She'll never know."

With a small, uncertain finger, Daisy touched each sweet as she counted aloud. "One. Two. Three. Four. Five."

"And in this group?"

Daisy's lips moved as she counted them quietly to herself. "Six."

"Well done, you. Now how many in both groups together? Together, five and six are . . . ?"

"Daisy," Rosamund snapped.

Startled, Daisy snatched her hand behind her back. "Yes?"

"Millicent's vomiting up her innards. You'd better see to her."

As her sister obediently retreated, Rosamund approached Alexandra. "I know what you're doing."

"I never imagined otherwise."

"You won't win."

"Win? I'm not certain what you mean."

"We will not cooperate. We are not going away to school."

Alex softened her demeanor. "Why don't you want to go to school?"

"Because the school won't want us. We've been sent down from three schools already, you know."

"Don't say you'd rather remain here with Mr. Reynaud. If it were up to him, you'd have only dry toast at every meal."

"We're not wanted by Mr. Reynaud, either. No one wants us. Anywhere. And we don't want them."

Alexandra recognized the defiance and mistrust in the girl's eyes. A dozen years ago, those eyes could have mirrored her own.

A tender part of her wanted to clutch the girl close. *Of course you're wanted. Of course you're loved. Your guardian cares for you so very much.* But to lie would be taking the coward's way out, and Rosamund wouldn't be fooled. What the girl needed wasn't false reassurance—it was for someone to tell her the honest, unflinching truth.

"Very well." Alex folded her hands on the desk and faced her young charge. "You're right. You've been passed around from relation to relation, sent down from three schools, and Mr. Reynaud wishes to rid himself of you at the first opportunity. You're unwanted. So what you must decide is this: What do *you* want?"

Rosamund gave her a suspicious look.

"I was orphaned, too. A bit older than you are now, but I was utterly alone in the world, save for a few distant relations who paid for my schooling—on the condition that they would never have me in their sight. It wasn't fair. It was lonely, and my school-mates were cruel, and I cried myself to sleep more evenings than not. But in time, I realized I had an advantage over the other girls. They had to worry about catching a husband to help their families. I was indebted to no one, I answered to no one, and I needn't meet anyone's expectations of what a young lady should or shouldn't be. My life was my own. I could follow any dream, if I was prepared to work hard for it. Do you hear what I'm saying?"

Rosamund gave no acknowledgment, but Alex could tell the girl was listening. Intently.

"So what is it you truly want? If you could have any life you wished, what would it be?"

"I want to escape. Not just this house, but England."

"Where do you mean to go?"

"Anywhere. Everywhere. I'd take Daisy with me. We'd travel the world, wearing trousers and smoking cheroots and doing as we pleased."

Alexandra had been hoping to hear "I want to be a painter." Or a French-trained chef, or an architect. Whatever pursuit Rosa-mund named, Alex could build lessons on its foundation. But she was quite certain Mr. Reynaud would not approve of lessons in cheroot-smoking. Alex wouldn't have known how to give them, anyway.

"That sounds like a grand life indeed," she said, "but how will you support yourselves?"

"I'm perfectly capable of looking after us both." Rosamund cast a glance at the table. "So you can clear away your nine sweets and leave us alone."

"You know very well there are eleven sweetmeats."

"Are there?"

Alex looked. Sure as could be, two sweetmeats were missing. The girl had managed to steal them, right from under her nose, and one of the two was already across the room in Daisy's hands. Alex could hear the paper crinkling as the younger girl unwrapped it.

"Rosamund, may I tell you something? You will find yourself reluctant to believe it, but it's the truth."

The girl gave a lackadaisical shrug. The warmest gesture she'd made toward Alex so far.

"I like you," Alexandra said. "I like you very much indeed."

Chapter Nine

$\mathcal{A}$lex woke to darkness.

Disorientation wrapped her brain like a fog. She sat up and shook her head, trying to clear it. Her heart pounded. Perspiration glued her shift to her chest. Worst of all, her stomach pitched and rolled. As if she were at sea.

Dread rose within her, quickly transforming—thanks to Nature's least helpful of alchemies—into panic.

She fumbled blindly, finding nothing familiar. Her hands grasped bedclothes of the softest flannel. Definitely not her own. Her feet found a solid floor, but as she stood, the floorboards didn't creak beneath her weight.

Then her knee collided with a chest of drawers. Ouch.

The pain gave her racing thoughts a jolt. *Calm yourself, Alexandra.* She pressed one hand to her belly and mentally sank through each solid, immovable layer beneath her feet. Wooden floor. Stony plinth foundation. Cobbled London street. The same layer of grainy, musty earth that Romans had packed beneath their sandals, and the bedrock Atlas, supporting the city on his shoulders.

There, now. You're fine, you ninny.

She wasn't lost at sea. She was in the Reynaud residence. And she was a governess.

An underqualified, ill-prepared, and thus far unsuccessful governess, but a governess nonetheless.

When she swallowed, her tongue rasped against the roof of her mouth. She was also a thirsty governess.

By now, Alex's eyes had adjusted to the dark. She went to the washstand and lifted the ewer. It was light in her grip, no sound of sloshing. Empty. Drat. Tomorrow she'd be certain to set a cup of water aside before she retired, but that wouldn't help her now. She supposed she might ring for a maid, but she hated to bother the staff. She squinted at her compact traveling clock on the washstand. Already five in the morning. She could wait another hour until sunrise, couldn't she?

Her parched throat objected. No, she couldn't wait. To most people, the sensation of thirst was an inconvenience. But then, most people didn't know the minute-by-minute torture of going without water for days at a stretch.

Alex slid her feet into a pair of worn slippers and made her way out of the bedchamber, through the corridor, and down the stairs with silent footsteps. Being small-statured had a few benefits, and stealth was one of them.

In the kitchen, she found the kettle on the stove. It still held some cooled water. She gulped down one cupful, then a second, and yet another still.

Once her thirst was slaked, she turned to make her way back upstairs.

Thump. Thump.

She eyed the closed door to Mr. Reynaud's private retreat.

Thump. Thump. Thump.

The dull rhythmic sound ceased, and then started anew, and despite her misgivings, Alex put her ear to the door.

Now the thumping sounded more like banging. Something hitting the wall, again and again. Not just banging, but intermittent grunting.

She shouldn't be listening to this, but she couldn't pry her ear from the door. The sense of sordid fascination was irresistible.

All went quiet once again. She pressed her ear tightly to the door and held her breath, eliminating the distracting sound of her own inhalation. Then:

Bang-bang-bang.

Crash.

And a deep, harsh sound that was part growl, part barbaric shout.

She clapped a hand to her mouth. She was so absorbed by the struggle not to laugh, she didn't notice the heavy footfalls until they were just on the other side of the door. The door latch turned.

No time for escape.

The door swung open.

She jumped back, clapping both hands over her eyes. "I didn't see anything."

"I SWEAR IT," she said. "I didn't see anything at all."

Chase stared at his governess. She stood there with a finger-blindfold clamped over her eyes, dressed in a simple shift. Shadows skimmed contours of the form beneath it. "I should think snooping is beneath you, Miss Mountbatten."

"I'm sorry," she said, still covering her eyes. "I'm so sorry. I only came down for a drink of water, I promise."

"Pressing one's ear to a door would seem an ineffective way to quench thirst."

Her shoulders wilted. "I didn't mean to intrude. And I didn't see anything, hand to my heart. I'll be going to my chamber straightaway." She covered both eyes with one hand and groped comically with the other. "Turn me around, if you would?"

"Are we playing blindman's buff?"

"No." Her throat flushed red. "Turn me the other direction. Toward the door. Point me back the way I came, and I'll go up to bed."

Chase went to the basin and worked the pump handle. The scene was so absurd, he'd nearly forgotten the throbbing pain in his hand. "I can't send you to bed yet. I'm in need of your assistance."

She swallowed audibly. "Assistance?"

"I can't deal with this one-handed."

She reeled a step in retreat, colliding with a shelf of copper butter molds, setting them a-rattle. Even though she'd backed herself into a corner, she still wouldn't lower her hands from her eyes. "Can't your . . . your guest provide you some relief?"

His guest?

"I don't have a guest."

A single finger peeled away from her face. He caught a glimpse of dark eyelashes through the gap.

"I thought you were entertaining a visitor," she said.

He looked at the door to his retreat, then back to her. "Why would you think that?"

"I heard . . ." She swallowed and whispered faintly, ". . . banging. And groaning."

Good God.

He chuckled. "If you hoped to hear something salacious, I'll have to disappoint you. I was hanging paneling. On the wall. With a hammer and nails. And I seem to have sliced my thumb. Hence the groaning."

"Oh." She lowered her hands and gave a nervous laugh. "Thank heavens. What a relief. I mean, I'm not relieved about your wound, of course. I'm sorry about that. I'm just glad you're not—"

"Bare to my skin and covered in well-earned sweat?"

"Erm . . . yes."

He gritted his teeth. He would have loved to draw out the amusement, but his thumb wouldn't be ignored any longer. "The cook keeps a bit of plaster up there." He jutted his chin toward a high shelf atop the cupboard. "If you'd kindly fetch it for me."

She didn't do as he asked, but approached him and had a look at his wound. "You can't just smear plaster over this."

"It's a small wound."

"But a deep one. It must be cleaned thoroughly."

"It's fine."

"I've seen wounds like this one fester. Bigger and stronger men have succumbed to less."

"It's truly none of your concern," he said, growing testy at the suggestion of her tending the wounds of bigger and stronger men.

"It *is* my concern. If you die of gangrene or lockjaw, I'll never be paid."

Fair enough. He offered her his hand for dressing.

She washed the wound thoroughly with boiled water from the kettle and strong lye scullery soap. He winced. *Damn, bugger, blast.*

Then she slipped the flask from his waistcoat pocket. "May I?" Having uncapped it, she lifted it to his lips. To his quizzical expression, she replied, "You're going to want it. This will hurt."

Chase took a sip. He wasn't about to admit any pain, but he wouldn't refuse a swallow of good brandy.

As he watched, she poured a stream of amber spirits directly into his wound, letting it trickle until it overflowed. Then she pressed the wound to purge more blood and did it again.

On the outside, Chase was determined to look manful and impervious to pain.

On the inside . . . *Christ.*

When she capped the brandy and set the flask aside, he exhaled with relief.

She turned to search the kitchen stores. "Now for some vinegar." *Bloody hell.*

He winced as she began her fresh round of torture. "How are the girls' lessons coming along?"

"Slowly. I've been attempting to earn their confidence, but they have the sort of wounds that won't be easily healed. How long ago did their parents die?"

"I've no idea," he admitted. "I don't even know if they're orphans. They could be illegitimate."

"They're not . . . ?" She broke off, abandoning the query.

"Mine?" He shuddered at the suggestion. "I would still have been at school when Rosamund was born. It's true that I possess a natural talent for seduction, but I wasn't *that* precocious. All I know is that their father never claimed them, and the woman they called mother died three years ago, and they've been passed around relations and schools ever since."

She clucked her tongue. "Despite all their mischief, I pity them."

You ought to be pitying me, he thought.

Having a woman this enticing living under the same roof was a constant temptation. And Chase battled temptation with approximately the same success as a seagull battling the Royal Navy.

Out of sight was not out of mind. At night, he found himself thinking of her. Upstairs, alone, in the dark. But worse by far were the mornings. For God's sake, he began each day holding her hand. That, and trying like hell to make her laugh. He hadn't managed it quite yet, but most days he wrangled a reluctant smile. That alone was worth four flights of stairs.

Just yesterday, Rosamund had woken him with a single word: "Tapeworms." He'd all but leapt to his feet with delight.

It wasn't entirely desire, but it was partly desire. He knew an innocent outward appearance often concealed a tightly coiled spring waiting for release. In the dark of night, with that virginal shift unbuttoned and that plait of dark hair unbound, Alexandra Mountbatten might prove surprising.

No sooner had he conjured the image than she untied the strip of linen holding the end of her plait. As her hair came unbound and fell loose, he stared at a lock of black satin dipping to graze the slope of her neck.

She pursed her lips and blew over his wound to dry it.

God Almighty.

"There's no doubt that they're clever," she went on, winding the strip of linen about his thumb, "but life's taught them some difficult lessons. One only needs to look at Millicent to know Daisy's hurting. It's obvious from spending mere minutes with Rosamund that she's learned to be wary. She won't lower her guard easily. It will take time and patience to gain her trust."

"You have until Michaelmas."

"*We* have until Michaelmas." She deftly tucked the strip of linen in on itself, securing the binding.

"Disciplining children is not among my talents. That's why I hired you to take them in hand."

She looked up at him. "Maybe they don't need to be taken in hand, but taken into someone's heart."

Heart? He tugged his hand from hers. "Oh, no. Don't get ideas."

"Goodness. Heaven forbid that a woman have ideas."

"Ideas are all well and good, but not *those* ideas. I know that look in a woman's eye. I've seen it before, many times. You think you can convince me to settle down."

"You don't need to settle down. My father was a sea captain. I was raised on a ship, sailing the globe. We were the least settled family in the world, and yet I never doubted his love for me."

"Wait. You were raised aboard a *ship*? Sailing the *globe*?"

She paused in the act of packing up the unused salves and plaster. "I probably shouldn't have mentioned that."

"No, I think you should have mentioned it. And long before now."

"Does it truly matter? Perhaps I had an unconventional upbringing, but that doesn't mean I can't perform my duties. I had a full education. Here in England, at a proper school. I . . . I did warn you I wasn't gently bred, and you said you didn't care." Her voice went small, but resonant with emotion. "Mr. Reynaud, I need this post. Please don't sack me."

"Don't be ridiculous. I have no intention of sacking you. That's not what I meant."

"It isn't?"

"No. You should have told me straightaway because you should tell everyone straightaway. If I had your life story, it would be the first thing I mentioned to anyone. 'Hullo, I'm Chase Reynaud. I learned to toddle aboard a merchant ship, and the Seven Seas rocked my cradle. And have I mentioned that no tropical sunset could compare with your beauty?' The women would fall into bed with me."

"Don't they fall into bed with you anyway?"

"That's true. But they might do so a half minute faster. Over months and years, those half minutes add up. So let's hear the rest of the tale."

She put away the soap and vinegar. "My father was American. After the Revolution—"

"The rebellion," he corrected.

"—he became a seaman. He'd worked his way up to first mate when they anchored in Manila harbor. Theirs was one of the first ships to open trade with the Philippine Islands. Aside from the Spaniards, of course. Anyhow, they anchored for a few months. That's where he met my mother. And they fell in love."

"She was a Spanish colonist, then?"

"Mestiza. My grandfather was Spanish, but my grandmother was native to the island."

Fascinating. This information solved a few mysteries that had been lingering in Chase's mind. Life on a trading ship would have taught her the value of goods—everything from the ribbon around her neck, to telescopes and comets. He supposed her mother had blessed her with that bounty of dark hair and her delicate snub of a nose—and her father was likely to blame for her stubborn, independent streak. Those Americans just wouldn't be told what to do.

"So if your father was American, and he met your mother in the Philippine Islands . . . how did you come to be living in England?"

"That's a long story."

He looked pointedly at his bandaged hand. "I won't be doing any more work tonight."

She paused. "After they married, my father sailed back to Boston. He promised to return once he'd found a partner and bought a ship of his own. It was only supposed to be a year, but in the end, it took him more than three. When he finally returned, he found that my mother had died. He was no longer a husband."

"But he'd become a father."

She nodded. "Most men would have left me to be raised by my mother's family, but my father would have none of it. He took me aboard his ship, and off we went. The *Esperanza* was our home for the next decade. He'd named it for her." She smiled a little. "The same way my mother had named me after him. His name was Alexander."

"That's appallingly romantic."

"Isn't it? And if you think that's treacly, wait for this part. My father went down with the *Esperanza* in a storm. Died in the embrace of his true love, you could say. And that's how I ended up in England."

"Hold a moment. There are a few bits missing from that story."

Such as the part that would tell him who to blame for stranding her in a strange country, alone. And whether that someone was still alive and available to be pummeled.

She changed the subject. "How did *your* parents meet?"

"Let's see." Chase drummed his fingers on the table. "My father was a second son. He had connections, but no money. He found a young woman with money, but no connections. He proposed, she accepted, they were married. A year later, I came along. And then we all lived miserably ever after."

She was quiet for a moment. "I like my story better."

"I like yours better, too. But coming back to the matter at hand, my history should only underscore the point. I've no idea what a family looks like. I cannot be a satisfactory guardian. Hell, I don't even have *dogs*. Commitment isn't in my nature."

"You're simply too virile to be tied down, is that it?" Her eyes teased him. "Must be all those antlers."

"Don't make light of it," he said in a warning tone. "And while I'm on the subject, it's inadvisable to wander the house at night in the home of a known rake. Your reputation could be compromised."

"I'm not worried. You said the thought of seducing me would never even cross your mind."

"Yes, but sometimes," he murmured, "a man acts without thinking at all."

He leaned in as if drawn to her, trying to convince himself that a kiss would be for her own good. Just a little one, of course. A mere brush of his lips on hers. It wouldn't be *so* very terrible of him. It would be a *tiny* bit terrible of him, and that was the point. To put the punctuation mark on his warning. *Beware. Turn back. Here there be monsters.* He'd be doing her a favor, really.

Right. He'd bedded Venetian acrobats less flexible than his morality.

She put a hand to his chest. "Wait."

Wait, she'd said.

"Wait" wasn't "stop."

"You can afford to act without thinking," she went on, "but I have to reason things through."

"Reason things through," he echoed, nonplussed.

"Whenever I'm faced with a decision, I consider the arguments for and against."

"Remind me. What decision are you facing?"

"Whether or not to allow you to kiss me."

He stared at her.

"That was your intent, wasn't it? To kiss m—" She paled in horror. "Oh, Lord. It wasn't, was it? I've misunderstood."

"No, no," he assured her. "It was my intent."

"Oh." She exhaled, and the pretty flush of pink returned to her cheeks. "That's good."

"Is it?"

"I'm not certain yet. The 'against' pile is rather large." She plucked lumps of sugar from the sugar bowl and began counting them into a heap on the worktop. "I'm your employee. You're my employer *and* a shameless rake. You're clearly trifling with me. I might lose your respect. I might lose respect for myself. I might give you the idea that I'm willing to allow further liberties—which I am not."

"I never imagined you were."

"But in the 'for' pile . . ." She gathered a cluster of sugar lumps with her right hand, adding them one by one. "If it would be just the once—"

"It would be."

"—with no further entanglement . . ."

"I despise entanglements. The mere thought of them makes me itch."

"And you must have accumulated some talent for kissing, considering your history. So I suppose I could do worse."

Hold a moment. *Worse?* He couldn't let that pass unchallenged.

He lowered his voice to a seductive drawl. "Sweeting, you'd be hard-pressed to do better."

"Precisely," she agreed, matter-of-fact. "I may as well have a pleasant experience for my first kiss."

Chase couldn't believe what he was hearing. Her first kiss? What a travesty. That lush, rosy mouth was eminently kissable.

She bit her bottom lip, as if she could sense him staring. "Goodness, I suppose it could be my *only* kiss. That's rather lowering to contemplate, but the possibility can't be discounted. Another lump in the 'for' heap, isn't it? Knowing that even if I die a spinster, I won't be an unkissed one."

He watched her slide another sugar lump into the pile. "If you truly make all your decisions this way, you must drive shopkeepers mad."

"I don't typically ponder them aloud." Her face flushed.

"Far be it from me to stop you. I have a stake in the conclusion." He plunked his elbow on the worktop and propped his chin in his hand, studying her. Her little one-person debate had him riveted. As did her fetching features when she was deep in concentration.

As many women as he'd charmed and seduced in his life, he could honestly say he had never, ever encountered a woman like this one. Her background wasn't the half of it.

She rolled a sugar lump back and forth with the tips of two fingers. He wanted to suck those slender fingers into his mouth and run his tongue over them, between them, lapping up the sweetness until she gasped with forbidden pleasure. The fantasy was so vivid, he could taste it.

Good God.

Chase straightened, cleared his throat, and rapped his knuckles against the worktop in an affable manner. "Let me know when you have your answer, then. I'm available Thursday next, if that suits."

With her eyes still trained on the sugar, she signaled for a pause. "One moment."

Naturally, the answer would be in the negative. No woman of her sense, given the opportunity to consider the matter fully, would weigh both sides and arrive at acceptance. That was why he sent his conquests spinning off guard with charm and flattery, why he dazzled them with lush surroundings and sparkling wines. Why he kept his liaisons to one night, and no more.

Because if a woman looked too close and thought too long, she would see the truth: He was a despicable, shameless cad. Alexandra Mountbatten knew it. She'd understood him from the first. Her answer would be no.

So why was he holding his breath in anticipation?

Perhaps the brandy had muddled his senses.

Or perhaps he couldn't help wondering how it would feel for a rational, clear-eyed woman to see him—truly *see* him—and still find him worth the risk.

His heart clawed up his throat and battered his eardrums, and all because a tidy little governess was taking longer than usual to reject him. Absurd. Stupid, really.

At last, she put an end to the suspense.

"I don't want you to kiss me," she said, "now that I've thought it through."

See? There it was. She was clever enough to see the black, rotted mess where his soul ought to be, and she wanted no part of it.

She lifted her tiny, delicate hand to his cheek. Not to deliver the slap he deserved, but in an exploratory caress. Her gaze drifted over his face like an apple blossom, finally coming to rest on his mouth.

"I think . . ." She wet her lips. "I think I'd rather kiss *you*."

And before Chase could begin to reckon with the shock of those words, she did.

Chapter Ten

*T*he moment she touched her lips to his, Alexandra knew she'd made a severe miscalculation. Her carefully tallied sugar lumps were merely sweet piles of lies. By insisting on taking the lead, she'd told herself she could satisfy her curiosity *and* retain control.

Control. Hah. She couldn't control something she scarcely understood. No more than a landlocked, untraveled farmer could board a Yankee clipper and set a course for the moon.

Alexandra hadn't the faintest idea how to navigate passion.

However, within moments he began to lead the way.

Her kiss became his. A series of light, teasing brushes of his mouth against hers. He tasted her upper lip, then the lower. Taking his time, as though the kiss were a puzzle. As though he found her compelling. Fascinating.

And then he nudged her lips apart and swept his tongue between them.

Oh. Oh, dear.

Alex was startled by the intrusion, reeling with sensations, but she didn't dare pull away.

To the contrary. She dared to move closer.

This was her first kiss. Good or bad, awkward or accomplished, she'd remember it for the rest of her life. But more than that, she wanted *him* to recall it, too. He'd forgotten her after their chance meeting in the bookshop. This time, she was determined to etch herself on his memory. No matter how many kisses had come before hers, or how many would come after—this one, he would remember.

No shyness. No hesitation. She meant to give as good as she received, or die of mortification trying.

As he deepened the kiss, she leaned into the embrace, sliding her hands up his shoulders until her fingertips met at the nape of his neck. He wore his hair clipped short there, and she teased her fingers through the dense fringe.

He moaned softly, and the sound was pleading. Resonant with longing. Vulnerable.

Then, with a growl, he caught her up in his arms and lifted her body against him. Her thin shift might as well have been nothing. Her toes barely scraped the floor. His tongue stroked hers in a bold, suggestive rhythm, and she couldn't catch her breath. Heat built between their bodies, welding them together. His uninjured hand gathered to a possessive fist, gathering and twisting the back of her shift.

He wasn't leading any longer, but overwhelming her instead.

Perhaps that was his intent. To hide behind intimacy. Draw her close as a way of holding her at a distance. Strange. She would have to ponder it further, once pondering was a viable option again. At the moment, his kisses were erasing her mind.

That was probably just what he desired.

Abruptly, he set her back on her feet. As they parted, her impulse was to lower her eyes and back away slowly. However, she forced herself to stand her ground and meet his gaze. She'd given it her best effort. She'd always have that much. If he found nothing memorable about this encounter, at least she would know that she'd held nothing in reserve. There was pride in that.

She searched his face for any hints of approval or disdain. His expression, however, revealed nothing but confusion.

He blinked down at her. "Christ."

As reactions went, she couldn't decide how to interpret blasphemy.

Maybe he didn't know, either.

He took her hands from about his neck, placed them back over her eyes, turned her by the shoulders, and guided her out the kitchen door. "Go back to bed, Miss Mountbatten. This never happened."

THIS NEVER HAPPENED.

Not for him, perhaps. But for Alexandra . . . ? That kiss had happened. Really, truly *happened*, in every part of her body. In the days to come, the kiss occupied almost all of her mind, as well.

She now understood why his attentions as a lover were in such great demand. All reason had deserted her when his lips touched hers. Only feeling had remained. Heat and scent and strength and taste.

He'd tasted like . . . she couldn't name it, precisely. What was the taste of a deep, masculine growl? Part brandy, part sin . . . and wholly intoxicating. Just the memory sent a languid drunkenness seeping through her limbs.

She gave her thoughts a shake.

She had to stop thinking of it and put the encounter behind her. Ever since last autumn, she'd been wondering how kissing him would feel. Now she knew, and her curiosity was satisfied. For him, it amounted to nothing. A boring evening at home.

This never happened.

She must concentrate on her duties instead. This was a brief period of employment. She had a future to finance.

"I'm hemming a handkerchief, Daisy. Would you like to join me?"

Daisy looked at her older sister. Rosamund shrugged in silent, grudging permission, as though to say, *If you must.*

"Now, then." Alex beckoned the younger girl closer. "Why don't you have a go?"

Daisy obediently took the half-finished work from Alex's hand. Her stitches were hesitant and clumsy, but Alex showered her with praise and encouragement when she reached the corner. "Well done, Daisy."

"No it's not. It's all crooked."

"But an excellent start. No one should expect perfection on the first attempt. All you need is a bit of practice. After the edges are done, I'll teach you to embroider letters. We'll begin with this one." She traced a letter in marking chalk. "Which letter is that?"

"D."

"And can you guess why I'm going to teach that one first?"

The girl smiled shyly. "Because it's for Daisy."

"Exactly so." Alex was pleased. One letter of the alphabet learned, five-and-twenty to go. She would celebrate the smallest of victories. "And once you learn to embroider, you'll be ready to take on all sorts of projects. Tablecloths, serviettes . . ."

"Serviettes?" Rosamund groaned. "Why would we embroider little flowers and monograms on scraps of cloth meant to catch spittle and dribbled soup? It's repulsive, if you think about it."

Alex had never considered it that way, but now that Rosamund mentioned it, it *was* a bit disgusting.

"It's not all embroidered serviettes," she said. "There are countless practical applications for needlework. Every girl should learn to mend a garment."

"And why don't boys learn to mend theirs?"

"Some *do* learn. It was a man who taught me to sew."

Rosamund arched an eyebrow in skepticism. "Truly?"

"Truly. I was raised on a ship. No ladies aboard."

"Tell us more," Daisy urged. "And not about the sewing. Tell us something exciting."

"What is there to tell?" Rosamund said. "She didn't meet with any mermaids."

Alex hesitated. Relating the story to Mr. Reynaud had been imprudent enough. She was supposed to be transforming these two girls into young ladies. Telling her charges about her own wild childhood would scarcely aid her goal.

And if she failed, she wouldn't be paid.

That was it, then. No tales of the high seas.

Mrs. Greeley came to her rescue. "Miss Mountbatten, you have callers. Two young ladies. They're outside, on the pavement. I would have asked them to wait on you in the drawing room, if not for the . . ." Her nose wrinkled in disgust. "The animal."

Two young ladies and an animal? That could mean only one thing.

"Thank you, Mrs. Greeley." Alex rose to her feet. "Rosamund, if I go down to visit my friends for a half hour, may I trust that I'll return to find you, your sister, and this room unscathed?"

"Don't worry. I'm still putting the final touches on our escape plan. We're not going anywhere today."

"Good." She added under her breath, "I think."

She hurried downstairs and out the front door to find her friends waiting in the center of the square. Nicola, Penny, and a nanny goat exploring the green on a collar and lead, like a lapdog out for a constitutional.

Alex flung her arms around each of them in greeting. Penny gave the most marvelously tight hugs, and Nicola always smelled like burnt sugar. Alex's heart wrenched. She hadn't realized how deeply she'd been missing her friends.

"It's so good to see you both. Why have you come?"

"Emma's had her baby." Nic held up an envelope. "The express arrived this morning."

"That, and Marigold needed a graze." Penny scratched the nanny goat between her ears.

Alex whisked the letter from Nicola's hand, unfolding it to read for herself. It was so brief, scanning the contents took but a second. "Oh, it's a boy," she said. "How wonderful. I assume he'll be called Richmond, as it's the courtesy title. There's no mention of his Christian name."

"It's a terrible letter," Nicola said. "Ashbury wrote it. Never trust a man to write about babies."

"No descriptions whatsoever." Penny sighed. "How are we to know what he looks like? Which of his parents does he favor? What about his temperament?"

"He's probably pink, wrinkly, bald, and hungry, like all new-

born babes. I doubt he's had time to declare a political affiliation."
Alex folded the letter and gave it back to Nicola. "We'll have to be
patient. Emma will write when she's well rested, and she'll tell us
every detail."

"Speaking of details," Nicola said meaningfully, "I believe a
certain governess owes us a few."

"Yes." Penny released Marigold's leash and took Alex by the
arm, dragging her to the nearest bench. "Tell us everything."

They didn't have to ask Alexandra twice. She unburdened herself of a fortnight's thoughts. She told them all about Rosamund
and Daisy. The daily doll funerals, the petty theft, and the five
accomplishments she had been given ten weeks—now eight—to
help them master.

"The poor dears are hurting," Penny said. "They need snuggles,
not lessons."

"I know. But preparing them for school is the task I've been
employed to complete. If I don't succeed . . ." Alex propped her
elbows on her knees and let her chin fall into her hands. "They've
no interest in needlework. They're immune to bribery. And how
am I supposed to teach Daisy penmanship when she doesn't even
know her letters?"

"I wish we could be of more help to you with the governessing,"
Nicola said, "but traditional ladylike accomplishments aren't our
strong points, either."

"I know," said Alex. "That's why I treasure you."

They were friends precisely because they *didn't* fit in with the
finishing school set. They were different, and unashamed of it. The
same could be said of Rosamund and Daisy. The world would try
to tell them they weren't good enough, and Alex hated participat-
ing in that effort.

Penny lunged to catch the goat's leash. "What of the Bookshop
Rake? Has he confessed his love for you yet?"

"No," Alex replied. *"No."*

"That disavowal was entirely too vehement to be believed."

"I spend my days with the girls in the schoolroom," she insisted. "I scarcely cross paths with the man."

Except for a few minutes every morning, when he holds my hand in his. Oh, and that one foolish, fumbling kiss in the kitchen.

"Come now," Penny wheedled. "We're your closest friends. If he's romancing you, you must tell."

Nicola groaned. "If he's harassing her, you mean."

"There is nothing to tell," Alex insisted. "Nothing romantic. Nothing villainous. Nothing at all."

Alex didn't even consider her statement to be an untruth. *This never happened*, he'd said. And so it hadn't. That kiss in the kitchen was the last time she would let herself be carried away. From now on, practicality reigned.

"Believe me," she insisted once more for good measure. "I'm more likely to find my future in the stars than in the arms of Chase Reynaud."

Nicola perked. "Oh, I nearly forgot." She untied her bonnet and removed it carefully, withdrawing a packet wrapped in brown paper, which she handed to Alex. "I finally got the lavender-vanilla shortbread right. Took me seven attempts, but at last I made a batch that didn't taste like soap."

Alex accepted the packet. "You carried them here in your bonnet?"

"The goat kept trying to snatch them from my hand, and Penny said she's not allowed sweets. When are you sending that animal back to the country, anyway?"

"When she's healed, of course. Marigold has sensitive digestion."

"Obviously," Nic said dryly, looking on as Penny coaxed the animal away from a half-eaten shrub. "A delicate stomach indeed."

Clutching the packet of shortbread in both hands, Alex kissed Nicola on the cheek in farewell. "Thank you. This was precisely what I needed."

"It's only shortbread," Nicola said.

Alex smiled. "Never underestimate the power of biscuits."

ONCE HER FRIENDS had gone, Alex hurried upstairs, entered the nursery, and went directly to the slate.

Seven attempts. Nicola had needed seven different attempts to make edible shortbread before she'd found success. Alex needed to follow her example. These five subjects chalked on the school-room slate weren't the right recipe for an education. They were like Nicola's first six batches of lavender-vanilla shortbread. Put together, they tasted like soap.

She wiped the slate clean. "No more maths and etiquette. We have a new set of lessons."

"What are you on about?" Rosamund asked.

"You wanted to buck all the rules, Rosamund? See the world? Be free? Then you have only one option." She wrote a single word at the top of the slate and underscored it with a thick, decisive line. "Piracy."

"Piracy?" Rosamund sounded skeptical, but intrigued.

"These are your new lessons." Alexandra wrote five topics on the board. "Log keeping. Plunder. Navigation. The Pirate's Code." She ended the list. "And needlework."

"Needlework?" Daisy made a face. "Why would a pirate need serviettes?"

"They don't. But every sailor, law-abiding or otherwise, must know how to work a needle and thread. On the open sea, no one else is going to mend a sail or darn a sock."

Rosamund's suspicion won out. "Never mind her, Daisy. It's only a trick."

Alex forged ahead, pretending not to hear her. "We'll have our own ship. Right here in the nursery. I'll be captain, of course. Rosamund, you're first mate. You'll be responsible for log keeping and the money."

"What about me?" Daisy asked.

"You," Alexandra said, crouching close, "will be our quarter-master. That means you'll ration food and water for the crew. And since we're so undermanned, you'll also take on the most important duty of all: ship's surgeon. There are oh so many diseases and maladies that afflict pirates. Scurvy, malaria, tropical fever . . ."

Daisy's eyes lit up. "Plague?"

"Yes, darling. Even plague."

Poor Millicent had rough seas ahead.

Alex stood. "What say you, Rosamund? Are you joining our crew?"

Rosamund peered at the slate. "How do you mean to teach us all those things?"

"Personal experience. From the time I was younger than either of you, I was climbing the ratlines. I know how to set a course to Barbuda, I know the worth of a Spanish *real* in shillings, and I can barter in Portuguese."

"Does our guardian know you're proposing this?"

"Not at all."

"He's not going to like it."

Alex lifted one shoulder in a shrug. "Pirates don't ask permission."

She'd been hired to teach these girls, and she meant to fulfill that duty. Her financial circumstances wouldn't allow her to do otherwise. But she was going to accomplish it on her own terms. Rosamund and Daisy needed encouragement, not etiquette. Confidence, rather than comportment.

And whether Chase Reynaud wished it or not, Alexandra would make certain they received it. She would not participate in transforming them into well-mannered, empty-headed, docile young ladies who wouldn't cause him any trouble.

She'd help them become women who couldn't be ignored.

"Well, Rosamund?"

After a pause, Rosamund set aside her book. "Very well."

Alexandra suppressed a triumphant grin. The girl was humoring her, and probably out of sheer boredom, but it was a start. "Then we have a great deal to do. To start, we'll have to rig our ship." She went to the window and yanked the curtain from its rod. Not precisely sturdy canvas, but for their purposes, it would make an adequate sail. She looked at Rosamund. "Do you know where we might find a coil of rope?"

Chapter Eleven

$\mathcal{L}$ ie back on the bed for me."

From his seat on the edge of the mattress, Barrow regarded him. "That is not in the terms of my employment."

"Just do it, will you?"

Barrow complied. "Mind, I am only doing this because it's five o'clock, and I value being on time for dinner more than I value my pride."

"No, no. Not like that. On your side, facing me. Prop yourself on one elbow and rest your head on your hand."

"Are you going to draw me like one of your French girls?"

"And keep your boots off the mattress. It's new. Finest quality a shameless rake can buy."

Barrow rolled his eyes.

"Now." Chase lifted a gilt-framed mirror and positioned it on the wall opposite the bed. "Tell me, can you see yourself?"

"Partly."

"Which parts? The good parts?"

"That's it." Barrow rolled to a sitting position. "I'm done."

"Come along, man. I can't do this by myself."

"Well, I can't run the Belvoir estate by myself. You're the one with power of attorney." He sighed and gave in. "A few inches to the left. Now up. A bit more. No, no. That's too much."

Chase strained under the weight of the mirror. "Hurry up, would you?"

"Tilt it forward a smidgen . . . There."

"Took you long enough." Chase drew a nub of chalk from his pocket and marked off the corner. Then he set the mirror down with a groan of relief.

"Now," Barrow said, "we need to discuss the land steward at Belvoir Manor. He might be a wizard with crop rotation, but he can't write a report worth sheep dung. You need to pay him a visit yourself and sort matters."

Chase checked his marks with a level, then hammered two hooks into the wall. "We have a hundred other matters needing attention. The planting's done for the summer anyhow."

"In point of fact, the planting was not yet done when I first raised the subject. In February. You've been avoiding the discussion for months."

"I have not been avoiding the discussion." He hefted the mirror again, hanging it on the hooks. "I've been avoiding my uncle."

"The duke's too ill. He won't even know you're there."

"He'll know I'm there," Chase said softly. "He always knows I'm there."

Eager to change the subject, he turned and propped his hands on his hips, surveying his handiwork. The Cave of Carnality was finally complete. Now it could start living up to its name.

"Very well," he told Barrow. "I'll make the journey to Belvoir soon."

"Excellent. I will pin a date to that promise, I hope you realize." Barrow rose from the bed, reached for his hat, and headed for the door. "But it will wait for tomorrow. I'm late getting home as it is."

"Give Elinor a kiss for me."

"The hell I will," Barrow said, shutting the door behind him. "Find your own wife."

That wouldn't be happening. But a little matrimony had never stood between him and a kiss.

God, that stupid kiss. Days ago now, and he remembered the taste of Alexandra as clearly as he recalled his own name. Fresh and sweet. Like cool water straight from a mountain stream.

Enough.

He left the retreat through the kitchen, locking the door after him, and mounted the stairs to his bedchamber, intending to change for the evening.

He hadn't even reached the first landing when a piercing cry pulled him to a halt midstep. It was followed by a blood-chilling scream. Not a girlish scream, but a womanly one—coming from the direction of the nursery.

Alexandra.

He jogged up the remaining flights of stairs, pausing on the third landing for breath. The silence was ominous.

Dear God, they'd killed her.

He took the last flight of stairs at a sprint, rushed down the corridor, and flung open the door to the nursery, steeling himself for the sight of her bloodless corpse splayed on the floor.

The scene that greeted him, however, was anything but lifeless.

"Ready the cannon."

They took no notice of his entrance. Chase used the following moments to survey the nursery. At least, it had been a nursery. He wasn't certain what it had become since Millicent's funeral early that morning.

The girls' beds had been pushed side by side, with a gap of merely a few feet between them. The curtains had been removed from the windows and strung from the bedposts. Standing amid it all, Daisy squinted into a spyglass fashioned from a discarded paper cone, and Rosamund brandished a crescent-shaped object that resembled nothing so much as a cutlass.

Millicent sat on the opposite bed, wearing a paper sailor's hat and, as was her usual, an unsettling smile.

Rosamund slashed her blade through the air. "Fire."

From behind them, Miss Mountbatten made a series of the most fantastic noises. A boom, then a whistled glissando, followed by a rumbling crash that she accompanied with a brisk shake of the bedpost.

The girls gave a rousing cheer.

"Dead-on hit to the broadside," she declared. "Bring the ship about and ready the plank."

Rosamund yanked on a curtain tie, and a white "sail" unfurled from the top of the bed frame. Meanwhile, Daisy reached for a board that looked to have been ripped from a crate and cobbled together with rope.

"Ready for boarding!"

She scrambled from one bed to the next and held the cutlass to Millicent's throat. "Hand over the plunder!"

Chase had seen enough. "Ahem."

All three of them froze. Four, if he counted Millicent. The room went silent, save for an audible gulp from Miss Mountbatten.

"What is going on here?" he demanded.

Daisy spoke first. "Millicent's been wounded." She drew the "blade" across the doll's neck. "Kerchief, please. She's losing a great deal of blood."

Chase ignored the doll's death throes and stalked across the room to have a word with his governess.

"I can explain," she said.

"You had better."

"The girls and I . . . Well, we're playing a game, you see."

"You weren't hired to play games."

"But this is an educational game."

"An education in cutlasses?"

She bit her bottom lip. "Only partly."

Her eyes flitted toward the slate, and he followed her gaze. "Piracy?" He read the word aloud with horror. "You're instructing them in *piracy*."

"It isn't how you're thinking. I—"

Chase caught her by the elbow and guided her to the far side of the room. He needed space to berate her properly. "You are meant to be teaching them to be proper young ladies."

"They're not ready to be young ladies. They're girls. They need to play, and they've forgotten how."

"They need to learn their lessons. Letters, numbers, stitching samplers with misshapen flowers and dire Bible verses."

"They *are* learning." She directed his attention to the world map on the wall, where a series of pins guided a string from England to the West Indies. "We've plotted a course to Tortuga. There's geography." From there, she walked to the slate and pointed to a stack of figures. "Calculated the length of the journey, how many days it will take. How many rations we'll need aboard. That's arithmetic. I've even taught them a bit of French."

Chase read aloud from the board. "'*Donnez-nous le butin, ou nous vous ferons jeter par-dessus bord.*' What does that mean?"

She hedged. "Hand over the booty, or you'll walk the plank."

"Millicent's dead," announced Daisy. "It will have to be a burial at sea."

Chase rubbed his temples. "Right. This little game of yours stops. At once."

"If I'm the governess, I must be allowed my own methods."

"I'm your employer. You'll do as I instruct."

"Or what? You'll hire another of the candidates queuing up for the post?" She made an exasperated gesture. "I'm succeeding where all the others have failed. How many is it you've been through again?"

"Fifteen," he replied. "But I can always find the sixteenth. London is rife with women who'll happily submit to my wishes."

"No doubt it is. I'm not one of them."

They stood locked in a stalemate. Dangerously close together. Perhaps it wasn't that he was unwilling to step aside. Maybe he didn't want her to get away.

Maybe he wanted her closer.

No sooner had the thought crossed his mind than he got his wish. He felt a tight cinch about his rib cage. She made a startled cry.

In the space of a moment, they'd grown very close indeed. Indecently close. Chest-to-chest close. And if not for a few layers of fabric . . . the kind of closeness that meant skin on skin.

God.

Baffled, he attempted a self-protective step in retreat. A force resisted. "What the devil?"

His hellion wards collapsed on the bed with laughter.

He looked down. They'd been tied together with a length of rope. Tied and knotted, it would seem. Apparently while he'd been lost in her fiery eyes, the girls had managed to loop a rope about the two of them—and then cinch it tight.

"Oh, dear."

"You little . . ." Chase wriggled, attempting to turn and chastise them. He succeeded only in craning his neck. "Come back here at once."

"Daisy, do you think there's cake in the kitchen?"

"I heard there's jam, as well."

The girls linked hands and skipped toward the door.

"Don't you dare." Chase hopped in their direction, dragging Miss Mountbatten with him. "Get back here, or I'll—"

Or he'd what? Shut them up in the nursery? Send them to bed without their tea? He'd tried all those punishments, to no avail. His well of threats had run dry.

"Rosamund!" he bellowed.

"Oh, I answer to Sam now."

"Sam? Where did this come from?"

"It's right there in my name. Ro-SAM-und."

"You can't answer to Sam. That's absurd."

"It's not absurd at all. Ask Miss Mountbatten. Her friends call her Alex. I want to be called Sam." She beckoned to Daisy. "Come along. The kitchen is just waiting to be plundered. Maybe there's custard."

They disappeared, shutting the door behind them.

Chapter Twelve

Chase strained in the bindings, attempting to wriggle loose. His movements only seemed to make the ropes tighter.

To add to the predicament, all that wriggling began creating other problems. Virile-man-with-a-functioning-cock problems.

Be calm, he told himself. This was hardly his first time dealing with an unwanted cockstand. He could coax it down.

Cricket. Think about cricket. That's what they say, isn't it?

Unfortunately, Chase didn't know much about cricket. His knowledge began and ended with heavy balls and long, rigid bats—not particularly helpful right now.

"How the devil did they manage to do this?" he asked.

"Knots were among our pirate lessons."

He rolled his eyes. "Of course they were."

"They're an essential part of seamanship," she said, as if this should be an acceptable excuse. "I'll have us out of this in a trice. They've only learned the simplest types so far, and they made the mistake of leaving me one hand to untie it." She moved her free hand along the rope lashing them together. "Now where is the knot?"

"At the small of my back, unfortunately."

She had her arm around him as far as she could reach. As if they were locked in an embrace.

"Just a little further. Aha." Her fingers traced the contours of the knot where it lay against the small of his back. "A simple reef knot. I'll have it loose in moments, if I can just . . . find the proper . . . angle."

She moved up and down, sliding along his body to angle for a better grip. If he had any hope of subduing his swelling erection, it quickly evaporated.

No cricket could save him now, unless he took a bat to the head.

ALEX FELT IT. The thick, hard ridge pulsing and growing against her belly. Her fingers froze in place. She'd already been over-whelmed by the scent and heat of him, and the solid wall of his chest. But this? The crude, unmistakable proof that he was feeling it, too? It set her brain spinning.

Thank heaven he was so tall. At least she was staring, crimson-cheeked, into his waistcoat rather than his face.

Ignore it, she told herself. *Think of celestial navigation.*

But his swelling groin proved difficult to ignore. Its size was an inconvenient wedge between them, making it even harder for Alexandra to work the knot loose. She would have a devil of a time freeing it with one hand.

"Perhaps we should talk."

"Yes," she jumped to answer. "Let's talk."

"So your friends call you Alex."

"It's simpler. Alexandra is quite the mouthful. And your friends call you Chase, I gather."

"It's Charles, properly. But ever since school, I've answered to Chase."

"Ah. So your schoolmates gave you the nickname."

"No, I chose it."

"You chose your own nickname?" She laughed to herself. "That is a bit pathetic, I'm sorry to say."

"The name didn't fit my lifestyle. Charles is dull. Chase sounds roguish. Exciting. No woman wants to cry out, 'Oh, Charles! Yes, Charles!' in bed. I mean, would you?"

"Er."

"Forget I said that."

Alexandra would try, but she doubted she would succeed.

"Tell me about your schooling," he said.

"My schooling?"

"Boring lessons, grim schoolrooms. If by chance you had any dour, dried-up, snaggletoothed headmistresses, I'd love to hear about them right now. In detail."

"My least favorite teacher wasn't dried up or ugly at all. She was quite pretty, as a matter of fact, but she would spank us for misbehaving."

"Really," he said, groaning weakly.

"A smart thwack of the ruler, straight on the backside."

"On second thought, let's not talk."

She managed to snag a fiber of rope with her fingernail. "I think I'm making progress."

"Thank God," he breathed.

"I'm not certain I can loosen it without a bit more slack. Is there any way you can press just a bit closer? A few moments, no more. All I need is a half inch."

He made a strangled noise. "If you must, but do it quickly. Otherwise we're going to move a good seven inches in the wrong direction."

"What?"

"Never mind."

Alexandra leaned in, turning her head so that her cheek rested on his chest. His chin settled atop her head, heavy and square. The hollow thump of his heartbeat drummed in her ears and echoed in her belly.

For a moment, she forgot all about the knot. And the nursery, and the children, and anything else in the world that wasn't his hard, lean male body. She was wrapped about him like a sailor lashed to the mast in a storm. And then his hand gripped her hip and pulled her closer still. As if they were lovers in an embrace.

He exhaled a shaky breath. The sigh gave her just enough space to work with. She wiggled her trembling fingers into the loop of rope, then pulled.

There. The knot was undone, and so was she.

They weren't prepared. Pressed together so closely, they had all the stability of a lawn bowls pin. The sudden release sent them toppling, and his grip on her backside meant she tumbled with him.

And landed atop him, as they hit the floor with a thud. He cushioned the fall, taking the brunt of it.

"Oof."

Alexandra levered herself on her elbows. "Are you injured?"

"No."

"But you thunked your head." She felt his skull. "Say something."

"Ouch."

She laughed, both relieved and nervous.

"Now I know what that dratted doll feels like."

"Are you hurting terribly?"

"Tomorrow I will be. At the moment, I'm fine."

"You're certain? Perhaps I should—"

"Alexandra." He cupped her chin and forced her to meet his eyes. "Enough."

Goodness. The sound of her name from his lips, in that forceful, husky voice . . . He still clutched a handful of her backside.

"I know you don't approve of the piracy game, but it's the one way I've found to reach them. Daisy's struggling with her lessons. She can scarcely read. Rosamund is so protective of her. Her instinct is to push me away rather than risk being hurt. They need patience." She paused. "More than that, they need to feel safe and loved."

"I've told you. I cannot give them that."

"You could if you tried."

"I thought you understood this from the very first day. I'm a bitter disappointment, remember. A poor excuse for a gentleman. A man incapable of understanding the consequence of stockings."

"But you're also a man who holds a little girl's hand and eulogizes her doll every morning. A duke's heir who builds cozy window seats and bookshelves by hand for his orphaned wards."

"How did you know that?"

"I guessed. Downstairs, you were hanging your own paneling. Thank you for my verandah, by the way. You're good with your hands."

"You don't know the half of it," he growled. He gathered another handful of her bottom and squeezed.

An electric thrill forked through her. After zinging wildly all over her body, the sensation settled in her nipples, drawing them to tingling points.

"See? Don't waste your time attempting to 'reform' me. It's a lost cause." He muttered, almost too low for her to hear: "I'm a lost cause."

A lost cause?

That wasn't the sort of conclusion one came to on one's own. Someone had taught him a lie, etching it not only on his mind, but in his soul. Whoever it was, Alexandra despised them—on behalf of Rosamund and Daisy, and on behalf of Chase Reynaud himself. She couldn't allow such a falsehood to pass unchallenged.

"Chase." She softened her touch, smoothing back his hair. "No one's a lost cause."

His eyes held a clash of emotions. Doubt, mixed with a desperate yearning to believe. Denial, warring against desire. Push, tethered to pull.

Don't imagine things, she told herself. In all likelihood, his eyes merely reflected the confused emotions in her own.

His grip on her bottom went firm as a decision. Her breath caught. In a flash, he'd rolled her onto her back, pinning her beneath him.

"Listen to me," he said. "If I were any sort of decent man—one who could be trusted to care about anyone other than himself—I wouldn't have a governess flat on her back, beneath me, on the nursery floor. If you refuse to believe that, I'll have to teach you a lesson."

She gave him a teasing smile. "What if I teach you one first?"

She kissed him square on the forehead.

He kissed her back, square on the lips.

And the passion of it took her breath away.

Chapter Thirteen

*C*hase kissed her forcefully, to prove what he was. There was no tenderness in it, only punishment. A good lashing with his tongue rather than a switch.

If everyone else was playing pirate, he was going to play pirate, too.

Pirates took. They seized. They plundered.

He kissed his way down her neck—her delicate, lovely neck—while he skimmed his hand the full length of her torso, tracing the contours of her body through the thin muslin of her frock. The embrace he meant to be punishing became much too tender.

"Alexandra," he whispered.

Her friends called her Alex, but he wasn't her friend. He was her employer, her superior in society, and a practiced rake. One who could ravish her right here, right now on the creaking schoolroom floor, amid the scattered books and slates and chalk.

Instead, all he wanted was to kiss her for hours. Days.

Every woman was unique, but she was just so *different*. Strange and brave and clever. She made him different, too. For once, he wanted to slow down, take time to explore and notice everything about her, rather than hide from himself.

Her tongue shyly caressed his. Each light, teasing pass was a gift. Her first tastes of passion, and she shared them with him. Freely. Sweetly.

In her arms, he could almost dream he deserved it.

No one's a lost cause.

He'd never wanted to believe anything more. But she didn't know—couldn't begin to understand—how far he'd strayed from the path of respectability.

Chase was so lost, he'd fallen straight off the map.

He broke the kiss and rose up on one elbow, needing to see her. She stared up at him with dark, glassy eyes. Her lips were plump and reddened from his kisses.

"By God, you're lovely."

Her skin warmed with a bashful glow. If she'd been lovely a moment ago, she was radiant now.

And he was in very deep trouble.

The moment was precipitously ruined by the sounds of two girls crashing up the stairs. He and Alexandra were barely able to scramble to their feet and straighten their clothing before Rosamund and Daisy barreled into the room. Each girl had a slice of cake in one hand and a jam-stuffed roll in the other.

"Boo." Daisy used her sleeve to wipe jam from her mouth. "You escaped."

"We'll practice our knots and do better next time," Rosamund told her sister.

"There will be no next time," Chase said sternly. "No more piracy." He waved expansively at the piratical decor. "In fact, tomorrow I am going to take all—"

"He's going to take all of us on an outing," Alexandra interjected.

"An outing?" Rosamund sounded incredulous.

Chase was incredulous, too.

"I thought we weren't allowed outings," Rosamund said.

"You are absolutely correct," Chase replied. "And that is why I'm—"

"He's making an exception tomorrow," she interrupted.

Oh, now *really*. This was an act of shameless betrayal.

Daisy cheered as she bounced on the bed. "Where are we going?"

Chase stood tall. "I am *not* t—"

"Mr. Reynaud's not telling." His treasonous governess spoke over him once more. "He said it's meant to be a surprise. Isn't it wonderful?"

Chase glared at her.

She smiled back.

He left the room on an exasperated curse.

Very well. If they wanted an outing, he would give them one. And it would be highly educational.

"THE TOWER OF London," Alexandra mused aloud. "A bold choice. So much rich history. We can view the crown jewels."

"Jewels are not on the schedule. I have a specific history lesson in mind."

They proceeded directly to Beauchamp Tower, where Chase—she couldn't think of him as Mr. Reynaud any longer—marched them up a spiraling stone staircase.

They emerged onto a floor shaped rather like a flower. A round space in the middle, with small alcoves sprouting from the center, like petals.

Daisy popped in and out of each alcove, skipping in circles. "What is this place?"

"It's a prison," Rosamund answered. "This middle here was for the gaolers, and those little bits you're dancing around were cells."

"How do you know?" Daisy replied.

"Because this is the Tower of London, ninny. If you don't believe me, ask the prisoners who left their marks." Rosamund pointed at letters carved into the wall. "See, here." She traced another mark, a bit higher. "And here."

"Everywhere," Daisy said, turning in place.

Hand-etched graffiti crammed every bit of stone that a man could conceivably reach. Sometimes, merely initials or a date. In other places, elaborate crosses had been chiseled in bas-relief. Bible verses stretched for yards across the walls.

"Why would they do that?" Daisy asked. "It's terribly naughty."

"They were *criminals*," Rosamund said. "They didn't care about right behavior."

"People want to leave a mark on the world," Alex said. "It's human nature. Some are remembered by their accomplishments, or their virtues. Others live on through their children." She trailed her fingers over Daisy's back as she strolled by. "And if he has none of those to leave behind, a man carves his name into the wall. We all want to be remembered."

"Oh, they were remembered—as criminals." Chase stood in the center of the room. "Do you know who ended up in a prison like this one, girls? Murderers. Traitors."

"And pirates," Rosamund finished dryly, having caught on to her guardian's lesson.

"Yes. And pirates. A few hundred years ago, you'd have been brought in through the river entrance, dragged up to one of these cells, and left to rot for a year or five. Only straw for your bed. Crusts and weak soup, no meat. You'd have been crammed in with other unwashed prisoners. Covered in filth, lice, rats, disease."

"Disease!" Daisy cheered. "Which ones?"

"Very, very boring ones," he said. "And don't *cheer*. It was misery. Now if all that wasn't bad enough, once you were convicted in court?" He drew a finger across his neck in a throat-slicing gesture.

"Beheading," Daisy said, awed.

"Right out there in the yard. That's if you were of noble birth. The rest were hung by their necks, and their heads went on pikes by the river as a warning. All the blood dripping down. Eyes pecked out by ravens."

Hands behind her back, Alex ambled over to stand by her employer. "Surely there are less gruesome ways of teaching history, Mr. Reynaud."

"Surely there are less irritating methods of teaching geography than piracy."

She had no answer to that.

"Be grateful I didn't choose an outing to the Fleet." He crossed his arms over his chest and addressed the girls. "Now. I expect that this little visit will have cured you both of your criminal behavior. There will be no further stealing, piracy, or . . . dollicide. Not unless you want a scene like this one in your future."

"In our *future*?" Rosamund looked around the ancient cell, considering. "Locked in an upstairs room, given only crusts to eat, and plagued by disease. Seems rather like the life we have now. We may as well have a few high-seas adventures while we can." She beckoned to Daisy. "Let's go see the menagerie."

Chase tipped his head back and gave an exaggerated groan of despair.

"Wait." Alex rummaged in her reticule. "You'll need a shilling each for entrance."

Rosamund rattled two coins in her hand. "Our guardian gave us the coins already." She cast a cheeky smile at his pocket. "In a manner of speaking."

Daisy skipped to follow her sister, singsong chanting all the way down the stairs.

Alex moved to follow them. She only made it two and a half paces before his deep voice arrested her progress.

"Not yet, Miss Mountbatten."

"I should follow the girls. It isn't safe to leave them without supervision."

"They're fine," he said. "Rosamund won't let Daisy out of her sight."

"Oh, I know the girls will be safe." She gave him a deceptively carefree smile. "It's the lions and tigers I'm worried about."

"You're not going anywhere." He pulled her into one of the room's stone alcoves. "I need a word."

He needed a word. Which word, she longed to know. Could it possibly be "lovely"? Because that was the only word she'd been able to think since the previous night.

By God, you're lovely, he'd said.

He called you lovely! her brain had sung. And it hadn't stopped singing ever since. *Lovely. Looov-eh-leeee. Lovely lovely lovely lovely. L-O-V-E-L-Why? Because he finds you lovely. Also, lovely.*

"I could have told you this outing wouldn't work the way you hoped."

"Since I hired you, Miss Mountbatten, nothing has gone the way I hoped."

"Try to see the positives. Rosamund and Daisy are bold, clever, resourceful girls. Even if the mischief *could* be beaten out of them—and I suspect there's a solid chance the rod would splinter first—their spirits would be broken, too. What a tragedy that would be."

"Oh, yes. A tragedy indeed."

His ironic tone didn't fool her. Alex was coming to see the fondness he harbored for his wards. If he didn't care about them, he wouldn't bother to try.

"They're *children*. They have a natural curiosity about the world, and a desire to learn. They merely need the encouragement and opportunity. The freedom to pursue their own interests. Aren't you concerned with the improvement of their minds?"

"I'm chiefly concerned with the improvement of their behavior. They must learn to move in society. My duty as guardian is to provide Rosamund and Daisy with a secure, comfortable future. A young woman's best hope at such is to marry, and marry well."

She lifted an eyebrow. "The same way your parents married well?"

"Oh, I'll make certain they do better than my father. They could scarcely do worse. But in general, yes. That is how the English aristocracy works."

"Perhaps the English aristocracy needs to do better."

He made a derisive sound. "I'm flattered you think I've the power to change the world."

"I don't think *you* have the power to change the world," she replied. "I think Rosamund and Daisy do. If given the chance."

"Is that so." He drew closer. "And how are *you* planning to change the world, Miss Mountbatten?"

"I couldn't tell you, Mr. Reynaud. At the moment, I'm too busy changing the sky."

After staring into her eyes for an eon or two, he sighed dramatically. "You are the worst example of false advertising. I was led to believe I was hiring a prim scold. Then I learn you're *remarkable* and *bold* and *interesting*."

Well, Alex thought, that stupid song in her brain had four words now.

She stammered, "I wish you wouldn't say things like that."

"I wish you didn't make me think things like that. So we're square."

"We should go after the girls."

"Yes, we should."

Neither of them moved.

Alex bit her lip. "We're going to kiss instead, aren't we."

He caught her in his arms. "You're goddamned right, we are."

Chapter Fourteen

Chase kissed her with the desperate fervor of a man going to the gallows. Grappling and moaning, pressing her into the wall at her back.

He palmed her breast—the warm, gentle swell he'd felt melting against him last night. She'd made him so damned hard then, and his cock seemed determined to outdo itself today. Her leg wrapped over his. He kissed his way down her neck—her impossibly delicate, lovely neck—until the collar of her jacket halted his progress.

He felt a twinge of conscience. Most people would think he didn't have a conscience, but he did. It surfaced about as often as the lost island of Atlantis, but he did possess one, down deep.

And it was bellowing at him now.

Then she arched her back, pressing her breast into his hand, and made a soft, pleading moan.

Conscience? What conscience? Lock the prison bars and throw away the key.

God, this place did something to him.

The infamy of centuries swirled in the air. Imprisoned ghosts rattled their chains. He felt the echoes of suffering ages past. The weight of guilt. Crushing regret. Hunger, and yearning, and loneliness. All the same miserable emotions that held him captive, late at night.

Chase had spent years locked away inside himself. And all too often, holding a woman in his arms felt like his only escape.

But this . . . this was different. Alexandra was different. This wasn't a moment he'd be wishing to erase from his memory later. On the contrary. He yearned to etch the shape of their entwined bodies into the stone, amid all the names and dates and Bible verses, and leave a mark that time couldn't erase.

What was it she'd said? *We all want to be remembered*? Well, Chase wouldn't be inventing a steam-powered phaeton. No monument would be raised to his heroics, and he'd vowed not to father any children of his own. But even if all that survived of him was this embrace, that would be a legacy he could reflect on with pride.

On this site in 1817, Mr. Chase Reynaud gave Miss Alexandra Mountbatten the most passionate, erotic, bone-melting kiss in recorded history.

As he kissed her deeply, he lifted her, parting her slippers from the floor and pinning her hips to the wall with his own. She stared at him, her lungs working for breath, eyes glassy. He reached between their bodies, finding the buttons of her jacket.

He began to undo them, slipping them free one by one. The task was easily done, and he knew the reason why. She had only the one jacket, and she'd worn it so many times that the buttonholes had gone slack. This tangible evidence of her poverty was convenient, he supposed. Many men of his station would view it as permission to make free with her favors. However, it didn't strike Chase that way. As he slipped the final button loose, he felt resentful and protective.

She deserved better. A young, unmarried woman of her class lived with the specter of danger, and a threadbare jacket made for a pitiful shield. He wanted to peel the garment from her, cast it aside, and offer himself instead.

Chase wasn't good for much, but he could stand between her body and the world.

He cupped her breast through the light muslin of her day dress. He found her nipple and rolled it beneath his thumb, teasing it to a hard peak.

"Chase."

The pleading note in her voice made him wild. He stole inside her open jacket, shoving aside the virginal white fichu, then worked his fingers beneath the muslin of her frock. He knew the layers of a woman's clothing as well as he knew his own. Better than his own, truthfully, since he had a valet to assist with his own attire.

He eased one of her frock's sleeves down over her shoulder. The strategy gave him just enough space to reach beneath her stiffened stays and linen shift. With a deft, well-practiced motion, he lifted her breast, liberating it from her stays.

Her eyes fluttered closed. She bit her lip, sealing in a gasp. He would have liked to hear her moan and cry out with pleasure. But there was something about the silence that was just as erotic, if not more.

Breathless, he cradled the soft weight in his hand. Caressing, treasuring. She was so small and slightly built. Her heartbeat thrummed like a bird's beneath his palm.

Holding her breast was like holding her heart in his hand.

And that scared the life out of him.

Guarding her body was just basic masculine impulse. But he couldn't take responsibility for her heart.

He broke the embrace with uncharacteristic brusqueness, setting her back on her feet. A bewildered look moved over her face as he rearranged her clothing. He regretted causing her any confusion or disappointment, but this time he'd gone much too far.

More accurately, he'd drawn too close.

He cleared his throat. "Alexandra, this . . ."

"Never happened," she finished. "I know." Her lips curved in a smile, but her eyes weren't in on the joke. She was hurt.

He felt small enough to disappear into a crack in the wall. Well, she couldn't be surprised. She had no illusions about the sort of man he was. Not when it came to women, anyway. She'd had ample evidence of his rakish history from the start.

Apparently, it was Chase who needed the reminder.

Very well, then. He would go out on the town, find a sophisticated, beautiful, willing woman, bring her back to his retreat, put that new mattress to the test—and rid himself of the desire to paw at the governess like a slavering hound.

And he would do it tonight.

Chapter Fifteen

"Come have a look at Mars."

It was a clear, dark night, and Alexandra had invited the girls to join her for a bit of stargazing, well past their bedtime. A lesson in celestial navigation, she called it. In truth, it was a bribe to get them into their baths and nightclothes, then brush and neatly plait their hair. The girls' hair smelled clean and fresh, and as she bent over Daisy's shoulder to help her find the red planet, she drank in the innocent scent. A tender, warm emotion spread through her chest.

In just a few weeks' time, she'd grown to care for these girls. Deeply. By helping them, it was as though she could reach back through time to her younger, newly orphaned self and clasp that girl in a hug laced with assurance. *Don't be afraid. I know it's hard now. So very hard. But you're stronger than you know, and it will all come right in the end.*

But as she wrapped her arm round Daisy's shoulders and pressed her nose to the girl's sweet-smelling crown, Alex was a little bit afraid, herself. When the girls went away to school, would anyone be there to hug and soothe them then?

"I can't make it out," Daisy said. "It's all muzzy."

"Truly? Let me see." Alex replaced her young charge at the eyepiece. "Perhaps I need to clean the lens."

Before she could take a proper view, however, they heard the sounds of a carriage drawing up alongside the house.

A quick peek out the window confirmed Alexandra's suspicions. Mr. Reynaud had rolled up to the house in his phaeton—and he wasn't alone. Light, feminine laughter floated up through the night air and swooped through the open window, uninvited. Alex wanted to swat that laughter like a pesty gnat.

"Oh, Reynaud," the lady said coyly. "You *are* a devil."

Blech.

He handed the lady down from the high-sprung carriage. As she alighted, the woman "stumbled." Mr. Reynaud caught her in his arms.

Alex rolled her eyes at the transparent ploy.

She was so distracted watching them, she hadn't realized she wasn't alone in her spying. Rosamund had swung the telescope to point down toward the street. "Enemy craft sighted to starboard. And la-di-da, isn't she a fancy one."

"Give that here." Alex took control of the telescope and had a look for herself. Once she'd adjusted the instrument, she could make out the lady as well as if they were standing mere inches apart. The woman had golden hair tucked in an elegant upswept style, and she wore a gown of deep purple satin with matching elbow-length gloves. Jewels sparkled at her throat.

Daisy leaned over the window ledge. "She's rather beautiful."

"Take care, Daisy," Rosamund murmured. "Or else Millicent might contract the pox."

Alex was aghast. "You shouldn't speak of such things," she whispered. "You shouldn't even *know* of such things."

"I've chased away every governess and been sent down from three schools, but that doesn't mean I haven't had an education." Rosamund smiled. "And you told us yourself, ten is old enough to be a ship's boy. They see a great deal more."

From the street below, Alex heard a deeply male murmur of seduction. She couldn't make out distinct words, but their intended effect was plain.

She burned with indignation. The *scoundrel.* How dare he parade his paramours directly beneath the noses of two innocent children. Well, perhaps one innocent child and one Rosamund.

"That's enough." Alex closed the telescope. "To bed with you both."

Both girls stamped and pleaded. "Not yet."

"We'll continue another evening." Alex herded them to bed. "I can't permit you to witness this, and—"

Another giggle from the street below.

Alex cringed at the sound. "I just can't. To bed with you, then."

"No." Daisy stood firm. "Are we pirates, or aren't we? Pirates don't retreat."

CHASE ATTEMPTED TO extricate himself from Lady Chawton's arms. She'd had one or three too many glasses of champagne tonight, and her embrace was all gloves and no dignity.

"I," she said in a breathy voice, "am going to do the most wicked things to your body. All. Night. Long."

"*All* night?"

"Yes."

Chase sighed. He didn't have "all night" in him. His plan had been "some of the night."

And as of this moment, he was leaning toward "none of the night."

This wasn't turning out the way he'd hoped. Winifred was beautiful, no question. Witty, too. They'd been flirting for years at balls and parties, bringing their sensual tension to a slow simmer. Yet he'd always held off on making an advance. On reflection, he supposed—and God, it was a worrisome thing to admit—he'd been saving her for a special occasion.

Or, in this case, an emergency. He had never been in such desperate need of a good, hard bout of bedsport.

Now he teetered on the brink of calling it off. He just wasn't in the mood, for some reason.

No. For *one* reason.

A small reason, really. One with black hair and eyes that swallowed up rooms. A reason possessing the most tender touch he'd ever known and a voice that curled softly in the air, like smoke.

"Reynaud?"

He snapped to attention.

Winifred pouted. "Do let's go inside." She snuggled closer and gave a dramatic shiver. "It's cold."

The night was unseasonably warm, even for July.

"Perhaps you're taking a chill, darling." He motioned for the groom to remain, rather than leading the team back to the mews. "If you're ill, I'd better see you home. We can do this another night."

"Don't be a bore." She looped her arms around his neck and swayed like a pendulum in his arms. A pendulum on opiates. "You've kept me waiting a long time for this. Far too long."

"Then what are a few days more? The waiting will make it all the sweeter." He tried to peel her gloved fingers from the back of his neck, but just when he'd worked one hand free, the other clamped down. He began to wonder if her purple gloves were adorned with octopus suckers.

"What a cruel tease you are." She leaned forward, falling against his chest, and whispered vampishly in his ear. "Be careful, or I'll tease you back." With a satin-gloved finger, she traced the whorls of his ear. A pleasant enough sensation, but it didn't precisely send lust bolting to his groin. Then she slipped her finger *in* his ear. All the way to the knuckle. Probing and wiggling.

She murmured, "Do you like that, you naughty boy?"

Actually, no. No, he didn't.

He batted her hand away, and her finger dislodged from his ear canal with a popping sound.

That was enough. The evening was over.

First, Winifred was drunk.

Second, her sexual overtures were decidedly strange. Chase didn't mind strange. In other times and other places, he'd enjoyed far stranger. But not tonight.

Third, and most importantly, he couldn't get Miss Mountbatten out of his mind. Oh, he could coax himself to *try* panting and sweating her out of his bloodstream. But that wasn't his style. Chase liked to think he possessed too much respect for women to make love to one while thinking of another. He had too much pride, as well. Halfhearted encounters would tarnish his reputation—one he'd polished to a glossy sheen with hands and lips and tongue.

He put his hands on her shoulders and pushed, applying just enough force to put distance between them. "Listen, Winifred—"

She shushed him by putting a finger to his lips. The same finger that had mere moments ago been knuckle-deep in his ear. "Not another word until we're inside, naked, and I have my mouth on your—"

Chase would never learn precisely where Winifred meant to place her mouth. Before the lady could finish her thought, she gave a shriek piercing enough to cut glass, and he found himself sputtering with shock.

Cold. That was the first decipherable sensation.

And after cold, wet.

A deluge of water had sloshed over them both. He slicked his hair back with both hands and looked up. He spied Rosamund and Daisy hanging over the window sash far above. Each girl held an empty bucket in her hands.

"Ever so sorry!" Rosamund called down. "We needed to bail out the bilgewater."

"Too many rats," Daisy added, hand cupped around her mouth. "There's plague aboard."

"Oh, those little . . ." Chase completed the thought with a growl. They had better run and hide, or he would show them the meaning of *plague*.

Winifred hadn't ceased shrieking. Her once-artfully arranged golden ringlets were now plastered to her face, obscuring her eyes. She swiped at them with gloved fingers, all the while vibrating with shock.

Chase saw his narrow window of advantage, and he took it. He shook his arms free of his topcoat and draped it over her shoulders, turning her to face the phaeton. To the groom, he said, "Lady Chawton will return home at once."

What with the added weight of water, and her unwillingness or inability to assist, it took Chase and the groom several failed attempts and a final *one-two-three-heave!* to boost poor Winifred into the phaeton. Chase fought back clouds of purple satin and netting, stuffing them into the coach and slamming the door.

The groom took the driver's seat, and Chase gave the lady's address. "Lovely spending time with you," he called out, raising a hand in farewell.

Then he turned on his heel and jerked open the door.

Four flights of stairs. Chase stomped on each riser with deliberate, ominous slowness, giving those hellions time to hear him coming and quake with mounting dread. "Rosamund and Daisy Fairfax!" he bellowed. "Pack your things for Malta!"

However, he never made it as far as the nursery. Just as he reached the third-floor landing, he found his march of doom intercepted.

By Miss Alexandra Mountbatten.

Chapter Sixteen

*H*e looked like a wet cat, Alex thought. A wet, angry, ferocious, wild, and very, very large cat. Such as a tiger or a lion or a jaguar or—

"Miss Mountbatten," he snarled. "Kindly step aside."

"Wait." She stretched her arms from the banister to the wall, obstructing his progress. "It wasn't their fault."

"Not their fault?" He flung a gesture at the ceiling, spraying her with water. "Are you telling me this is a mystery? That some unknown culprits are at large? Well, let me call in the Bow Street runners."

Alex retracted her arm barrier and wiped the anger-propelled droplets from her face.

"Rosamund and Daisy were hanging out the window," he went on. "Holding pails. It was, most assuredly, their fault."

"Yes, but only partly. I was there, and I didn't stop them."

"You didn't stop them." He pronounced each word as a separate count in a list of felony charges.

"No, I didn't. Because I—" Her courage faltered.

Because I was jealous. Irrationally, unspeakably envious in a way that made my toes catch fire.

"Because I believed you deserved it," she said, lifting her chin. "How dare you conduct your amorous liaisons right under their noses."

"That's none of your concern."

"The children are my concern. Don't think they don't know you bring women into that . . . libertine lair."

"Libertine lair? Oh, that's a new one." He brushed past her, stalking down the corridor and disappearing into what she supposed must be his own bedchamber.

After a moment's hesitation, Alex followed him, charging through the door and shutting it behind her. They were a full two floors below the nursery and at the opposite end of the house—but she lowered her voice anyway. "We're not finished discussing this."

"There's nothing to be discussed. I *know* I'm a terrible guardian. I *know* this house is a masonry monument to scandal. That's why I employed you. You're meant to teach them proper behavior. Not plague me."

"*Plague* you? When have I plagued you?"

"Aside from right now?" He tussled with his waistcoat buttons. "Only every hour of the day and night since you walked through my door."

"I can't imagine what you mean."

He gave her a skeptical look. "Really. So all that rolling around on the schoolroom floor and groping in the Tower of London didn't give you the slightest hint."

Alex was coming to recognize his strategy—revealing his naked desire in an attempt to hide his heart and soul. She wouldn't be fooled this time. "You said . . ."

"I know what I said." Swaggering strides brought him close. "I said the thought of seducing you would never cross my mind." He swept aside her plaited hair and bent to whisper darkly in her ear. "I lied."

He retreated. She was rooted to the floor.

"The thought had crossed my mind before I even made you that promise. And since then, so many thoughts have crossed my mind, my brain is the Charing Cross of filth. A riot of lewd fantasies. You're naked in nearly all of them, and ever since a certain incident in the schoolroom, a fair number feature ropes."

Well, then.

Alex needed a moment to recover from that.

Perhaps two moments.

Or a year.

But he didn't allow her another second.

"Why do you think I brought Winifred home? I thought I could purge a certain governess from my mind." He cursed under his breath. "And see how well that worked. I can't even muster the decency to drive you from this room."

Alex's mind reeled. He'd been thinking about her that much, and in that way? She didn't dare plumb the meaning behind it. Instead, she said, "This plan of yours doesn't sound very fair to Winifred."

"Yes, I realized that." He flung aside his unbuttoned waistcoat and pulled his damp shirt over his head, tossing it on the heap. "I was on the verge of sending her home when the girls doused me with"—he swept his hands down his muscled, glistening torso—"whatever this is."

"Leftover bathwater."

"Whose bathwater?"

She bit her bottom lip at the corner. "Mine."

He laughed bitterly. "Of course. Of course it would be yours. I knew I smelled orange-flower water."

Orange-flower water. He knew her *scent*?

Don't make anything of it, she told herself. Naturally, he knew her scent. He likely recalled the scent of every woman he encountered, in the same way a wine merchant could taste cherries or lavender in a bordeaux. One of those talents gleaned from vast and varied experience.

"I suppose I now understand how you can be so callous about your wards," she said. "Given the way you carry on with women, you doubtless have a dozen illegitimate children you're ignoring, too."

"You're wrong. I do not."

He snagged a towel from the washstand and gave his hair a good rubbing. Alex gawked, transfixed by the way his arm muscles bunched and flexed.

"How could you be certain you have no offspring?"

"Because I am excessively careful not to create any."

"No sponge or French letter is that effective."

"Which is why I don't rely on them. I simply don't put myself in that position."

"What position?"

"Any position that requires insertion of my . . ." He waved vaguely toward his loins. ". . . male member."

"Male *member*. Are we discussing a Masonic society, or are you referring to the penis?"

He stared at her.

"We are adults. If you're going to discuss such matters, you may as well use the proper words. I would never have supposed you to be prudish."

"I'm not *prudish*. I'm protecting your delicate feminine sensibilities."

"I never acquired many of those. And considering that it was pressed up against me the other day, I should think we've moved beyond euphemisms. So go on, then. We were discussing your penis."

He set his jaw and stepped toward her. "Since you're so fond of bold language, we are discussing my cock. And the fact that I never thrust it ballocks-deep in a woman's tight, wet cunny. *That* is how I'm certain I have no bastards in the world."

She was shocked into silence for a moment. Shocking her was, of course, what he'd intended. The entire scene was scandalous in the extreme—a governess, alone with the master of the house, in his bedchamber, while he was bared to the waist—and he knew it. He wanted her to feel intimidated. He wanted to avoid her questions, and possibly his own answers, too.

With a smile and a bow, he crossed to a low cabinet and withdrew a decanter of brandy.

"You—" She shook her head in bemusement. "You can't mean to say you're a virgin."

"No, I don't mean to say that. I had my share of indiscretions when I was younger." He paused to pour brandy into a glass. "But not anymore."

The low timbre of his voice seeped into her bones.

"I live by one rule," he went on. "No attachments. I don't keep mistresses. I won't risk siring bastards. I refuse to make myself a slave to mercury cures, either. Because inevitably, whether I deserve it or not, the Libertine Lair will become the Duke Den. I'm a poor excuse for nobility, but the least I can do is keep the estate unencumbered by bastards or blackmail, and keep myself free of the pox. So I refrain from—"

"Intercourse."

"Fucking. Yes." He downed a swallow of brandy. "If you think I've taken you into confidence, don't flatter yourself. My abstention is no secret. Why do you suppose I'm so popular with ladies? I've cultivated other talents."

"What other—" She caught herself, but it was too late. Her ignorance had been exposed. Much like his bare, sculpted chest.

"So, the governess has a few delicate sensibilities after all. There are other ways to give and take pleasure, Alexandra. A great many ways." His gaze swept her. "Shall I teach you a lesson?"

Without taking his eyes from her, he drained the last of his brandy.

Alexandra found that her reserve of courage was similarly drained. She didn't know where to look. Her gaze kept landing in the worst possible places. The heap of his discarded clothing. The closed door. The bed.

"Daisy needs spectacles," she blurted out.

And then she turned and fled.

Chapter Seventeen

"The girl ca—" Daisy stopped and tried again. "The girl cat-cheese . . ."

"Catches," Alex gently corrected.

"The girl *catches* the fish."

"Very good, darling. Go on."

Now that she'd been fitted for spectacles, Daisy was flying through her primers. Her mind had connected the letters and sounds long ago. She simply hadn't been able to *see* them.

The primers *had* needed a bit of editing. As originally written by a certain Mr. Browne—who suffered an appalling lack of imagination—the boys did everything interesting and the girls never left home.

Nothing that a few snips of the shears and a couple dabs of paste couldn't manage.

Daisy turned the page. "The boy wa-shes the dish."

"Excellent."

Rosamund was making strides, too. Or if not making strides, at least she'd stopped mulishly blocking the road. The girl had already been a voracious reader, and her command of numbers was well beyond her years. She scarcely needed any lessons. What she needed were the sorts of things she'd never ask for and only would occasionally, grudgingly accept. Things like praise and warm pats on the shoulder. Alex was still working up to hugs.

All in all, she was encouraged. There was still a great deal to accomplish by summer's end, but both Rosamund and Daisy were on their way.

And then there was Chase.

His amorous liaison with Winifred may not have come to fruition, as it were, but it seemed to have had the intended effect. Chase now avoided Alex with unqualified success. Save for the perfunctory morning condolences (scrofula being the latest ailment to claim poor Millicent's life), she hadn't seen him in a week.

Therefore, neither had the girls.

Rosamund and Daisy could memorize the encyclopedia, and they still wouldn't truly be ready to leave for school—not unless they knew they had a loving home to come back to. There was only one person who could give them that. And when that person wasn't working with Mr. Barrow, he was hammering at something in his Rake Room.

Alex knew they had an undeniable attraction, but she couldn't be so irresistible as *that*. Perhaps she could find some way to render herself entirely undesirable. Daisy might have a noxious skin condition to recommend.

"What's this?" Daisy twisted on Alex's lap. She plucked at the ribbon tied about Alex's neck and pulled the beaded cross pendant out from beneath her fichu. "You never take it off."

"The beads were a gift from my mother." Alex untied the ribbon from behind her neck. "You may look, if you wish."

Daisy ran her fingers over the tiny red beads. "Why aren't they on a proper chain?"

"Governesses can't afford gold chains."

Nevertheless, Alex kept them as secure as possible—individually knotted, on a ribbon that she faithfully replaced every three months, lest it fray.

"They're *corales*," she told Daisy. "Red coral beads. Where I was born, mothers make a bracelet of them and tie it around their baby's wrist." She reached for Millicent and demonstrated, wrapping the ribbon around the doll's arm where the carved wooden hand met the batting-stuffed arm. "Like so. It's for protection."

"Protection?" This skeptical inquiry came from Rosamund. Apparently, she'd been paying attention from across the room. "Protection from what?"

"From all sorts of terrible things. Sickness. The evil eye. An *aswang*—that's a witch. There are all manner of fearsome creatures. Take the *manananggal*."

"Magana-what?"

"*Manananggal*." Alex made her voice dark and mysterious. "She's a lady vampire who can cut herself in two. Her legs remain rooted in the ground like a tree stump, and the rest of her flies out into the night. Her intestines unwind like a string behind her, and she goes hunting for mothers and their children. She lies on the roof of a house, and uses her long, long tongue to reach her sleeping prey, probe down their throats, and suck out their blood."

"I shan't be frightened of those," Daisy said. "The intestine is only twenty-six feet long, and the Philippine Islands are much farther away than that. No mana-thinggum could possibly reach us."

"Perhaps not."

"I have a necklace from my mother, too." Daisy scampered to the trunk that served alternately as treasure chest and Millicent's burial vault. Rosamund looked on, wary, as her sister sifted through the contents and retrieved a small, gilded box inlaid with French motifs painted on porcelain.

Once she'd returned to the bed, Daisy opened the box and drew out a gold pendant on a slender chain. "Here."

"Oh, that's lovely," Alex said.

"It's a locket," Daisy said proudly. She picked open the latch to display a painted miniature. "That's Mama."

Alex took the pendant in her hand, holding it closer for examination. "How beautiful she was."

"Oh, yes. She was *very* beautiful. She was brilliant at singing and cards. And clever, too. She always knew just how to make you feel better, if you had a stomachache or cough."

"It would have been better if she hadn't known," Rosamund said.

"Why would you say that?" Alex asked.

"That's how she caught her death. She was helping nurse the neighbor's boy when he was ill with the putrid throat. He got better, but not before making her sick. She wasn't so very clever after all."

"She *was*," Daisy retorted angrily.

"She ought to have never gone. Anyone could see what would come of it. It was stupid of her."

"Rosamund," Alexandra said gently.

Daisy jumped to her feet. "You can't say that. Take it back."

"I shan't take it back." Rosamund tossed aside her book and stood. "It's the truth. Mama was stupid and reckless. She cared more about mending the neighbor boy than she cared about staying alive for us."

"That isn't so," Daisy yelled through tears. "You're mean and spiteful and I hate you."

"Well, I hate *her*." Rosamund tore the necklace from Daisy's hand and threw it across the room. It bounced off the wall and clattered to the floor. She stood there for a moment, breathing hard and staring at the wall. Obviously struggling not to cry.

Alex approached her gingerly. "Rosamund."

"Don't." The girl flinched, recoiling from the touch. "Don't touch me. Leave Daisy alone, as well. Don't pretend to mother her. You're leaving at the end of the summer. And when you've gone, we won't miss you at all."

Rosamund ran from the room. Daisy had retreated to a corner, where she curled her knees to her chest, buried her head in her arms, and sobbed.

Alex wanted to soothe them both, but she knew well from her own youth that the loss of parents couldn't be healed with biscuits or hugs. The girls needed time, and they needed to know they were safe. Safe to rage or shout or cry, without being told to hush. With her, they needn't pretend they weren't hurting inside. If nothing else, she could give them that—for a few more weeks, at least.

She found the locket and turned it back and forth in her hands. Thankfully, it appeared undamaged from its disastrous flight across the room. The hinge had been tweaked, but she was able to bend it back in place with a bit of gentle manipulation. After replacing the necklace in the French inlaid box, she returned it to the trunk at the foot of the bed. In digging for her treasure, Daisy had made quite a jumble of the playthings and blankets that filled the chest. Alex pulled it all out, planning to fold, sort, and organize the contents as she replaced them.

When she reached the bottom of the trunk, however, she found a mysterious bundle, roughly the size of a teapot. It had been tightly wrapped in oilcloth and bound with a length of twine.

Which was tied with a cat's-paw knot.

Alexandra ran her fingers over the twine, considering. Children needed privacy, just as adults did. Poking through the girls' secrets could damage what fragile trust they'd built. She decided to replace the bundle beneath the other contents, close the trunk, and say nothing about it.

And then she changed her mind.

An anxious weight had settled in her stomach, heavy enough to pin her to the floor. She wouldn't rest easy until she learned what was in the bundle.

With a quick look over her shoulder, she picked apart the knot with her fingernail and carefully unfolded the oilcloth. What she found inside made her heart wrench.

Everything two girls might need, should they wish to run away.

Money, chiefly. Alex did a quick counting, and the total was above ten pounds. That was an impressive number of coins, no doubt pilfered one by one from Chase's pockets and carefully hoarded over the months.

Oh, Lord. Rosamund was always making quips about her "escape plan," but Alex had believed her to be joking. The preparation reflected in this bundle was serious indeed.

Aside from the purse, Alex found a tiny book of coaching timetables, maps of London and England, a flint and tinderbox, a pocket knife, a ball of twine, and a compass. The same compass that had gone missing a few weeks ago. Apparently, it hadn't gone missing at all. It had joined the rest of Rosamund's cache.

Last, she found a simple sewing kit. Needle book, thread, and a small pair of shears. Her lips curved in a bittersweet smile. At least she'd convinced Rosamund of the value of needlework.

Alex hastily remade the bundle, careful to replace the objects as she'd found them, and tied the twine with an identical knot. She reburied the packet at the bottom of the trunk and closed it.

One thing was clear. She would have to redouble her efforts with Chase. She didn't want to betray Rosamund's fragile trust by telling him about the bundle, but there was more at stake here than he knew. Rosamund was capable and determined, and if she decided to take Daisy and run away, no headmistress would be stern enough to prevent them, nor quick enough to track them down. They had squirreled away enough money to take them anywhere in England. Possibly farther.

If Chase wasn't careful, sending the girls to school could mean losing them. Forever.

Chapter Eighteen

*W*ith a satisfying *whack*, Chase drove home the final nail.
There.

He pulled his shirt over his head and used it to mop his face before casting it aside. Then he stood back to admire his work.

His gentleman's retreat was, at long last, complete. Ready to be christened. By this point, he'd been presented with a myriad of options for its title: Cave of Carnality, Libertine Lair, Rake Room, Passion Palace.

Lately, it had been the Self-Pleasure Sanctum. He'd shared it with no one but his hand since Alexandra Mountbatten arrived in this house. To be truthful, even on those occasions when he satisfied himself, she was still there—in spirit. In fantasy.

It was as if the moment she'd strolled through that door, her dark hair neatly pinned and a weathered satchel in hand, she'd claimed the place. As he looked around at the products of several weeks' labor, the space that was meant to have hosted a succession of meaningless encounters . . . it had meaning.

There was the chair where she'd been sitting while she enumerated the many deficiencies in his character.

There was the stretch of paneling he'd been hanging when he sliced his thumb and surprised her in the kitchen, and she'd given him the most stirring kiss of his life.

There was the glassware rack he'd pieced together on a night when he'd been aching with want, lost in fantasies of tying her naked to a bedpost mast and licking her body from bow to stern.

She was in every nook and niche of this room. He was having difficulty imagining sharing it with any other woman. If he didn't act soon, the Den of Deviance would be boarded up before it had even opened for visitors.

Alexandra, Alexandra. What the hell am I going to do with you?

Nothing, of course. He couldn't do anything with his tempting little governess, and that was his bloody problem.

Someone rapped at the door. When he didn't answer it directly, the rapping became pounding. Whoever was standing out on the street sounded equally as desperate as Chase felt. He made a vow to himself in that moment.

If the person on the other side of that door was a willing woman, Chase was going to haul her inside and make hot, sweaty love to her. End of discussion.

When he opened the door, he was instantly reminded why he should never, ever make vows.

The woman standing on the other side of the door was Alexandra.

"Do you have company?" she asked.

He shook his head.

"Good."

She entered without waiting for his invitation, breezing past him and into the center of the room. "So sorry to intrude. I went out on the green to track a celestial object that was passing out of my view upstairs. In my haste, I locked myself out of the house. The night is unusually cold. Thank goodness you were awake." She looked around her. "And alone."

She wore only her nightclothes, and her arms were crossed over her chest to soothe her shivering. Good Lord, he'd seen her in her shift entirely too many times. All he could think of was seeing her out of it. He'd spent days struggling to banish this fantasy from his mind, and it was all for nothing in the end. She stood before him, a dream come to life, and he was seized with desperation to take her in his arms and hold her tight, lest she vanish.

He plucked a blanket from the chaise longue and wrapped it about her shoulders, in the interests of self-preservation.

"So was it a comet?" he asked.

"Not this time, I'm afraid." She hesitated, looking him over. "I'm glad to see you."

His heart made an embarrassing, giddy flip.

"We haven't spoken in some time," she said. "And the girls have been missing you."

"Is that so?" he said in a low, flirtatious drawl. "And you, Miss Mountbatten? Have you been missing me, too?"

She looked away, flustered.

He was a coward, burying that question beneath jaded swagger when he secretly longed to hear the answer. For his part, he'd been missing her intensely.

She turned her gaze about the room. "My goodness. You've been busy, haven't you? So many improvements. Have you done all the labor yourself?"

He shrugged modestly. "Most of it."

All of it, but he didn't want to sound as eager for her admiration and approval as he felt. He'd been telling himself he'd done all this building to take his mind off her, and now he wondered if he'd been telling himself a lie. Maybe he'd done it *for* her. Not to seduce her, but to impress her. She'd complimented his carpentry, after all. Even named it as one of his redeeming qualities.

You're good with your hands.

Her gaze landed on the hammer and nails he'd just set aside, and she walked toward his just-finished project—a wide, tall cabinet with two shuttered doors.

"Is this a new wardrobe?" She put her hand on one of the door handles.

Bloody hell.

"Alex, wait." He lunged forward just as she gave the handle a pull, catching her in his arms and drawing her to the side. Just in time. The contents of the cabinet fell forward as designed, spilling into the center of the room and landing with a crash.

His heart pounded from the urgency of whisking her to safety. It pounded even harder from the thrill of holding her in his arms.

She didn't seem in a hurry to leave his embrace. Instead, she stared at the room's new centerpiece and gave a little laugh. "Oh, my. Now that is impressive."

ALEX WAS AWESTRUCK.

A bed.

Really. A secret, stashed-away *bed*. This was beyond antlers, beyond bawdy house paintings and velvet draperies. He'd tucked a mattress and bed frame in the cabinet, standing it on end so that when the doors were opened, the bed folded down from the wall—ready for use.

It was ingenious in its sheer depravity.

His strong arms remained about her. She probably ought to express some thanks for his swift move to save her from being crushed by the thing. But at the moment, she was too transfixed by his invention. Extricating herself from his embrace, she strolled around the perimeter of the bed, peeking under the frame and investigating the mechanics.

"Did you devise this yourself?"

"I'm not the first to think of a folding bed, if that's what you mean—but I made my own customizations for this one."

"Where did these wooden legs come from? The cabinet's not deep enough to fit them."

"They're tucked under the bed frame. When the bed is lowered, they unfold to support it."

"Remarkable. And it's even made up with bed linens." She trailed her fingertips over the satin sheets. When she came to the end of the bed, she peered at the back of the cabinet. "Oh, look. There's a mirror. You truly are shameless, aren't you?"

"Never claimed otherwise." He moved behind her, stepping into the reflection. "There's meant to be a strap to secure the thing. Keep that sort of accident from happening. But I hadn't installed it yet. I only completed the thing today."

If he'd only completed it today, and he didn't have company tonight . . . that meant the bed hadn't yet been used.

Good.

The thought of him occupying this bed with another woman made her tremble with envy.

She wanted him for herself.

There was no denying it any longer. Only deciding what—if anything—she meant to do about it.

Alex regarded herself in the mirror, consulting her conscience. In years to come, her memory of the next few moments would either be cause for pride and satisfaction, or a source of profound regret. One way or another, her life would be altered forever.

"The other night, in your bedchamber . . ." She turned to face him. "You told me there were many ways to give and receive pleasure. A great many ways."

He nodded slowly. "Yes."

She steeled her nerve. "Teach me a lesson."

As Chase stared at her, Alex's nerve endings tied themselves into knots. Individually. By the time he finally spoke, she was nothing but human carpet fringe.

"You can't mean that," he said.

"Before you argue, let me assure you—I've thought it all through."

He looked dazed. "But of course you have."

Alex navigated around him and went to the well-stocked bar. "Let's count the advantages." She slid a whisky decanter toward one end of the counter. "There's too much tension between us. If we can dispel it, why shouldn't we? We're both adults." She sent a bottle of champagne to join the whisky. "You're frustrated"—a jug of apple brandy—"and I'm curious."

He had no response.

"You said yourself, you're scrupulous about preventing conception and disease. That does away with those risks on my end." She moved a few more bottles to join the rest, then stood back. "Look at the tally. The conclusion is obvious."

He blinked at the row of bottles and decanters. "What I'm concluding here is that I should send you to bed and then get roaring drunk."

"Don't be absurd. I can't think of any disadvantages at all, unless . . ." She gave him a coy look and pushed a wine bottle toward the "against" direction. "It might be bad?"

With a huff, he crossed to the bar, grabbed the wine bottle, and plunked it down solidly among the "for" arguments. "It would *not* be bad."

"Or maybe . . ." She reached out and nudged the bottle back toward the negative side. "Maybe you don't want me. I know you could have your choice of lovers."

"Bloody hell." His hand closed over hers in an iron grip, keeping the bottle in place. "You know that's not the source of my hesitation. I haven't wanted any woman with the fierceness I've been wanting you. Not in . . ."

She clung to the end of that sentence by her fingernails. Not in what?

Not in weeks? Not in months? Not in years, decades . . . a lifetime?

Instead of finishing the thought, he left her hanging. Impossible man.

He released her and ambled to the other side of the room. "Alex, lovemaking is something you should explore with a husband. Or at least with someone you love."

"But *you're* not married. *You're* not in love."

"No, and I don't intend to be."

"Then why are liaisons acceptable for you, but not for me? It can't be because I'm a woman. You take women as lovers all the time."

"Not inexperienced women."

Inexperienced? Now that was too much. She'd endured more in her lifetime than he could possibly imagine.

"You don't know what I've experienced in my life. Just because I'm a virgin, that doesn't mean I haven't lived. I've earned the right to make my own choices, thank you."

He rubbed his face with his hand.

Alex went to him. "I know there'll be no promises," she whispered. "I don't expect them."

"You *should* expect them." His arm tightened around her waist, and his intent gaze swept her face before settling on her lips. "You deserve them. I've been shameless, letting you squander your first tastes of passion on me. Someday you'll meet a man who has it within him to promise you the world. And the moon and stars and a few comets, too."

Curious that he should mention comets. At the moment, her heart threatened to burst from her chest and blaze a flaming arc across the sky.

"Well . . ." She made a show of looking about the room, craning her neck to search the corners. "Unless you see that man standing about, I'm content to be with you."

"Alex . . ."

Undeterred, she swept a touch along his cheek, treasuring the dark growth of whiskers there. Then, turning her hand over, she laid the backs of her fingers to his neck. In her best attempt at playing the seductress, she traced them downward in one long, sinuous, unbroken caress, past his Adam's apple and down through the notch carved at the base of his throat.

By the time her fingers reached his breastbone, she'd reached the end of her bravado, too.

His heart pounded fiercely beneath her touch. Breath rose and fell in his chest. The rest of him remained so quiet and still, Alex's insides began to quiver with doubt.

Please, she silently begged. *Take the reins. Make the next step. Don't force me to crawl farther out on this limb.*

After an eternity, it seemed her choices were to act or spend the rest of her life staring numbly at the dark, flat circle of his nipple.

She summoned the last of her courage and lifted her head. "Cha—"

His mouth fell on hers before she could even complete the syllable. As his hand fisted in her hair and drew her into the kiss, sweet relief melted through her bones.

Breaking away, he loomed over her, filling her vision with his raw, masculine presence. She couldn't see anything else at all.

Only him.

When he spoke, his voice was so perilously deep it needed a fence and a warning signpost. "If it's a lesson in pleasure you truly want . . ."

"It is."

"Then it's a lesson you'll get."

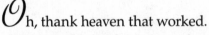
Chapter Nineteen

*O*h, thank heaven that worked.

In a single, fluid motion, Alex found herself swept off her feet and deposited on the bed. He laid her down on her back, and then he joined her, stretching out on his side and propping himself on one elbow.

"As I told you, there are a great many ways." He nuzzled her neck and ran his fingertips from her wrist to her elbow. "Perhaps you've discovered one or two of the ways yourself. In bed, in the dark, with your hands beneath your shift. Or in that orange-flower-scented bath, with no shift at all. Exploring all your body's secrets, learning where the pleasure gathers and how it breaks."

She nodded, dizzy with sensations.

"It's different," he murmured, "when the touch belongs to another. Anticipation lays a fuse through your veins. The slightest caress is a spark."

Good Lord. That was one lesson Alex didn't need. He'd scarcely touched her, and she was ready to explode.

His hand settled on her belly. "If you wish me to stop at any time, you've only to say it. Do you understand?"

She couldn't respond. She couldn't breathe.

"Alexandra." He tilted her gaze to his. "When I ask a question, it needs an answer."

Somehow she managed to nod. "I understand."

"Good." His gaze dropped to her breasts, glassy with desire. His murmured words sounded miles away. "Good."

His hand, strong and callused from work, claimed her breast. Kneading and shaping her through the thin veil of her shift. He pulled the fabric tight, and her dark, hardened nipple stood out in relief.

He dipped his head, swiping his tongue over the aching, needy peak. She gasped with the keenness of the sensation.

As he shifted his hand to her other breast, he dropped hot kisses on her lips, her neck, her ear. "I have to see you." His whisper stirred her hair. "Alexandra. Let me see you."

She nodded.

He raised his head, gazing down on her as he plucked at the buttons down the front of her shift. The first slipped free easily. He pressed an openmouthed kiss to the patch of skin he'd revealed.

When his fingers moved on to the second button, however, he stilled. "I have a better idea."

"You do?"

He rose up on his knees beside her, hooked his thumbs into a gap between the lowermost buttonholes—and yanked, ripping the two sides of her shift apart. Buttons went flying.

She stared up at him. "Why?"

"So I can buy you a new one. One that's warmer, finer. As lovely as the woman who wears it." He pushed the ruined garment down her shoulders. "Besides, I've always wanted to do that."

"It was rather arousing, I must admit."

The curl of his lips was wolfish. "Good. Because I have no regrets." His gaze roamed her exposed breasts, making her tender flesh ripple and quiver. "God, you're beautiful."

Instead of stretching alongside her, this time he lowered himself atop her. He weaved his legs with hers, pressing a broad, muscled thigh directly against her sex. As pleasure jolted through her, Alex gasped.

Suddenly, he was everywhere. Licking and suckling her breasts, drawing a hand down her body to gather the hem of her chemise, rubbing his thigh against her cleft in an exquisitely maddening rhythm. Desire raced through her body like a pack of wild, hungry beasts. No part of her was safe. She had nowhere to hide.

It occurred to her, rather belatedly, that perhaps she ought to be doing something, too. She slid her hands to his shoulders, clutching him tight.

Then he slowed, easing his weight from atop her body and sliding one hand under her shift. His fingers climbed the trembling slope of her inner thigh, dragging the frail linen with them.

As he moved his hand to her center, his gaze held hers. His fingertips brushed—lightly, gently—along her cleft.

Oh, sweet heaven above.

He explored her with that same light, gentle touch. Not invading her body, but waiting for its soft, wet invitations. His thumb covered the swollen bud that was the center of her pleasure, and she felt his fingertip ease inside her.

Alex tensed and made a faint, whimpering sound of bliss.

He paused. "Still a yes?"

She bit her lip and nodded. "Yes."

Yes.

He watched her responses so intently, she grew self-conscious and had to close her eyes. In the dark, her awareness narrowed to that sweet, pulsing pleasure between her thighs. It flickered, expanded, glowed blindingly bright . . . until—

Yes.

And *yes* and *yes* and *yes.*

He caressed her as she came floating back down to earth, running his fingers through her unbound hair and murmuring words that she couldn't quite catch—but they sounded warm and approving.

When she opened her eyes, he kissed her forehead. "That was magnificent."

"I think I'm supposed to be the one saying that."

"Well, you can say it, too, if you like." His mouth widened into a lopsided, cocky grin. "I'm not stopping you."

Alex rolled onto her side and gave him a coy smile of her own. "You are magnificently arrogant. But apparently the arrogance is well deserved."

She reached for him, skimming her fingertips down the expanse of his chest and hooking her fingers under the waistband of his trousers.

He put his hand over hers, halting her progress.

"Don't you want . . . ?" She darted a gaze at the pronounced tenting of his trousers. "I mean to say, it would seem you *need* some relief of your own."

"Pleasuring you was pleasure for me. I don't want you to feel you must reciprocate out of obligation. Lovemaking isn't a market trade. Not the way I go about it, anyhow."

"I don't feel any obligation. I feel curious. You promised me a lesson. But I know my own body already. I don't know yours." She placed her hand over the bulge in his trousers, cupping his hardness and tracing the shape of him through the thick wool. "May I?"

He groaned. "Do with me what you will. I've no strength left to protest."

She found the buttons of his trouser falls and undid them one by one. Once the last button slipped loose, however, her courage faltered.

What came next?

Was she meant to push his trousers down, or pull his erection out? Did she grasp it by the tip or by the root? How was she supposed to react on introduction? Ought she compliment its noble shape, or ooh and ah over its size?

Alex was totally unaware of lovers' etiquette. She feared she'd do it all wrong.

Sensing her hesitation—or perhaps simply too impatient to indulge her dithering—he took her hand and guided it inside his trouser falls, introducing her by touch rather than sight.

Oh, this was so much better.

Her first impression was the softness. She hadn't been expecting such a silky, smooth quality to meet her touch. As she ran her fingertips along his length, lightly tracing him from root to tip, he drew a shaky breath. Then she curled her fingers around his shaft, squeezing tight and letting his hardness fill her grip.

He lifted his hips, pushing his trousers down to his thighs. His cock sprang free, jutting into plain view. She continued her explorations, fascinated by the ruddy hue of the tip, and the veins that wound around his shaft and shivered under his skin. Even when his breathing grew harsh and fast, he allowed her to stroke and touch him as softly and slowly as she pleased.

She looked up to find him watching her, his brow furrowed and his jaw tight.

She bit her lip, feeling unsure. "Is it . . . ?"

He nodded curtly. "It is."

"Am I . . . ?"

"Oh, yes. You are." He reached to caress her cheek, and his thumb traced the shape of her lips. "You are perfect."

Her chest swelled with relief, and not a little bit of pride.

A drop of moisture welled at the tip of his cock, and she covered it with her thumb, spreading it in circles around the broad, smooth crown. His cock jumped in her hand, and the muscles of his abdomen went hard as cobblestones.

He squeezed his eyes shut and muttered a curse. As she touched him again, his hips bucked and his shaft pumped into her hand.

Alex had never felt more powerful. Even in her ignorance, she could reduce this powerful man to a single raw, quivering nerve. She had him, quite literally, in the palm of her hand.

"Teach me," she whispered. "Teach me what to do. What you like."

He reached down and covered her hand with his own, guiding her into a rhythm of tight, swift strokes. Pumping faster and faster, until their linked hands were a blur. She watched his face contort, flashing back and forth between pleasure and pain. His head was thrown back, and his eyes closed tight.

He seemed to have gone somewhere else, somewhere inside himself. She wondered where his mind had traveled. Whether he was with her, or with someone else. Or perhaps he'd been transported to a place where there were no names, no faces—only sensation.

A low, primal growl forced its way through his clenched teeth.

His body shuddered with release. Warmth spilled over her fingers. He released his grip on her hand, and she caressed him— equally fascinated by the softening of his cock as she had been by the hardness.

"Alexandra," came the hoarse whisper. His hand drifted to her hair, and he tangled his fingers in her unbound locks, drawing her down for a kiss.

Wherever it was he'd journeyed to, he'd returned. He was back in the here and now, with her.

As his breathing returned to normal, she considered her options. Mutter a word of thanks and flee to her room? Pretend to fall asleep and sneak out in the middle of the night? Both of those seemed beneath her dignity.

Instead, she rolled onto her side to face him. If she avoided him now, it would only grow more and more awkward. What had just happened between them would need to be confronted, discussed.

He stared at the ceiling. "That was . . . unbelievable."

She smiled, thrilled by his evident satisfaction and more than a bit proud of herself.

Until he went on.

"So ill advised," he continued, groaning. "Inappropriate. Unforgivable of me." He stood, hiking his trousers, and reached for a handkerchief to wipe away the evidence of their encounter. "I'm sorry, Alexandra. You should go up to your room, and we'll agree that this never—"

"Don't." She sprang to her feet. "Don't you dare say this never happened. It *happened*. I'm glad it happened. I want it to happen again."

"Truly?"

Could that be a hint of anxious uncertainty in his eyes?

Surely not. Infamous rakes weren't anxious or uncertain with women. Certainly not with women like Alex.

"Truly," she assured him. "I want this."

I want this. I want you. I want to feel wanted. Even if it's only for a short while.

Alexandra knew she was ignoring several possible disadvantages to this *affaire* she'd proposed. There were dangers, certainly. He understood how to prevent both pregnancy and emotional entanglement. She, on the other hand, could only be assured of avoiding the first. After the bookshop, she'd spent months infatuated with him on the basis of a mortifying wreck of a conversation, green eyes, and a charming smile. After a summer of sensual "lessons," she shuddered to think what fancies could bloom in her imagination.

Dreams were only that—dreams. She would have the rest of her life to forget them.

But mercy. For as long as she lived, she didn't think she'd forget the sight before her eyes now.

As she watched, Chase lifted the far edge of the bed, hefting the heavy mattress and frame onto its end to return it to the cabinet. The powerful muscles of his arms and shoulders were on dazzling display.

Flexing.

Straining.

Licked by amber tongues of candlelight.

Lord, he was a beautiful man.

His low grunt of effort pulled her out of her reverie.

Ho there, Alexandra. Perhaps you ought to help?

She rushed to help him shove the mattress back into place, fold the bed frame's wooden legs, and lock the cabinet. Having managed it, they turned to face one another, each resting one shoulder against the closed cabinet doors.

"So we're agreed? On continued . . . lessons?"

He studied her face. "If you're certain you want them."

"Quite certain. It makes sense. The only alternative is to avoid each other all the time, growing progressively more frustrated. That's not good for anyone in the house." She swept a gaze about the room. "And thanks to your industriousness, we do have a secluded, private place for liaisons."

"I'll need to rename it."

"Cave of Carnality doesn't suit anymore? I thought you'd ordered the plaque."

"If I'm giving you lessons, I think it needs something more . . . tutorial in nature. School of Sensuality," he proposed. "Climax Classroom. Perhaps the Office of Orgasms?"

"Anything's an improvement over the Virility Vault." Alex smiled. She'd missed this back-and-forth with him. She looked at the fireplace mantel. "I don't suppose you might take down the antlers?"

"What do you have against antlers, anyway?"

"I just think they could be replaced with something more welcoming. A nice landscape, perhaps." She gave him a teasing look. "Or maybe a sampler in needlepoint? The place could use a woman's touch."

He took her by the waist and pulled her flush against his chest. "There's only one thing in this room that needs a woman's touch."

Oh, that seductive growl in his voice did unspeakable things to her.

"Of course," she said in her firmest governess voice, "it goes without saying we must be absolutely, entirely discreet."

"Don't worry. They'll never know. Why do you think I installed new paneling? To prevent any sound from escaping. The drapes are heavy enough to keep light out, and in. And that door"—he tipped his head toward the kitchen entrance—"has three locks."

Apparently, none of those three locks was engaged at the moment. The door swung open.

"Mr. Reynaud? Miss Mountbatten?" Daisy rubbed her eyes as she stumbled into the room.

Alexandra deftly sidestepped, putting distance between her and Chase. She wrapped her arms about her torn nightclothes. "Daisy. You surprised us."

"I couldn't find you."

"And now you have. Let's go back up to bed."

The girl looked from Alex to Chase. "Why are you down here in the middle of the night?"

"Oh, we were merely talking. About . . ." Alex rummaged through her brain for a topic. "Needlepoint."

Which would have been an excellent reply, had Chase not simultaneously said, "Antlers."

Daisy's face scrunched with confusion.

"Antlerpoint," Chase said with authority. "It's a traditional handicraft in the Finnish Lapland."

Alex looked at him. *Antlerpoint?*

He shrugged. "I've been looking into the schools there, as you know. So it's an important educational matter. One that couldn't wait until morning."

Alexandra went to her young charge. "Why are you out of bed, darling?"

"Millicent has a small bowel obstruction."

"Goodness. We'd better make her an infusion of buckthorn, now hadn't we?" She looked cautiously at Chase. "Would you care to join us for a cup of tea?"

"Thank you, no."

The words had Alex feeling deflated. Perhaps Daisy's interruption had changed his mind, and he'd be calling off their arrangement before it had scarcely begun.

Instead, he searched out and lifted his hammer. "I have a lock to install. The fourth."

"Oh." Alex smiled and nodded. "Good."

Chapter Twenty

$\mathcal{A}$lex woke in the night again—trembling all over, her lips cracked with thirst.

Somehow the episodes came and went in an insidious rhythm, disappearing just long enough that she could almost forget and feel safe, before crashing back with a cruel vengeance. The past had a hold on her, and she'd long given up on breaking free. The best she could do was keep a full glass of water next to her bed. She hastily drained the largest share of it—saving a little bit to wet a cloth and dab the perspiration from her neck.

Dawn had begun its slow creep through the house. She wouldn't be able to fall asleep again, and her charges wouldn't wake for a few hours more—she hoped.

Since she was awake, she decided to dress and have a stealthy wander downstairs. Even after all these weeks, there were parts of the house she still hadn't explored.

Namely, the library.

The room called to her. Any roomful of books called to her, but this particular library wailed like a bevy of sirens.

Maybe—just maybe—somewhere in those shelves was her lost copy of Messier's *Catalogue of Star Clusters and Nebulae*. The book he'd absconded with after their collision in Hatchard's. The one she'd imagined him to have kept tucked in his breast pocket for months, desperately hoping to see her again.

At the memory, she inwardly cringed.

She began her search on the lowest shelf, scanning the full breadth of the bookcase before working her way upward. By the fourth shelf, she was straining on tiptoe to make out the titles. The fifth—and topmost—was hopelessly beyond her reach.

She looked about for a book stair or stepstool, but her search proved fruitless. Undeterred, she pushed an ottoman toward the shelves and climbed atop that.

Much better.

"Good morning."

Alexandra lost her footing on the ottoman. Her hands closed on the bookshelf. For a moment, she dangled, feet twisting in the air. There was only one option—to let go and drop to the floor. Her body would survive the fall, even if her dignity didn't. It was only a matter of two feet to the ground.

Go to it, then. The longer you dangle, the more ridiculous you look.

However, in the same instant that she released her grip, the shelf—already groaning with books—caved under the added weight of her body.

She fell to the carpet in a heap. And then a shelf's worth of books fell atop her.

Alex curled into a ball, tucked her head beneath her crossed arms, and waited for it to be over. She winced as volumes pelted her from above. A few of the weightier tomes landed with a force hard enough to make her yelp.

At last, the blows came to a halt.

She cautiously lifted her head and peered upward. Perhaps the bookcase had vomited up the last of its leather-bound knowledge.

No. It hadn't. There was one book more. A formidable, encyclopedia-sized volume bound in crimson leather. And as she watched with horror, it slid off the unhinged walnut shelf— plummeting directly toward her head.

Alexandra ducked, squeezed her eyes shut, and braced herself for the worst. However, instead of the skull-crushing *thwack* of oblivion, she heard only a soft *thud*.

"Good God. Tell me you're alive under there."

"I am," she said weakly. Though she rather wished she weren't.

As deaths go, it would have been a kind one. There were worse ways to meet one's demise than being buried alive in literature. Daisy could have named dozens of them.

As she attempted to sit up, Alex found herself aided by a large, strong hand hooked under her upper arm.

Chase.

He cast aside the book he'd caught, and Alex watched it land atop the heap. He must have caught the thing an instant before it bashed in her brains.

It wasn't an overstatement to say he might have saved her life. At the very least, he'd saved her a splitting headache.

He crouched before her. "Anything broken?"

"I don't think so."

He searched her gaze. "What month is it?"

"July."

"And what day of the week?"

"Wednesday."

"How many tiny buttons on the back of your frock?"

"I don't know. Who counts such things?"

He shrugged unrepentantly. "I do."

"Of course you do." She tucked a stray wisp of hair behind her ear. "I'm fine, thank you. You merely startled me."

"I expect so. Chase Reynaud, in a library? Searching for missing estate ledgers, no less? Who *wouldn't* topple with surprise."

"I didn't mean to say—"

He brushed off her attempt at an apology. "I've also been drinking wine and entertaining a great many impure thoughts, so it's not a complete break with character." He lowered his voice to a teasing murmur. "If you were looking for the erotic novels, they're hidden behind the books of sermons." He nodded toward the opposite side of the library. "Second shelf from the bottom, over there."

Her cheeks flushed. "I wasn't looking for those."

"I wouldn't think less of you if you were. I read them all the time."

"I don't think they'd suit my purposes today. I was searching for new reading material for the girls." She knelt and began to gather the fallen books.

He joined her in the effort. "Why? I purchased a great many books for the schoolroom, months ago."

Yes, I know. I was there, in Hatchard's. You made me drop all my books then, too. I was probably even wearing the same frock.

Alex absorbed the timely reminder. No matter what they were doing in the dark of night, nothing else had changed. They had a temporary physical arrangement. She mustn't hope for anything more.

"Rosamund's read all the books ten times over, and Daisy needs something different. Something suited to her interests."

He stood to have a look at the broken shelf. He teased the splintered wood with his thumbnail. "Rotted through," he pronounced. "I'll have to replace the plank."

"Good. Then I needn't apologize. Instead, you can thank me for finding your next project." She drew to her feet. "Look," she said, flipping through the plates of a human anatomy book. "This would be perfect for Daisy, budding physician that she is."

"Budding gravedigger, I think you mean."

"Just look at the detail in these illustrations." She moved closer, angling her body so that he could peer over her shoulder.

He reached over her arm to turn the page. As he did so, his forearm grazed her shoulder. His breath caressed her ear.

Alex stared at the line drawing of the respiratory system. Perhaps the illustration could help her identify exactly which features of her own anatomy were failing her—because his proximity made it difficult to breathe.

"I took an interest in anatomy as a youth," he murmured. "Continued my studies all the way through university."

"Truly?"

"Oh, yes. I found it fascinating. But I did the majority of my learning from life, rather than books." He took the volume from her hand, closed it, and set it aside. "Do you know, I think it's time for another lesson."

With that, he turned her toward him and captured her mouth in a searing kiss. His hands made possessive sweeps, caressing her breasts and thighs and hips. Awakening her body the way dawn woke the earth.

When he lifted his head, his eyes had a devilish gleam. He nudged her backward until her spine met the library shelving.

Then he sank to his knees.

CHASE'S SKIN TIGHTENED with anticipation. He'd been waiting for this.

"Chase," she whispered. "Chase, get up."

Get up? The hell he would. He was just getting started.

He gathered her skirts with both hands, hiking them high enough that he could dive under. Her frothy petticoats drifted down around him. They smelled of starch and soap, that faint hint of orange-flower water—and the intoxicating feminine musk of her skin. The draped fabric around him was the hushed, sacred temple of a pagan goddess, and he was a supplicant on his knees.

However, the offering he had in mind would be no sacrifice.

He slid his hand down one of her stocking-clad calves, bent her leg at the knee, and hooked it over his shoulder. That accomplished, he reached to grasp her by the hips and tilt her pelvis forward.

There. Now she was open to his view, to his touch. To his kiss.

He nuzzled the slope of her bare thigh, reveling in the satiny texture of her skin against his cheek. Beginning at her garter, he trailed kisses upward in an arrow-straight path to her cleft.

Her thigh tensed.

She squirmed in his grasp. "What are you doing?"

Chase decided demonstration was the most useful answer. He ran his thumb down the seam of her sex, parting her with a gentle touch. Then he leaned into her heat, sweeping his tongue along the sweet, silky furrow.

Her hips jerked, and she kicked him in the kidney. "Chase." Her hands patted around his back and shoulders, meeting atop his head. She gave him a shake. "*Chase*. We can't do this. Not here."

"Certainly we can." He wasn't sure if his words reached her, given that his voice was muffled by her skirts and his mouth had more pleasant tasks at hand than enunciation. He explored the treasure before him with slow, gentle passes of his tongue, giving her time to adjust to the sensation.

She gasped and bucked. "This is so very wrong."

Beneath her skirts, he grinned. "That's what makes it so very good."

"A servant could come by at any moment."

"Then stop interrupting."

Her fingers still clutched at his hair, but she ceased struggling.

With that, he returned to his task. He found the swollen bud at the apex of her cleft and fluttered his tongue.

Her breath escaped on an erotic sigh.

That's it. Surrender to the pleasure. Surrender to me.

He slid his hands to her bottom, clasping tight with both hands and drawing her closer, the better to kiss, lick, suck, nibble. Using her reactions as his guide, he learned the ways to make her sigh, moan, whimper, and dig her fingernails into his scalp.

"*Chase.*"

Hearing his name from her lips was the most heady triumph of all. It told him he wasn't an anonymous lover to her, but a man— one with whom she would share her most intimate places and sensations. A man she deemed worthy of her body and her plea- sure. Even if he could never be worthy of her heart or her hand, this was enough.

At least, he would tell himself it was enough.

She began to roll her hips, seeking more contact, wanting it faster. A muscle in her thigh quivered. He knew she was close.

Come, he silently willed. *Come for me.*

A few more flickering pulses of his tongue, and she went over the edge. She came with a series of shuddering whimpers, brac- ing herself on his head and shoulders. He didn't let up until her pleasure eased, and even then he couldn't tear himself away. He pressed his mouth to her inner thigh, sucking and biting until a bruise rose on her tender flesh.

There, now he'd left his mark: *Chase Reynaud was here.*

Once her breathing slowed and the leg draped over his shoulder went limp, he extricated himself from beneath her skirts and carefully rose to his feet, making sure to support her weight as he did so.

God, she looked beautiful. Throat flushed, chest heaving, her glazed eyes looking up through thick, dark lashes. Her hair had been mussed in the back, from where she'd reeled and rubbed against the shelves. The early-morning light painted her skin with a palette of golds and rosy pinks.

"You," she sighed, "are terrible."

"You"—he pressed his lips to her forehead—"are delicious." He kissed her cheek. "Beautiful." Then the corner of her lips. "Irresistible."

He leaned in, hungry for more.

She put her hand to his chest, holding him in place.

He took a step back, then cocked his head and searched her expression. "Is something the matter?"

"No." She wet her lips. "Not really. It's only . . ."

"Dropsy."

Chase wheeled about, searching for the source of this abrupt diagnosis. *What?*

Rosamund stood in the corridor. "It's dropsy today," she repeated. "The funeral is prepared."

"Right." He ran a hand through his hair. "Miss Mountbatten and I were just . . ."

"Looking through books," Alex finished.

"Well, yes." Rosamund gave them a quizzical look. "That is what one does in a library, isn't it?"

"Precisely," Chase declared. "Go on, then. We'll be up directly."

Once Rosamund had left, he and Alex exchanged looks of relief.

"That was close," he said.

"Much too close."

"I concur."

"If she'd been three minutes earlier, Chase. Just imagine."

"No," he clipped. "I refuse to imagine. You can't make me." He stood aside for her to precede him as they left the room.

"You're right. There's no use fretting over it now." She repinned her hair as they went. "Dropsy, really? I thought that was an old person's disease."

"Well, you know what they say. Only the wood die young."

She stopped in the middle of the corridor and burst out laughing. "That," she wheezed, "was dreadful. Criminally bad."

"It made you laugh, didn't it?"

Finally.

Chapter Twenty-One

*C*hase? *Chase.*"

Chase tore his gaze away from the clock. "Hm?"

"And . . . ?" Barrow gave him an impatient look. "What did you want to do about the mining interests?"

"Which mining interests?"

"The ones we've been discussing for the past hour. The coal in Yorkshire. Is this jogging your memory?"

"Right. The coal. Sorry."

Memories weren't Chase's problem. His mind was full to bursting with memories. The problem was, they were all memories of Alexandra beneath him, naked, gripping the bedsheets in ecstasy. Even if his body was in the study with Barrow, his mind was downstairs in his retreat. Which wasn't even his retreat anymore. Over the past fortnight, it had become *their* retreat.

Chase straightened in his chair and sifted through the report before him. "Hold on to the mines. The seam is nowhere near exhausted, and the demand for coal will only increase."

"Agreed." Barrow dipped his quill and bent over the writing desk. "Chase, I know how you feel about me meddling in your personal affairs, but this is different. You must put a stop to it."

"To what?"

"Whatever it is you're doing with Miss Mountbatten."

Chase looked up sharply. "What makes you think I'm doing anything with Miss Mountbatten?"

"Oh, come along." Barrow threw down his quill. "Whenever she's in the room, you steal hungry glances at each other. It's obvious."

"It is not obvious."

Barrow lifted his eyebrows, and Chase realized too late that he'd given himself away.

"That's not what I meant. It's not obvious because it's not happening."

"Work on that 'gentleman's retreat' seems to have stalled. You haven't demanded my opinions on satin bedding or erotic etchings in weeks."

"I was going to solicit your preferences on perfumed sensual oils," Chase said idly, "but then I decided not to spoil your Christmas present."

Someone knocked at the door.

"Cha—" Alexandra popped her head around the door. Her lips clamped shut, and her cheeks flushed pink. "Oh. Mr. Barrow. I didn't realize you were here. I beg your pardon for interrupting."

"Not at all," Barrow said. He slid a meaningful glance in Chase's direction. "We were discussing nothing, apparently."

"If that's the case . . ." Alex came out from behind the door and entered the room. "Mr. Reynaud, I thought you'd want to know that Rosamund and Daisy are ready."

Ready? Ready for what?

Once again, Chase had completely lost hold of his faculties. Because she stood in the doorway, dressed in a gauzy, daffodil-yellow frock, and the only readiness that mattered was how ready he felt to pull her into his arms.

She stole his breath away.

He rose to his feet. Etiquette didn't require a gentleman to stand when a member of his house staff entered the room. Alexandra knew it, and her expression reflected the awkwardness of his gesture.

But Chase was unrepentant. A man rose to his feet for a lady, his queen, or a divine being, and she was at least one of those—if not all three.

"I have them dressed and ready for the outing." When he didn't answer, she added, "You do recall promising them an outing? I spoke to you about it the other evening, and you said yes." Her eyes took on a saucy gleam. "Rather emphatically."

Cheeky minx. Only the Devil knew how many times she'd heard the word "yes" from his lips on any of several recent evenings. She must have tricked him into agreeing to this when he was insensate with pleasure.

He said, "Barrow and I have a great deal of business to attend to."

"Please. I've promised Rosamund and Daisy. The girls will be so disappointed."

She'd promised them? Damn it. Broken promises were something he avoided at all costs. And the simplest way to avoid them was to not make any in the first place. Tonight he would give her a stern talking-to about making promises on his behalf.

And perhaps a light spanking just to underscore the matter.

But that would be later. As for this afternoon . . . that fetching yellow frock just begged to be out of doors. He wanted to see the breeze whip the flimsy muslin about her legs, wanted to watch her untie the ribbons of her bonnet with a gloved hand and then give him a bashful smile.

And what he didn't want was to spend another afternoon in this study with Barrow.

"Give me an hour to make a few arrangements," he said. "Tell the girls we'll be going to the park."

She smiled. "Thank you, sir."

When she'd gone, Barrow turned to him and said dryly, "Oh, that wasn't obvious at all."

"Do you know, I've been thinking." Chase reached for his coat and hat. "We spend entirely too much time together."

"I can't disagree." Barrow tapped his quill on the edge of the inkwell and continued in a quiet, serious tone. "Be careful, Chase. She's not the only one who stands to be hurt."

"Don't worry. The girls have no idea."

"I wasn't referring to the girls. I meant you."

Chase snorted. "Now you're just being absurd."

"Am I?"

"Yes," Chase answered as he quit the room, sounding far more authoritative than he felt.

"ARE WE THERE yet?" Daisy dragged her feet along the well-trodden path.

Chase didn't even break stride. "No."

"You might slow the pace a touch," Alex suggested in a murmur. "For the girls' sake."

And for mine.

After trotting alongside him for nearly a half hour, she and the girls were breathing hard and perspiring in the summer's afternoon sun. They'd reached the halfway point of Hyde Park now, where the Serpentine widened into a lake.

"Are there ices in this park?" Rosamund asked.

"I've no idea," Chase replied.

"We were promised a treat. Not a military march."

Daisy halted in the path. "Millicent has dysentery."

Chase groaned. "She does not. She was perfectly well a moment ago."

"The grueling pace was too much for her. Now she could die at any moment."

Alexandra decided to intervene. "Here." She untied the ribbon knotted at her nape, removing her coral pendant and tying it about Millicent's neck instead.

"But that was your mother's," Daisy said.

"Millicent may borrow it for the day. It's especially effective against dysentery. And Mr. Reynaud promises to walk a bit more slowly."

"Actually, we don't have to walk much farther at all," Chase said. "There's your surprise, girls. It's waiting over there, on the bank."

When Alex saw what he'd pointed out, her stomach knotted. A neat little skiff bobbed atop the rippling water, tied to a tree branch at the side of the lake. The miniature craft had been gaily painted, and it boasted a crisp white sail and a jaunty red flag.

"You . . . you mean to take the girls sailing on the lake?"

"No, we're going to skate on the lake. Yes, sailing—if you can even call it that, on this small scale. And I don't mean to take only the girls. You're coming, too."

"Oh." Her throat worked, but it felt like trying to swallow paper. "That's kind of you, but I'll wait on the bank."

"Nonsense." He stripped off his coat and draped it over the tree branch before turning up his cuffs. "You must be dying to get on the water again. This is hardly a voyage on the open sea, but it's something. As close as I could give you at the moment."

The dear man. He'd arranged this not only as an outing for the girls, but as a gift to her. Now she could understand the reason for his determined clip through Mayfair and across the park. He'd been excited.

Inside, Alex wanted to weep. Everything in her screamed for escape. But how could she disappoint him?

Use your common sense, she told herself. *Be rational. As he says, this isn't a merchant ship bobbing about a wild, stormy sea. It isn't even a wherry on the Thames. It's a skiff on the Serpentine, on a Tuesday in August, smack in the middle of London. There isn't any true reason to be afraid, so stiffen up and get on with things.*

She took his hand.

His eyes warmed. "That's my girl."

Her heart flapped and fluttered like a loose ribbon caught by the wind.

The girls had climbed aboard the skiff and begun preparing for their maiden voyage as proper pirates. Millicent was placed at the fore of the craft, like a mermaid decorating the ship's prow.

As the girls unfurled the skiff's tiny sail, she kept watch on their every move. "Rosamund, come away from the side at once."

Chase stretched his arm across her back in a stealthy motion. "Take the afternoon off, Miss Mountbatten. I'm relieving you of your governess duties today."

148 *Tessa Dare*

She could take the afternoon off from being a governess, perhaps. But she couldn't take an afternoon off from being herself. She was still that shivering girl in the dark, caught between pelting rain and a hungry sea. She was still that stammering woman in Hatchard's, entranced by roguish green eyes and the scents of sandalwood and mint.

Alex was still Alex. Chase was still Chase. And she could no longer deny that she was mad for him, despite there being every rational argument against it. She'd been ensnared by infatuation the moment they collided in that bookshop, and now she couldn't imagine ever getting free.

This hopeless yearning would be the end of her. Or at least the death of her common sense.

"I brought provisions." He withdrew a tiny corked jug from his pocket and lifted it triumphantly. "There's grog."

The girls celebrated with rousing huzzahs. Chase unstoppered the jug and passed it to Daisy, who struggled to lift it to her lips.

"Don't worry," he whispered in Alex's ear. "It's just water and molasses."

"They'll have stomachaches."

Chase clasped the skiff's prow and grunted as he pushed the craft off the bank. The girls' second round of cheering was even more rousing than the first. He kept one boot firmly planted on the bank and had the other in the boat, keeping the skiff close.

Then he motioned to Alex. "Come, then. I'll hand you in."

She hesitated a few feet from the water. Panic rose in her breast. Her heart thundered so fiercely she couldn't hear anything but her own frantic pulse.

I can't. I can't do this.

"Truly, I'll wait here. It's too small for four."

"No, it's not," Rosamund argued. "There's plenty of room."

Daisy propped her hands on her hips. "Mr. Reynaud, you must make her come along."

"I agree. If she won't come willingly, piracy is the only choice." Chase lunged, took Alex by the waist, and lifted—parting her from the safety of the bank and swinging her into the boat.

"I can't," she said. "Please. I can't."

As Chase moved to deposit her on the bench of the skiff, she clung to his neck. From the boat, Daisy tugged at her skirts.

She began to thrash, unable to think of anything other than fighting her way back onto the bank. The boat only tipped further, making everything worse. In her scrambling panic, she made a wild kick.

A kick that connected with Millicent, sending her flying through the air.

The doll landed with a splash in the center of the lake.

Daisy shrieked.

At first, the doll's wooden head kept her afloat, and for a few seconds it seemed all would be fine—just row to the center, fish her out with a long stick, and she'd be only a bit worse for the adventure. She'd survived far greater trials.

But as her wool-batting body started to soak through, the unthinkable occurred.

The resilient, indestructible, death-defying Millicent—and with her, Alexandra's coral pendant—began to sink.

"No!" Daisy screamed. "She's drowning!"

Chase set Alex back on dry land. "Not on my watch."

He had his boots and his waistcoat off in a matter of seconds. A talent gained over years of hasty disrobing, no doubt. Once he'd stripped down to his shirt and trousers, Chase dived in.

He swam out to the center of the lake, making directly for the area where the doll had disappeared. Again and again, he dived beneath the water and remained submerged for long seconds before surfacing empty-handed.

Every time he sank out of sight, Alex held her own breath. Daisy was inconsolable. Even Rosamund clung to Alex's side.

Seven times now, and no result. He had to be growing fatigued.

Alex cupped her hands around her mouth to call to him. "Mr. Reynaud! Come back to the bank!"

"No," he shouted in reply, pushing his hair from his brow. "Not without that bloody doll."

He went under once again and this time he stayed out of sight for what seemed like ages. Alex was beside herself. He could have been overcome with fatigue, or fainted from lack of air, or become tangled in reeds . . . There were scores of ways a man could die in the water, and she'd witnessed far too many of them.

Dolls were replaceable. In some cases, resurrectable. Her *corales* might be all she had left of her mother, but they weren't flesh and blood. Nothing else mattered right now. Nothing but him.

"Chase!" she cried.

At last, he surfaced. Not in the center of the lake, but close to the bank, taking her unawares. He emerged from the water with a spray of fanfare, his translucent shirt pasted to his torso and his hair slicked back. Like Poseidon rising from the sea—hoisting a waterlogged doll in place of a trident.

Chase Reynaud, god of the Serpentine.

And oh, he looked ready to enjoy a bit of worship.

He grinned at her, the horrid man. As if he hadn't just given her the fright of her life, and the past ten minutes were an expected element of any outing in Hyde Park.

He presented the doll to Daisy. "She took in some water, but I think she'll pull through."

Instead of hugging the doll, Daisy attached herself to Chase's leg, clinging to him with all four limbs. Alex rather wished she could do the same.

Chase shook his leg, and Daisy held tight. He looked to Alex. "You're the sailor. How does one remove a barnacle?"

It FELT DAMNED good to be a hero for a change—even if he was a fleeting, insignificant one.

However, on the way home from the park, Chase's glow of triumph faded to exhaustion, both of body and of mind.

When they arrived back at the house, Alexandra herded Rosamund and Daisy up the stairs at once. "Baths first, girls. Dinner second."

Chase decided these were excellent ideas. Once he'd scrubbed the mud and lake water from his body, he took supper in his study and opened a bottle of claret to keep him company while he went over yet another folio of estate papers.

It was nearing midnight by the time Alexandra joined him. They seemed to have chosen similar activities—her plaited hair was slick from bathing and she carried a book tucked under her arm.

"Wine." She sighed. "What an excellent idea."

"Join me, please. Rescue me from the fluctuating corn prices of 1792."

He poured her a glass of claret, and she accepted it eagerly, downing half the glass in one go. He'd asked the servants to lay a fire tonight, even though it was summer.

"I wasn't certain you'd be coming down. I thought perhaps you'd have fallen asleep, too."

"It was quite a struggle to settle the girls into bed. An hour of reading from *Robinson Crusoe*, plus two dishes of custard each."

"Custard? I expressly made a prohibition against custard."

"Then next time you can put them to bed," she teased. "Since you know all the best methods."

"I suppose I can let it go. This time."

"Even after they fell asleep, my own nerves needed a bit of soothing." She traced the rim of her wineglass with her fingertip. "Nothing like an hour or two staring into the telescope for that. When I focus on the stars and the spaces between them, all my other cares fade into the dark."

Chase hated that she had other cares at all. He especially hated that so many of them were his doing.

"You are quite the hero now," she said.

"Bah."

"I'm so sorry about it. It was all my fault."

"No, it was mine. I shouldn't have tried to force the matter. I didn't realize how frightened you were." He cocked his head. "So tell me something. Why would a sea captain's daughter, raised aboard a merchant ship, be afraid of the water?"

Her terror had been palpable that afternoon. Hesitation would be understandable. Her father had been lost at sea. But true panic? Perhaps there was more to it than that.

He sensed she didn't want to answer the question. He decided not to press.

"I'm curious, too," she said. "Why would a man with a good heart, willing to dive into a lake to save a bedraggled doll, be afraid of raising two orphaned girls?"

"It wasn't only the doll."

"I know. Thank you."

She touched the coral pendant where it lay at the base of her throat. He was glad to see it where it belonged. She'd knotted it onto a new length of ribbon—this time, a rich sapphire blue.

"You're so good at this," she went on. "The comforting, the caring. You'll make an excellent guardian. Residing with you would be worlds better for them than any boarding school."

"Maybe they'll like school. I liked school."

"Naturally you did. Your school was mischief and sport and studies of actual subjects. Not embroidery and etiquette. You were taught to go out and conquer the world. They will be taught to live in a satin-lined pocket. I know. I attended one of these schools. And just like Rosamund and Daisy, I was sent there by relations who wanted nothing to do with me."

"This is different."

"Is it? You're rejecting them. Just as everyone else has done. Don't believe they don't feel it. And if you send them away, they are never going to trust anyone again. They just want your attention, can't you see? Even if they have to tie you with ropes or douse you with water, or devise a different death for a doll every morning. Sometimes I think Daisy does it just for the excuse to hold your hand once a day. And you ought to see the way Rosamund looks at you when you're too occupied to notice. She'd never admit it, but she's desperate for your approval." She reached for his hand. "Chase, they love you already."

The words rocked him. But they changed nothing. He could not, should not be responsible for anyone's well-being. Even if he cared for—or, God help him, loved—that person. To cave to his desire for companionship would be selfish in the extreme.

"It's impossible, Alexandra. Unthinkable."

She gave an exasperated groan. "You're always saying that."

"And for good reason," he said firmly.

"What good reason is that?"

"The last time I promised to look after someone, he ended up dead."

Chapter Twenty-Two

*D*ead?

Alex searched his eyes. Her impulse was to dismiss his words, assume he must be exaggerating. But his intense, defiant gaze spoke of something beyond accidents or misunderstandings. Regret. Guilt. Pain.

So much pain.

"Tell me." She made it a demand, rather than a request. Whatever secrets he had, he needed to purge them before they devoured him from the inside out. "Chase. Tell me."

The doorbell rang.

"Son of a whore," she muttered.

He was taken aback. "I've never heard you curse."

"I try to avoid using profanity. But I grew up around sailors. I certainly know how."

The late-night visitor abandoned the bell in favor of pounding at the door. Chase started toward the door as if to answer it himself, but apparently a servant beat him to it. The caller didn't wait for an introduction, but stormed directly into the room.

"Where's Alexandra?" he demanded gruffly.

"I have a better question." Chase stepped between Alex and the intruder. "Who the devil are you?"

Alex smiled. "He's the Duke of Ashbury."

Truly, it couldn't be anyone else. It wasn't as though there were two tall, dark, imposing dukes in England bearing scars on one side of their body from a misfired rocket at Waterloo. Ash's scarred face gave him an intimidating, even fearsome appearance. But Alexandra knew him to be tenderhearted beneath the scars, and utterly devoted to his wife.

He also made an excellent friend.

"Ash." Alex emerged from the shadows and rushed to him, giving him a hug before he could deflect it. "But why have you come to London? I hope there's nothing wrong with Emma or the baby."

"Emma and the baby are fine." He looked over her shoulder, sending a glare in Chase's direction. "As for what I'm doing in London, I'm here to plant my boot in someone's arse."

"I thought you'd given that up."

"I thought so, too. But this employer of yours has me coming out of retirement. I came as soon as I heard you'd taken up residence in this place." He walked past her to stare down Chase face-to-face. "You deserve to know what a worthless scoundrel he is, Alex."

"Yes!" Chase exclaimed. He reached for Ashbury's hand and pumped it in a vigorous greeting. "*Thank* you. I've been trying to tell her myself, but she won't listen."

Ashbury looked more than a bit thrown by Chase's invitation. He gave Alex a what-the-devil-is-he-on-about look.

Alex could only shrug in response.

"Be seated, the both of you." Chase went to the brandy decanter on the sideboard. "Ashbury, can I pour you a drink?"

"I brought my own." Ash pulled a flask from his coat pocket and uncapped it.

"Even better," Chase replied, pouring himself a brandy. "Do go on. Don't wait on me."

Alex sat on the divan, since she knew neither of the men would sit until she did. They might not be sterling examples of upright gentlemen, but they were perfectly capable of behaving themselves when they wished. Ash took an armchair.

Ash turned to Alex, ignoring their host and speaking in a low, serious tone. "Listen to me, Alexandra. This man is a known libertine. Even before my injuries, I knew of his reputation. Everyone knows. He is unwelcome in any good family."

"See?" Chase returned, pulling up a chair and joining the group. "Exactly as I've been telling you, Miss Mountbatten. I am the most wretched of rakes."

"I wasn't unaware of Mr. Reynaud's . . . popularity with ladies," Alex said carefully.

"Has he touched you?"

Oh, had he ever. But what happened between them wasn't any of Ash's concern. "Not in any uninvited manner."

"Are you certain?"

"Absolutely certain."

"Now, now." Chase shifted forward in his chair. "Be honest, Miss Mountbatten."

"I am being honest. Mr. Reynaud has not subjected me to any unwanted attentions, nor taken advantage of me in any way."

Ash looked suspicious, but he didn't belabor the question. "Regardless. His sexual escapades are merely the tip of the iceberg."

"Oh, I haven't even acquainted her with the tip," Chase said merrily. "Not properly."

"Just ignore him," Alex told the duke. "Go on."

"Three years ago, there was a sordid, suspicious business with his cousin."

"I'd been wondering when we'd get to this." Chase took a large swallow of brandy. "This is the good part. Pay attention."

Ash gave Chase an annoyed look. "Do you mind? We're having a conversation here."

"I presume you mean the old duke's son," Alex went on. "The one who would have been the heir, had he not died."

"The cousin didn't merely die," Ash said. "He was killed."

"Surely you're not accusing Mr. Reynaud of *murder*."

"He might as well," Chase said. "My cousin didn't die at my hand, but I killed him just the same."

Ashbury rolled his eyes. "If you're going to interrupt me every ten seconds, you may as well do this yourself."

"You know, that's a fine idea." Chase set aside his brandy. "I'll take over, Ashbury. There are a few sporting magazines on the tea table if you need to amuse yourself in the meantime."

Ash harrumphed.

Chase leaned forward, bracing his arms on his knees and folding his hands together. "He was the youngest of my three cousins, and the best of the lot. Meant for the church, not the dukedom. But my middle cousin died in the war, and the eldest had a riding accident not long after. And then suddenly . . . Anthony was the heir. Twenty years old, no experience of the world or preparation for the title. Still grieving for his older brothers, and so naïve. My uncle sent him to London for the Season. I was supposed to show him the town, give him some exposure to society, help him make friends. I promised I'd look after him. And . . ." He sat back with a sigh. "I failed."

"That's a generous summary," Ash put in.

"I'm getting to the details, Ashbury." Chase continued, "It's probably no surprise that my ideas of society and culture were somewhat different from my uncle's. I took my cousin around to the clubs. Pleasure gardens. The theaters, both respectable and less than so. He needed some true experience among his peers. Enough confidence to hold his own. One night, we began at the club. Then it was on to the opera dancers. By the time we arrived at the gaming hell, we were having a right jolly time. Looking back, he was deeper into his cups than I realized. I wasn't precisely sober, either. An alluring bit of satin skirt floated by. I was flirtatious; she was willing. I told myself Anthony would be fine. He had to learn to look after himself eventually, didn't he? So I left with her. And I never saw my cousin alive again."

Alex was tempted to offer some crooning words of sympathy, but she didn't want to interrupt him when he so clearly had so much more to say.

"He accused a man of cheating at the *vingt-et-un* table. The fellow denied it, but Anthony wouldn't let the matter go. It was the sort of row I could have smoothed over in a matter of seconds, had

I been there. But I wasn't there. So the argument escalated. They went outside and . . ." Chase rubbed his face with both hands, and when he looked up again, his eyes were red. "Had I been keeping watch on him as I'd promised, I could have saved him."

"Perhaps you didn't want to save him," Ashbury said. "It's rumored that you killed him yourself."

"*Ash.*" Alexandra was aghast.

"No one saw this 'fight' happen in the alleyway. Reynaud was conveniently nowhere to be found."

"I told you, I was with a—"

"A woman, yes. Which woman was that, again?"

Chase's jaw tensed, as though he didn't want to answer. "I couldn't give you her name. I never learned it."

"How convenient."

Alexandra spoke up. "Surely you don't believe he killed his cousin in cold blood."

"Perhaps not. But the suspicions are not wholly unreasonable. As next in line, Reynaud stood to benefit directly from his cousin's death."

"I should think you know better than to heed that sort of gossip," she said.

"He's only relating facts," Chase said. "I did directly benefit, and there are many who suspect that my cousin's death was no accident. And then I wrangled legal control from my uncle a few years later. Your friend is not the first to deem it remarkable that I went from fourth in line for the title to presumptive heir with power of attorney, in the span of a few years."

"Remarkable, indeed," Ash said.

"But don't believe the rumor that my uncle's illness is some sort of ruse. When he viewed the lifeless body of his third and only remaining son, he suffered an apoplexy on the spot. The old man's been paralyzed and unable to speak ever since," Chase said bitterly. "So you see, I couldn't have planned it—but if you're conferring with the gossips, it worked out well for me anyhow. Is there anything I've forgotten, Ashbury?"

Ash rose to his feet. "The bit where you're a base, rascally, cheating, lack-linen mate."

Chase snapped his fingers. "Oh, yes. That, too. Whatever it meant."

"Ashbury only swears in Shakespearean," she explained.

The duke turned to Alexandra and crossed his arms over his chest. "Alex, I hope you see him clearly now."

See him *clearly*?

The suggestion that Chase would devise a plot to kill off his cousin and wrest legal control from his uncle was absurd. She knew Ash loved Shakespeare, but this wasn't a performance of *Richard III*.

Not to mention—if the Duke of Ashbury meant to convince her Chase was a villain, he ought to have sent someone else. Someone without a history of inspiring wildly untruthful rumors.

"Reviled throughout London, hm? Sounds remarkably like someone else I know. And dearly care about. A duke who not so long ago skulked about London styling himself the Monster of Mayfair."

"That's entirely different."

"And yet the rumors were equally contrived and false." Alex shook her head. "You know, you two have so much in common. You ought to be friends."

"We are nothing alike," Ash sputtered.

"No one could possibly confuse us," Chase agreed.

"Of course not," Ash continued. "One of us is a repulsive monster, and the other was scarred at Waterloo."

She spoke over their protests. "You should see yourselves. You're giving me identical scowls right this moment."

"I am not *scowling*," the two men said.

In unison.

While scowling.

For her part, Alex couldn't resist a smug smile. "Well, you seem to share one thing in common—the belief that I can't be trusted with my own decisions. Ash, you don't need to worry. You know I've always been the most sensible of the group. I have a good head on my shoulders, and I keep my feet on the ground. I can take care of myself."

"You don't have to remain here with him, Alex. Come stay with me and Emma. We'd be happy to have you. And if you've developed a sudden passion for child minding, we can put you to work."

"I truly appreciate that. But I can't leave without completing the job I was hired to do. The girls need me. More to the point, they need him. He isn't . . ." She lowered her voice to a whisper. "He isn't what others think. He isn't what *he* thinks."

"You don't—"

"Please send my love to Emma and the babe. And my congratulations to the proud father, as well." She kissed his cheek. "Go home to your family."

At last, he relented.

Chase opened the front door in a clear invitation for the duke to leave.

Before departing, he addressed Chase. "If you hurt her, in even the slightest way, I will eviscerate you."

"Understood."

"I mean it, Reynaud. In fact, gutting would be too good for you. I will subject you to my cat."

"Your cat?" Chase laughed. "To mewl at me, I suppose."

"Trust me. We're not speaking of the average cat."

Alexandra spoke up. "I can attest to this."

"I'll strip you bare, tie your hands behind your back, smear salmon on your manly bits, and lock the two of you in a wardrobe. Once he's clawed your ballocks to shreds, I'll crush whatever remains of you to a bloody, formless pulp."

"Good Lord." Chase sounded a little awed. "That's remarkably vivid. Did you plan all this out just for me, or do you keep a list of gruesome threats to use as the occasion arises?"

"Just stay away from her, king of codpieces." He grabbed Chase by the front of his shirt. "Or I will make you wish you'd never been born."

Chase shrugged off Ash's grip. "Too late on that score."

Chapter Twenty-Three

*O*nce the Duke of Arse-bury finally left and took his feline torture plans with him, Chase turned to Alexandra. He crossed his arms. "Well, I hope that puts paid to the matter. Are you convinced?"

"Convinced of what, precisely?"

"That I am the worst of all possible guardians. That it doesn't matter what I wish to do, or even if I love those girls. If I care *about* them, I should not, must not take the responsibility of caring *for* them."

"Oh, that? No, I'm not convinced of that at all."

He smacked his hand to his forehead and groaned. "Alexandra, come *along*. I couldn't even look after a twenty-year-old young man. This wasn't a case of my cousin falling into a bit of youthful mischief. I failed to keep him alive."

Her look went soft, and her voice went softer. "Chase, I'm so sorry."

"Damn it, do not be sorry."

"Why shouldn't I be sorry? You lost your cousin in an act of tragic violence. It's natural to feel sympathy."

"Were you not listening? I gave my word to my uncle. I promised I'd keep close watch on him. I broke that promise—in the worst possible place, at the worst possible time. He was stabbed outside a gaming hell and bled to death in the alley. Alone. And where was I? In a seedy inn, in bed with a woman whose name I did not know. So don't make excuses for me."

She took a step in his direction. "I'm—"

"I mean it." He held her off with an outstretched hand. "Don't do it, Alex. Don't try to hold me with my head in your lap, and kiss my tortured brow and stroke my hair, and tell me I'm blameless and misunderstood."

Her nose wrinkled. "I hadn't intended to do any such thing."

"Oh," he said. "Well, then. Good."

Damn.

She sat on the divan and patted the space next to her, inviting him to sit, too. He found himself helpless to refuse. Unsurprisingly. He had never been able to resist a woman's invitation to closeness. That was the root of all his problems.

She angled to face him, propping her elbow on the back of the divan and leaning her head on her hand. She looked beautiful and thoughtful, and even more beautiful for being thoughtful.

"You made a mistake," she said. "And not a small one. A grave one, with terrible consequences. You broke a promise to your uncle, and you deserted your cousin when you ought to have stayed at his side. Did you wield the knife that spilled his blood? No. But you weren't there to prevent it, either."

He swallowed back a lump in his throat.

"If you feel guilty, I won't try to dissuade you. In truth, I'd respect you a great deal less if you *didn't* feel regret."

"What do you mean, you'd respect me *less*? When did you start to respect me at all?"

"I'm not certain. But it must have happened at some point. If it hadn't occurred beforehand, you rescuing Millicent from the Serpentine would have sealed my regard."

"That was sheer stubbornness. That cursed doll wasn't going to die for good. Not if I could help it."

She smiled a little. "I know. And that's why I believe you'll make the girls an excellent guardian. Because you've made mistakes and you've learned from them."

"I've learned, yes. I've learned that I'm not to be trusted with that kind of responsibility."

"Your only true responsibility is to love them. Everything else will fall in line."

She ticked off a sequence of statements on her fingers. No sugar lumps or liquor decanters about, he supposed.

"You care for them. They worship you. Financially, you can provide for their every need. They're bound to break things, and you'll get to hammer them back together." She was down to her little finger. "Without them in your life, you'll be alone."

That last one twisted like a dagger in his chest.

She held out her hand, fingers extended. "Look, Chase. It's as plain as the fingers on my hand. All you have to do is reach out to them. And then hold tight."

She didn't understand. Chase didn't doubt his capacity to love. Rosamund and Daisy had captured his heart within hours of entering his life. The problem was, he couldn't imagine ever ceasing to despise himself—and that was his downfall, again and again. Self-loathing was what drove him to the distraction of a woman's embrace. Not boredom, not lust. Concentrating on a woman's pleasure was the only way he could forget his shame. When a lover wrapped her legs tight about his waist, when he heard a husky, feminine voice begging him for more . . . for a few blessed minutes, he felt something other than worthless.

And then afterward . . .

Well, was there a word for being *less* than worthless? Because the moment lovemaking was over, he felt that.

No matter how many times he vowed that he'd stop—telling himself he ought to be man enough to shoulder his well-deserved guilt, rather than go burying it in the depths of a lady's bountiful cleavage—inevitably, he caved to temptation. The nights were too dark and quiet. Memories took advantage of the emptiness, rushing in to fill the void the way rainwater collected in a ditch.

The way blood filled the cracks between cobblestones.

The way handfuls of dirt filled a grave.

The clubs, the parties, the brandy . . . they helped, but they helped only so much. Perhaps he'd manage a week of celibacy, sometimes two. But in the end, he always gave in.

How the devil could he vow to take care of these girls? He couldn't even keep the promises he made to himself.

"Consider the rumors that swirl about me," he said. "How can I raise those girls in any respectable fashion when people believe me a murderer? You heard the duke. There's no denying that his death worked to my benefit."

"Very well," she said. "A good part of the *ton* doubts your character. Perhaps they even have reason to do so. But by withdrawing from polite society you've made certain they don't have any evidence to the contrary. Seeing you dote on a pair of young girls, and watching you encourage and protect them as they grow into remarkable young women . . . that would probably cause some to reconsider their opinions. Don't you think?"

Everything she said was so relentlessly logical. Of course it was. She was always sensible.

He hadn't realized how badly he'd been craving this. Someone who didn't have any wish to accuse him or forgive him, but to sit down and discuss the facts of the matter in a calm, rational way.

"If you give them the chance, people will see that you've changed, Chase. *You* will see that you've changed."

God. He wanted so desperately to believe her, and he almost could—here, now, staring deep into her lovely eyes and feeling her looking deep into his. He trusted her opinion of his character more than he trusted his own. She made him want to be better. She always had, from the first.

But when she left him, he'd be lost all over again. It would never work, unless . . .

Unless he didn't let her go.

Keep her close. Make her stay. Make her yours.

He dragged her into his arms and kissed her.

There was no more contemplation in his mind. No more logic or reason or sense. Only a wild impulse that roared to life inside him and pounded in his blood like an ancient drum. One his cave-dwelling ancestors likely pounded in some torch-lit mating ceremony followed by a buffet of raw antelope. Each beat resonated as a primal urge.

Want. Need. Take. Claim. Mine.

He laid her back against the divan, trailing a path of hot, openmouthed kisses down her neck, grazing her shoulder with his teeth. He hiked her nightclothes with one hand, pushing them up to her thighs and reaching beneath to find the heart of her. The place where she was wild and needing and uncivilized, too.

After parting her with a light, sweeping touch, he pushed two fingers into her heat. She wasn't as ready as he typically made her with caresses of both hands and tongue. But he had no patience for finesse tonight. He probed deep, relishing the tight grip of her sex and the gasps he wrenched from her throat.

He reached down to unbutton his trouser falls and free his cock. He slid the thick, hard shaft up and down her sex, grinding and rubbing against her until she was wet for him. Then he backed off to pump his hand over his length, slicking himself with her essence. With his hips, he spread her thighs wide and positioned the head of his cock at her entrance.

"Alex, please. Let me have you. Take me in."

"Chase, wait."

"I want you," he murmured. "I need this. To be inside you, make you mine."

Mine.

Once he'd spoken the word, it echoed in his every heartbeat.

Mine. Mine. Mine.

She put her hands on his shoulders and pushed him away. "I know you don't want this. Not really."

"The hell I don't." He thrust his erection against her thigh, offering her ample proof.

"That's not what I mean. I know how you feel about intercourse. Or fucking, if you want to call it that."

"I don't want to call it that." Not now, not with her. He pulled away from her, breathing hard.

"You always do this. Let your body take the lead when you want to hide your heart. Right now, you're hurting. I don't want to take advantage of you."

"You think *you* could take advantage of *me*." He chuckled. "Well, aren't you precious."

"Well, aren't you patronizing." She stood up, pulling down the hem of her shift and dressing gown. "Good night, Chase."

She left the room.

Chase let his head fall backward on the divan and stared up at the ceiling. She was wise to pull away, but wrong about who'd be taking advantage of whom. He would have been using her. Not in the same way he used his other lovers, but using her just the same. Pushing her to accept him, redeem him. Cover up all the sins and flaws he didn't want to face deep within himself.

God damn his eyes.

He needed to leave. Get out of this house, remind himself of who he was—before he hurt her in some irretrievable way.

Fortunately, Chase knew just the place.

Chapter Twenty-Four

A week spent in Hertfordshire was guaranteed to quash even the mildest erotic desires or romantic longings. At least, Chase had counted on it working that way for him. Clearly the local residents managed to persevere in marrying and procreating, but they weren't lodged at the Belvoir estate. They didn't spend their days trying to coax details of sheep manure and crop rotation from a skeptical land agent who'd managed the farmland for longer than Chase had been alive. They didn't spend their nights rattling about in a cavernous, half-empty mansion, followed by the eyes of disappointed ancestors hanging in their portrait frames.

And they didn't spend a tense hour sitting at the bedside of an aged, brokenhearted man who'd lost his powers of speech and movement but had retained the ability to fix Chase with a watery blue glare that shouted without words: *This is your fault.*

The neglected pasture, the empty silence, his uncle's bedridden state and lack of an heir.

This is your fault.

So no. He shouldn't have thought of Alexandra or the girls at all.

Damn it, his plan had failed miserably. All cursed week long, he'd fought the temptation to go back. It was like Reynaud House anchored one end of a rope, and he'd spent the week tugging at the other end, flexing every last muscle he had in resistance. All he'd earned for his trouble were aches.

Each evening, he fell asleep wishing Alex was nestled beside him.

Each morning, he woke wondering what Millicent had died of today.

During his ride back to London, it grew worse. A raincloud split directly above him, rinsing the sheep dung and dust off his back, and leaving him cold, shivering, and desperate to be home.

And by home, his heart meant with them.

Upon his arrival, Alexandra rushed to him with arms outstretched in welcome. God. He nearly dropped to his knees. The journey had rendered him weary, muddy—shed of all his dutiful intent. If she embraced him, he wasn't sure where he'd find the strength to resist.

He braced himself, hand on the staircase banister.

Instead of catching him in a hug, however, she circled him, thrusting her hands deep into his pockets with bossy movements. Her hands were full of small, round mysteries, and she stuffed them into every possible place, jabbing him in the ribs and chest.

"Sweetmeats for the girls," she explained, seeing his baffled expression. "So you don't return empty-handed."

He could only stare at her.

"You could have warned me you were leaving," she chided. "You should have at least warned *them*. Soothing their feelings wasn't easy. But I told them they must expect your absence from time to time. You're a duke's heir, an important man with duties and so forth." Once she'd deposited her candies on his person, she stood back and smoothed his lapels. "I taught them a song while you were gone. It's a sea chantey, but I took out the crudest parts. They're eager to sing it for you."

"I don't want to hear it."

"Perhaps tomorrow, then."

"No. Not tomorrow, either. Nor the day after that. I'm not going to applaud their songs, or stuff my pockets with candy and gifts."

"It's only a song and some sweetmeats."

"You know very well it's more than that."

Irrational anger built a blaze in his chest. He'd exiled himself for a week to *break* these ties, only to return and find she'd been undermining him all the while. How dare she lead Rosamund and Daisy to believe they could be a family? If he must hurt them, better it be now than later. The last thing he needed was Alexandra building up their hopes.

Or his hopes, for that matter.

He caught her by the arms. "I have never made Rosamund or Daisy promises. Not one. Now you've made them in my stead, setting them up for disappointment. If those girls get their hearts broken—no, *when* those girls get their hearts broken—it will be your fault, Alexandra. Not mine."

He expected her to wince. Shrink from him, wounded by his words.

Instead, she tilted her head and surveyed him with curious eyes. "Are you feeling well?"

"I'm fine. And I meant every word I just said."

"You don't look well. Your face is rather pale. Are you fatigued from the journey?"

"If I'm exhausted, the journey has little to do with it. I'm bone weary of having this conversation over and over again."

She pressed the back of her hand to his cheek. "You're feverish."

"I am not feverish, for God's sake."

Chase supposed his face *was* flushed with heat. And maybe her face *had* gone wavy at the edges. Perhaps his iron grip on the banister felt essential if he wished to remain standing. But all those things were entirely due to anger, not illness.

"Chase," she said tenderly, looping her arm through his. "I think you should go upstairs and lie down. I'll bring you some tea."

"Stop fussing over me." He shook off her arm and tromped up the stairs, at a great cost of effort. Someone seemed to have painted this staircase with treacle while he was away. "Haven't you been paying attention at all? I am infuriated. With you."

"Of course you are," she crooned.

Good God. What would it take to get this message across? Did she need it spelled out in maritime flag signals?

He stopped on the landing of the staircase, out of breath. "Don't want you here. Don't want them here. Going to put a sign on the door tomorrow. No Females Allowed. Not even doll ones."

"No females whatsoever? That might interfere with your plans for the Cave of Carnality."

"*You* interfered with my plans for the Cave of Carnality. Another thing I hold against you."

Her amused little smile made his head swim with frustration.

"This isn't serious, Alex. I am being funny."

"Oh, indeed."

God damn it. None of this was coming out right. His brain buzzed like a hive of wasps. His whole body hurt. "Stop looking at me that way," he growled.

"In what way is that?"

"As if you care."

"I do care."

"As if you expect me to care in return."

"Don't you already?"

"*No.*" He released the banister, drew to his full height, and marshaled all his remaining strength into making one last stand. "Come Michaelmas, the girls are going to school. You will be leaving my employ. I will bid all three of you farewell, and we will carry on with our separate lives. No attachments." He let the words fly like missiles. Gunshots, arrows. Meteors, comets. Dried peas launched through a hollow reed. Anything hurled far and fast enough to wound. "And our little lessons downstairs? Those are through. We are through. I don't know what kind of dream you've sold yourself on, but it is time to wake up. Nothing has changed. *Nothing.*"

He despised himself for putting it to her so viciously. But apparently, it needed to be done. Any alternative would have been crueler, on balance.

"There, now." He dragged air into his lungs. "I hope we understand each other."

She nodded. "I think we do."

"Good."

And then, to put an ironic punctuation mark on this little speech, Chase staggered two steps sideways and fainted at her feet.

"CHASE." ALARMED, ALEXANDRA shook him by the shoulder. "*Chase.*"

No response, other than a low mumble. Something about sheep and manure.

She loosened his cravat. Good heavens, he was burning up. His breath came in shallow rasps. He was even more ill than she'd thought.

Alex surged into action. What with waking the house, calling for physicians, boiling water for tea, and dragging some fifteen stone of weakened, feverish man to his bed, the next few hours passed in a rush.

The following days, however? They slowed to a snail's crawl.

The longer Chase remained ill, the further Alex slipped toward madness. The nature of her relationship with the master of the house was—she hoped—a secret to everyone but the two of them. She didn't have an excuse to visit Chase's bedchamber, let alone sit by his sickbed and keep a nightly vigil, as she yearned to do. Neither could she use the excuse of bringing the girls in to visit. Too much risk of contagion.

The situation served as a painful dose of reality. A reminder of her true status in his life. She'd fancied herself to be something more than just another of his illicit lovers, but she wasn't. Not really. Not in any way that counted now.

She couldn't lay claim to him.

Her only news came from overheard scraps of conversation and bits of information shared by the servants. The doctors came and went, they said. Mr. Reynaud wasn't improving. A pneumonia had settled in his lungs, and his fever hadn't broken.

Alex wore a brave face for Rosamund and Daisy, but fear tightened its grip on her heart. Chase was a strong, healthy man in his prime of life—but even strong, healthy men in their prime of life could be struck down without warning. She knew that all too well.

After three days, she couldn't bear it any longer. She waited until the house went to sleep and then took the chance of slipping into his bedchamber. There would certainly be a maid or footman present, watching over him. On the way, she sifted through a dozen pitiful excuses. Mrs. Greeley was calling, or a new poultice had been prepared, or she, the governess, had been charged with keeping watch for an hour, for some unfathomable reason in a house full of servants.

To her relief, she found him alone.

Alex rushed to his bedside. "Chase."

His eyelids fluttered, and he moaned through cracked lips.

"It's me. It's Alex." She stroked the sweat-dampened hair from his forehead. Sweet Lord, he was still on fire with fever.

She took a cloth from the washstand, dampened it with tepid water, and dabbed his brow and neck.

"Alex." He opened his reddened eyes, struggling to focus on her face. "Sorry, love. Can't lick your cunny tonight. I'm sick."

She laughed aloud, even as tears of relief came to her eyes. The real Chase was still in there somewhere.

"I know you're sick, darling. It's all right." She kissed his forehead.

The door swung open behind her. Alex leapt to her feet and wheeled about.

Mr. Barrow entered the room.

"I didn't mean to intrude," she stammered. "The children have been asking how he's coming along. I thought I'd—"

"Don't worry. No excuses needed. I know about the two of you."

She was briefly stunned. After a moment, she found her tongue. "I know about the two of you, too."

"He told you?"

"I guessed."

"I'm not surprised." He pulled up a chair, and they sat next to one another at the bedside. "You're clever. And he's not very good at hiding it when he cares for someone."

"No, he isn't. And you're too promising a solicitor to take this post without a compelling reason. No one would remain in Chase's employ unless they were either desperate for work, or cared too much about him to leave."

"So what's keeping *you* here?" Her voice was quiet, but steady. "Desperation? Or love?"

"To be honest, I've been asking myself the same question. A bit of both, I think."

Chase had lapsed back into a fitful sleep. His rattling breaths were an unsettling accompaniment to their conversation.

"He isn't getting better, is he?" she asked.

Mr. Barrow exhaled heavily. "No. Much as I hate to even countenance the idea, the lawyer in me is cruelly pragmatic. We may need to prepare for the worst."

A painful lump rose in Alex's throat. "What would happen to the girls?"

"For the time, they'd pass back to the old duke's guardianship, just like everything else attached to the estate. That is, until the next in line can be granted power of attorney."

"They've been through so much already. To thrust them into the unknown again, just when they've begun to feel safe . . ."

"I'd do my best to advocate for them. But in the end, the decisions wouldn't be mine."

"I know. And it isn't only being uprooted that would devastate them. They adore him."

"As do we all." He sighed. "God knows why. He's such a horse's arse."

"He truly is." A hot tear spilled down her cheek.

Mr. Barrow reached for her hand. "All this talk will likely come to nothing. He won't go easily. At school, he was always scrapping with the other boys. Most of the time, in my defense. Mind, he wasn't purely motivated by brotherly love. He copied all my schoolwork. Without me, he never would have passed an exam. But he knows how to put up a fight."

"Right now he's fighting with both hands tied behind his back." Alex sat forward, determined. "We have to even the odds somehow. We can't just sit by and watch."

"All the usual remedies have failed. Bleeding, purging, sweating him out, starving the fever . . . Nothing the doctors have tried has helped."

"Then we send the doctors away," she said firmly. "Whatever we try, we can't possibly do worse."

He looked at her and nodded in agreement. "Very well."

Alex drew to her feet and peeled the heavy wool blanket away from his body. "We have to bring down his fever first. Cool compresses, tepid baths. And he's been sweating so much, he must be miserable with thirst. We should be spooning him all the broth and tea he'll take."

"I'll ask Elinor about an aromatic poultice for his chest."

"Elinor?"

"My wife. Perhaps you'll meet her someday. The two of you would get on well." He lifted Chase's head so Alex could place a cool cloth beneath his neck. "Chase and I were born only three weeks apart, less than one year after his parents married. That alone should tell you how much my natural father valued his wedding vows."

"That must have been difficult for you."

"Not really. I had the better half of the bargain. My father stepped forward to marry my mother and raised me as his own, with love and principles. There wasn't any affection in the Reynaud house."

Alex paused. "Why are you telling me this?"

"Because when it comes to love, Chase has no idea what the devil he's doing. He's brilliant at caring for others. He's bollocks at letting others care for him."

Of course. Of course he was. For weeks, she'd been needling him to express love for the girls—but she'd been taking the wrong tack. Chase needed to believe he deserved their love in return.

But before all that, he needed to not die.

"Well." She plumped his pillow decisively. "He's going to be cared for now, whether he likes it or not."

Chapter Twenty-Five

$\mathcal{C}$hase drifted in and out of consciousness. Gentle waves lapped at his body. Fresh, cool water trickled between his lips. Soothing murmurs came and went. The scents of herbs and lemon hovered about him. And orange flowers. Always orange flowers. As if he were floating in a sea of Alexandra. Or drowning in it. He couldn't tell.

He woke in the morning—it had to be morning, what with the light stabbing him square in the eye—to find her asleep at his bedside, head buried in her arms.

"Alex."

"Chase?" She lifted her head. "Chase." She pressed the back of her hand to his brow. When she spoke, her voice cracked with emotion. "Thank God."

"I told you I wasn't ill." He struggled to a sitting position. "I suppose I just needed a good night's sleep."

She blinked at him. "A night's sleep?"

He rubbed his eyes and cursed. "Don't say you let me sleep through a full day and a half. Good Lord."

"Chase, it's been a week."

"A week? That's impossible." He noted her tangled hair and the dark circles haunting her eyes. "What happened to you?"

"If you think I look dreadful, you should see yourself. You had pneumonia. You were burning up with fever for days. No fewer than three physicians waited on you. You had everyone so worried."

"You needn't have been worried. I'm fine."

He scratched his jaw and found it thick with whiskers. A week. Bloody hell. He swung his leaden legs over the side of the bed and prepared to stand. He could do with a wash and a shave. Perhaps then he'd feel human again.

"Don't you dare." She laid her hand flat on his chest. "You're not yet ready to stand."

"I can determine that for myself, thank you." He brushed away her hand. Planting his feet on the floor, he shifted his weight off the bed and stood. For a fraction of a second, anyhow. Then his knees buckled, and he found himself seated on the bed again, with black and white dots swimming before his eyes. "I've determined I'm not yet ready to stand."

As he waited to regain sensation in his knees, he looked around at the bedchamber's new appearance. His bed hangings had disappeared, and the walls looked as though they'd been repapered. On closer examination, they'd been covered with sketches and letters—all of them in a child's hand. He pulled one from where it had been tacked above his headboard.

Dear Mr. Raynod,

Sam says evry time you kiss Miss Montbadin we have an outing. Pleas get well and kiss her soon.

Yours truley, Daisy Fairfax and Milisent Fairfax

P.S. I made a draring of a tyger, but it is not much good.

Alex peered over his shoulder. "Her writing is coming along well, isn't it? Even if her spelling needs a good deal of work. I quite liked the tiger."

Chase's stomach twisted in a knot, and it wasn't from hunger.

Alex reached for a paper at the bedside, unfolded it, and put it in his hand. "This one was from Rosamund."

Dear Mr. R.,

Miss M. says I'm to write a letter of confession. I took four shillings and a nacre button from your library desk, this Monday last. They have been returned. I am sorry to have committed such a grievous act. Please take mercy on your wayward ward. The Tower of London is much too poorly lit for reading.

Yours, etc.
Sam F.

"I suspect she took more money than that," Alex said, "but I only caught her with the four shillings."

"I see."

"Oh, I must send a note to John straightaway. He was here all night, and he went home to sleep. He'll be so relieved to hear you're awake."

Chase was confused. "John? Who's John?"

"Mr. Barrow."

"You're on a first-name basis with my solicitor?"

"No. I'm on a first-name basis with your brother. Ever since we gave the doctors the boot, we've been trading the watch back and forth." She reached for a cup. "Here, take some broth."

He pushed the cup away. "What are you doing?"

"You need nourishment to regain your strength. Perhaps I'll take the girls for ices and bring you some back? It will be some days before you can take solid food, but it would be a change from beef tea."

"It's not the beef tea," he said irritably.

Damn it, had his whole week in the country been for nothing? He'd meant to put distance between them. This was the opposite of distance. This was closeness. Intense, unbearable closeness unlike anything he'd ever known. The walls were closing in on him, with their sharp-toothed tigers and sweetly printed words.

"I told you in no uncertain terms we'd reached the end of this.

You, me, and the girls. Then I wake up to you fussing over me, feeding me spoonfuls of beef tea. Drawings of flowers and tigers and pirate ships all over the walls." He gestured angrily. "For Christ's sake, Alex. When are you going to give this up?"

She stood still for a moment, and then set the teacup down with a clatter. "'Why would a sea captain's daughter be afraid of boats?' You asked me that the day you left. Recall it?"

Chase was dizzied by the swift turn of conversation. "I suppose."

"I'll tell you why I'm afraid of boats. I lost my father when I was twelve years old. The *Esperanza* foundered in a storm. He threw a blanket over my shoulders and forced me to leave in the little captain's gig. Told me to row as hard as I could. He promised to call me back to the ship once it was safe, but the ship was breaking apart already. My father ordered the crew to the jolly boat. He kept trying until the end, making certain all his men were safe, but . . ." She swallowed hard. "As they say, the captain goes down with the ship."

God Almighty. How terrified she must have been.

"I tried to reunite with the rest of the crew." She shook her head. "But it was too dark, and the waves were too high. We were separated within moments, and I couldn't reach them. I called and called until I was hoarse. Perhaps they, too, foundered and perished. When the morning came and the sky cleared, I was alone. Drifting in the middle of the ocean. A crewman on an English brig happened to see me, and they came to my rescue. Ask me how many days I waited."

"Sweetheart, you don't need to—"

"Eight," she said. "Eight days."

Jesus.

"No provisions. Only a bit of rainwater. I can't describe it. The slow crawl of time when you're dying of thirst. Every breath, every swallow. It's all you can think of. Toward the end, I grew delirious, and that was a mercy. I still find myself back there in dreams. I don't imagine the boat, the storm. I only feel myself drifting in the dark, and when I wake, I'm desperate for water."

"So that night when you came down to the kitchen . . ."

She nodded.

"Alex, I'm so sorry."

"You don't need to pity me. I'm here. And I'm alive. So there's your answer, Chase. When am I giving up? I'm not. I did not give up on myself then. I am not giving up on you now." She smoothed her apron. "Now I'm going to tidy myself up, take the girls for ices, eat two of them myself, and not bring you any. When we return, I'll send Rosamund and Daisy in to visit you, and you *will* behave. Treat me as you like. But you will not belittle those girls for loving you. I won't allow it. And do not ever waste your breath again with more of that 'lost cause' nonsense. Consider yourself found."

"Wait." He tried to push himself to a stand again, but he'd wasted what strength he had in the first attempt. "Don't go. Give me a chance to—"

"Oh, and by the way." She stopped at the door. "While you were ill, you pissed yourself. Twice. Just so you know."

THE PIRATES HELD Chase captive, and this time there was no slipping the knots to escape. Over his days of slow recuperation in bed, he was indoctrinated in the Pirate's Code, fitted for a peg leg, and given a gold hoop earring. (God only knew where Rosamund had pilfered that from.) His tea and broth were served in ship's rations, on two-hour bells.

Alexandra had taught her sailors well. So well, in fact, that she never needed to join the work at all. Chase had the feeling he was being punished. And he had the feeling he deserved it.

What she'd given him, however, was an excellent motivation to recover.

By the fourth day, he'd had enough. If he had to listen to Daisy read that book about girls climbing towers and boys picking flowers one more time, he would go mad.

When the girls came in that afternoon, they found him out of bed, bathed, properly attired, and ready to do something, anything, other than convalesce.

"Oh, boo." Daisy pouted. "You shaved. You made a better prisoner when you were scruffy."

"It's just as well," Rosamund said. "Now that you're presentable, you can come with us to tea."

"Tea?"

"We're going to tea at Lady Penny's house," Daisy said. "We've been two weeks in a row now. She's Miss Mountbatten's friend, and she has a hedgehog. And an otter named Hubert, and a goat named Marigold, and a two-legged dog named Bixby, and a heap of other animals."

"Literally," Rosamund interjected. "Literally a heap."

"Today, I'm allowed to pet the hedgehog if I remember my manners. Also, Miss Teague bakes the scrummiest biscuits." She took Chase by the hand and tugged. "You should join us."

"I don't believe I'm invited," he replied.

"You can come. That is, if you wish." Alexandra stood in the doorway. She was wearing that fetching yellow frock again, and he suddenly felt starved for sunshine.

Starved for her company, as well.

"You're certain?" They locked eyes, and he searched her expression for hints to her true emotions. "I don't want to go where I'm not wanted."

"Lady Penelope would welcome you." She worked her fingers into her gloves with short, impatient tugs. "She takes in every creature that wanders past, no matter how ill behaved."

Chase knew the tone of a woman's enthusiastic invitation, and that was not it. Alex was clearly hoping he'd decline.

This afternoon, he'd be disappointing her hopes once again. "I'll order the carriage."

Chapter Twenty-Six

*A*lex cursed herself all the way to Penny's house. Why had she invited him? She'd been so relieved to see him well and strong again, she hadn't been thinking clearly. And she never dreamed he'd accept.

The carriage ride to Bloom Square wasn't a long one, and they arrived before she was ready.

Once Chase had helped her out of the carriage, she kept a tight grip on his hand. "Lady Penelope Campion and Nicola Teague are two of my dearest friends in the world."

"I understand."

She didn't think he did, not truly. "Penny and Nic . . . well, they're not the usual sort of ladies. They weren't among the finishing school set. If you are even the slightest bit teasing or unkind, I will rip that gold earring straight through your earlobe."

He cursed and fumbled at his ear until he'd removed it himself.

She shouldn't have mentioned it.

"One last thing," she muttered as Rosamund reached for the door knocker. "If Lady Penelope Campion offers you a sandwich— you will eat it. And you will like it."

"Why does that sound like a threat?"

She didn't answer. He'd learn soon enough for himself.

The door opened, and Penny greeted each of the girls with sound kisses on their cheeks. "Come in, darlings."

Then she noticed Chase, and Alex sent up a prayer. *Please, Penny. For once, remain calm.*

Penny threw her arms around Chase and caught him in a hug, rocking him back and forth. "I'm so relieved to see you. I've been desperately worried ever since I heard you were ill. Alex was beside herself."

Right. Brilliant.

"Come in, come in," she urged. "Nicola's already here. She's made teacakes."

Alex held the girls back. "Wait. You know they're meant to be practicing. Go on, girls."

The girls curtsied. Not especially smoothly, but they were improving. "Good afternoon, Lady Penelope," they said in a chorus of two.

"Rosamund, would you introduce Lady Penny to our guest?"

"Mr. Reynaud, may I present—"

"No, no. The other way around," Alex said. "You ask Lady Penelope if you may present him, because she's his superior in society." *And his superior in many other ways.*

"Alex, you know I despise that sort of thinking," Penny said.

"They need to learn. Their guardian wishes them to be proper young ladies." She turned to Chase. "Isn't that right, Mr. Reynaud?"

Rosamund began again, the promise of teacakes outweighing her impatience with the exercise. "Lady Penny, may I present our guardian, Mr. Reynaud. Mr. Reynaud, this is Lady Penelope Campion."

Chase not only bowed, but took her hand and kissed it with devilish charm. "Enchanted, Lady Penelope."

"Oh," Penny sighed. "You *are* wonderful. I knew you would be."

Etiquette lessons were left at the door. Penny's house didn't lend itself to propriety, anyway. The upholstery was shredded, and the carpet pattern was medallions interspersed with tufts of loose fur, and if a one-eyed kitten wasn't mewling and climbing the draperies, a yipping two-legged dog was racing around the room on its specially made cart.

Alex loved the place unreservedly.

Chase was introduced to Nicola, whose reception of him was

as icy as Penny's was warm. No kisses on the hand. Nic swiveled her gaze to Alex the moment he'd turned away and mouthed a simple *Why?*

Alex could only shrug.

They all settled themselves in the parlor. The girls dashed off to the back garden at once.

"Where are they going?" Chase asked.

"Oh, they've gone to feed Hubert his tea," Penny explained.

"Hubert?" he asked.

"The otter."

"Yes, of course. A beautiful creature, the otter."

"Isn't it, though? They're so affectionate. Hubert adores Rosamund and Daisy. We all do. You must be so proud of your girls." She lifted a plate and offered it to him. "Sandwich?"

Aha. Here was the moment of truth.

"This one is a new recipe of mine." Penny pointed at one half of the plate. "I call it tuna-ish."

"I'm . . . unfamiliar with that."

"Well, the tuna is a Mediterranean fish, and I had a letter from a cousin in Cadiz who told me it makes an excellent sandwich with a bit of soured cream. But I don't consume animals, so I made my own version. Instead of tuna fish, it's tuna-*ish*. The secret is in the brine."

She pointed at the other half of the plate. "And this is my usual specialty. Sham. It's everyone's favorite."

"Sham?"

"It's like ham. Only made from vegetables, all pressed together into a loaf and sliced thin. I've been told it tastes even better than the real thing."

Alex caught his eye.

Do not hurt her feelings. Do not. Or I will never forgive you.

"Lady Penny, that sounds delightful," Chase said smoothly, and for a moment even Alex believed him. "Thank you, I'll take two of each."

In the end, he ate *three* of each—and asked Penny for the recipes. He praised Nicola's baking and listened to her describe her latest fascination: the engineering challenges of tunneling under the Thames.

Even the hedgehog uncurled in his hand, offering her soft underbelly for a gentle stroke.

He didn't commit a single act of unforgivable behavior. With the exception of being unforgivably wonderful, perhaps.

As they hugged in farewell, Penny whispered a teasing question in Alex's ear. "So? How does it feel to be falling in love?"

Hopeless, Alex silently answered.

It felt hopeless indeed—because it was.

Chapter Twenty-Seven

*I*n the office the next morning, Chase clutched his side and groaned.

Barrow gave him a sidelong glance. "Is it the bank accounts?"

"No, it's the sham. Or maybe the tuna-ish."

"I won't ask."

"Good. I don't want to talk about it."

Barrow stretched his arms overhead and yawned. "You know, I've noticed that doll of Daisy's hasn't taken ill in weeks."

"I suppose my own bedridden state was entertainment enough."

"Hm." Barrow cast a pensive look out the window. "Speaking of beds . . . As far as I can tell, you haven't shared one with a woman in weeks, either."

"Oh, yes. I did finally manage a period of celibacy, didn't I? And all I had to do was nearly die." Chase narrowed his eyes at him. "What are you on about, then? Don't tell me you're going to badger me to keep the girls."

"I mean to suggest you should marry Miss Mountbatten. And then keep the girls."

What?

"That's impossible."

"Don't you love her? I think you love her."

Chase avoided answering that question, and he did so easily. He'd had a great deal of practice avoiding merely thinking about that question.

"It doesn't matter how I feel about her," he said. "I'm not marrying, ever. You know my reasons."

"Yes, but your reasons aren't good."

"I'm responsible for my cousin's death. I refuse to replace Anthony's legacy with my own sorry bloodline. The title should have been his." He hesitated, then decided to have out with it. "And if it couldn't be his, it might as well have been yours. You're the elder between us. We both have Reynaud blood."

Barrow sat back in his chair, crossing his legs. "So. We're going to talk about that now, are we?"

"We may as well." Chase gestured at all the paperwork around them, and the immense wealth and lands it represented. "You'd make a much better duke than I will. Are you certain I can't give this to you? At least half of it?"

"I'm afraid not. It's all entailed."

"Well, at least start embezzling or something."

Barrow chuckled. "I'll take that under advisement."

"I'm serious."

"Chase, you're going to make a better nobleman than half the peers in England. At least you look after your dependents. You know, it hasn't escaped my attention that since we took over all this, you've asked me to establish no fewer than six trusts and legacies for 'devoted servants.' I've seen your servants. They're not devoted."

Chase sighed. Difficult to argue that point.

"So I'm guessing I'm not the only bastard your father sired." After a moment, Barrow asked quietly, "What about the girls?"

"I don't know." Chase covered his eyes. "It's possible they're his, but I can't be certain. Doesn't make a difference, though. I intend to provide for them. School, dowries, trusts."

"So you can care for all your father's bastards, but not a family of your own?"

"Bloody hell, Barrow. I don't 'care' for all his bastards. It's just money."

Barrow's face went hard. "Oh, really."

"That's not what I meant." Chase cursed his thoughtlessness. "But this is a perfect illustration of the point. I am shite at caring. Friendship, maybe I can manage. But guardianship? Family? Absolutely not. After Anthony was killed, I took his body home to Belvoir. I'd sent an express in advance with the news, but somehow it hadn't yet arrived. My uncle only learned of it upon seeing the body. Do you know what it looks like when a person's heart breaks right in front of you?"

Barrow shook his head.

"Well, I do. And I never want to see it again."

They were silent for a minute.

"Chase, when you love someone there's always a chance you'll hurt them. But if you let them go, hurting them isn't a possibility—it's a certainty. I watched that woman spend day and night by your bedside while you lingered near death." He arched an eyebrow. "You pissed yourself, you know. Twice."

"Yes, I heard that," he said irritably. "Thank you for bringing it up. Again."

"Alexandra's in love with you. If you can't find it within yourself to love her back, then you'd better make that very clear. Sooner rather than later."

Chase nodded. As always, his annoyingly smug brother had the right of it. "I've promised them an outing to the British Museum tomorrow. I'll speak with Alexandra at the first opportunity."

AFTER A MERE two minutes in the Egyptian Room, Alexandra knew this outing was the most brilliant idea she'd had all summer.

"Look at them." She nudged Chase's arm. "Have you ever seen those girls so happy?"

"Of course they're happy," he replied, sounding markedly less enthusiastic about it. "Daisy is surrounded by death, mummies stacked three to a case, and even Rosamund couldn't dream of this much plundered gold."

"Just think of the educational benefits."

Daisy pushed up her spectacles and bent over a label on the

glass case of an intricately carved stone coffin. She sounded out the word, syllable by syllable. "Sar-co-pha-gus."

"Come look at this." Rosamund waved her sister over. "Before they wrapped the mummy, they took the organs out and stored them in golden jars." She pointed. "This one's for the brain. It says here they pulled it out through the mummy's nose."

"Ooooh."

Alex turned to Chase. "You can't deny that they're learning."

He only shook his head in response.

Secretly, Alex agreed with him somewhat. She, too, hoped the girls would develop other interests with time—or if not other interests, at least less morbid and criminal applications of them.

"May we go on to the South Seas curiosities?" Rosamund asked. "I want to see the maps and things from Captain James Cook."

"You may go ahead of us," Alex told her, "if you mind Daisy. We'll join you in a moment. And no running."

Once the girls had left the Egyptian Room, Alex maneuvered toward a quieter corner between galleries. "We should talk."

"I've been thinking the same."

"The summer's drawing to an end."

He nodded. "And so is our arrangement."

"Yes." She lowered her voice. "Promise me one thing, if you will. Wherever you send them to school, don't make them stay there over school holidays. If you won't have them at your house, send them to me. I stayed at school every holiday for years, and it was misery."

"Surely you didn't stay *every* holiday."

"Where would I have gone? I'd no family. There was one year another schoolgirl invited me to summer with her family at their country home. But in the end, it didn't come to pass."

She didn't tell him the rest of the story. That the schoolgirl— Violet Liddell—had spent weeks describing all the wonderful things they would do together that summer. Picnics and buying ribbons in the village and staying up all night, giggling. Alexandra had dreamed of it every night for months, imagining all the adventures she and Violet would have together. What she looked forward to most wasn't adventurous at all. Family dinners.

When the term ended and Violet's parents came to collect her, Alex was waiting outside with her trunk, dressed in her best frock and beside herself with excitement for the journey. She waited to be introduced to Mr. and Mrs. Liddell, but that introduction never came. Instead, Violet turned to her with a cruel smile and said, "I hope you have a fine summer, Alexandra."

And she climbed into her family's carriage and left.

Alex would never forget the shame of lugging her trunk back up to the attic dormitory one step at a time, while the other schoolgirls stood by laughing. They'd known what was coming. They'd all known.

"Just promise me," she said. "Easter, Christmas, summers. Don't leave them there. They need to feel that they have a home."

"Blast," Chase muttered, turning toward the wall.

"What is it?"

"I spied someone I know—and don't particularly like."

"Where?" Alex turned her head.

"Don't look," he hissed. "I'm hoping he didn't notice me."

She returned her gaze to what lay in front of her. "I'm hoping no one notices we're staring at a blank wall."

"Very well, have a look. But be casual about it. At the far end of the gallery. The shorter fellow compensating by means of an absurdly tall hat."

Alex turned in place, trying her best to look aimless about it. Although she wasn't certain it looked better to be aimlessly turning in circles than to be staring at a blank wall.

As she completed her circle, she caught sight of the man Chase had described. Her stomach churned.

"Tell me he's not looking this way," Chase mumbled.

"He's looking this way." Which meant Alex wanted to pick up her skirts and sprint in the opposite direction.

"Reynaud?" The voice carried from the other end of the gallery. "Chase Reynaud, is that you?"

Chase cursed under his breath. "No escaping it now." He turned and raised his hand in a halfhearted greeting. "That's Sir W—"

"Sir Winston Harvey."

"You know him?"

"I set the clocks in his house for three years."

"Then you know he's insufferable."

Her skin crawled. "Oh, yes."

In the distance, Sir Winston began taking leave of his current conversational partner—the quicker, presumably, to make his way down the length of the gallery to them.

"I'll go to the girls," Alex said. "They've moved on to the Grecian marbles."

"No, stay." He tugged her to his side, drawing her hand through his arm. "If you're here, he won't regale me with tales of his sordid brothel adventures. He seems to think I'll be impressed."

"I'd rather go with the girls."

"What did he do?" He must have caught the tense note in her voice. "Tell me."

"It was mostly just leering," she whispered. "A pinch or two. You know, the usual."

"The *usual?*"

"The usual for him. Chase, it was years ago. He won't even recognize me. Just let me go."

But it was too late. The man was upon them now.

No escape.

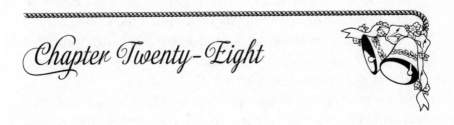

Chapter Twenty-Eight

$\mathcal{C}$hase had never been one for committing acts of violence. He wasn't opposed to a bit of vengeance, but somehow the opportunity had thus far eluded him. He always seemed to show up too late, after the damage was already done.

That was not the case today.

"Reynaud, you old cur. Haven't seen you about the clubs much of late." Sir Winston's attention slid to Alex, and he raked her with a lecherous gaze. "Good to know you're still in fine form. Who's this?"

"I'm just the governess," Alex quickly volunteered.

"You are not just the governess," Chase corrected. "You are not 'just' anything."

"Well, of course she's not 'just' the governess." Sir Winston gave him an unsubtle wink. "They never are, are they?"

Chase clapped the man on the shoulder, as if in appreciation of a good joke. And then, turning his back to the room, he drove his fist into the leering blackguard's gut.

Sir Winston's hat skittered across the floor.

The man himself was doubled over and groaning. "What the devil was that for, Reynaud?"

"You owe Miss Mountbatten an apology."

"An apology for what?"

"For insulting her today, to begin. And for taking liberties with her in the past."

"In the past? For God's sake, man. What are you on about? I've never laid eyes on the chit in my life."

Alex ducked her head, evading the gaze of the other museum-goers. She murmured, "I told you he wouldn't remember."

"But since you mention it," Sir Winston said jovially, "I wouldn't mind knowing her. When you're done with her, send her my way."

The man reached to pick up his hat.

Chase stomped on it. He held the man's gaze as he slowly and meaningfully lowered his boot, crushing the tower of felted beaver to a fuzzy burnt pancake.

There, you bastard. Try compensating with that.

"Apologize to Miss Mountbatten." He growled the words through clenched teeth. "Or by the gods of the Egyptians, I will pull your brain out through your nose and stuff you in that sarcophagus for the next three thousand years."

Sir Winston knew when he was bested. He straightened and bowed. "My apologies, Miss Montbarren."

"Mountbatten."

"Miss Mountbatten."

Once they'd watched that bit of human refuse depart the gallery, they collected the girls and left the museum. Rosamund and Daisy protested the hasty departure. While they waited on the carriage, Chase bribed them with oranges from a boy selling them on the street.

At home, the girls raced upstairs to mummify Millicent. Chase strode into his study. Alexandra followed him, closing the door after her and turning the key.

"The nerve of that blackguard." He jerked off his gloves and slapped them against the edge of the desk. "I'm sorry if he upset you."

"Perhaps Sir Winston Harvey upset me, but what you did was more humiliating by far. You made me a spectacle."

"Hold a moment. I'm not the villain here. That bastard deserved everything I gave him, and more. My only regret is that he had but one hat to crush."

"It's all about your pride, isn't it? Did you pause to consider my feelings at all?"

"Your feelings were my foremost concern. How dare he speak to you in such a manner. As if you were my—"

"Mistress?" she supplied.

That was the kindest way of putting it, he supposed.

"Naturally he assumed I was your mistress." She approached the other side of his desk and placed her hands flat on the top. "Do you know why? Because I *am* your mistress. And now that fact will be all over Mayfair by dinnertime."

"First, you're not my mistress," he said. "Second, don't worry about gossip. I highly doubt that Sir Winston Harvey will be eager to repeat the tale."

"No, he won't dare say a thing about you crushing his hat. He'll save all his venom for describing me. Lord, you are so naïve."

"*Me*. You're calling *me* naïve?"

"Yes, you. Chase, you are a wealthy, well-placed man. The heir to a duke. Society will forgive you anything. Women in my position are not so fortunate. We work for our living at the pleasure of the upper classes. The tiniest hint of scandal, and we are *ruined*. Unemployable, forever. That's the way English society works."

"Then English society needs to do better."

"Well, unless you intend to change it by the end of the summer, I'd thank you not to throw me under the wheels of a high-sprung phaeton." She crossed her arms and paced back and forth. "What if word spreads that your governess is really your mistress—"

"You're not my mistress."

"—and then Rosamund and Daisy aren't accepted to school? I'm counting on that extra two hundred pounds you promised me. I have to make a life for myself beyond this summer."

As if he would let her wander off penniless to starve. "You needn't worry about your wages. You know I'll take care of you."

"Really? How? You'll set me up in a little house in the country somewhere, with an income and a companion, perhaps. Like a *mistress*."

"For the last time." He came around the desk and seized her by the arms. "You are not my mistress."

"Then what am I?" Her voice quavered. "What am I to you?"

"You're . . ."

Everything.

A bitter smile curved her lips. "Don't strain yourself reaching for that answer."

"Bloody hell, Alex. I don't know what to call it." He pulled her close, crushing her body to his. "I just know I'll be damned if I'll let you go."

WHEN CHASE'S MOUTH crushed to hers, Alex crushed right back. Equal and opposite reactions.

The result was glorious.

In their time together, they had shared a great many kisses. Passionate kisses, tender kisses, stolen kisses, secret kisses . . . but if she'd known how thrilling an angry kiss could be, Alex would have started rows with him nightly.

They grappled and clutched, each punishing the other for unspoken sins. She'd missed his heat, his scent, his hunger for her. The way his hardness filled her hand, and the salt of his skin on her tongue.

It had been so long. Too long. His fault.

He gripped her bottom and lifted her, shoving her onto the desk. Papers and quills fell to the floor.

At some point they ceased fighting each other and began fighting the space between them. They became allies in the war on clothing. Buttons were battled; laces, conquered. Petticoats marched north. His shirt was the final white flag of surrender, fluttering to the ground.

When skin finally met skin, the heat was so searing, they gasped in unison.

His greedy mouth and hands pushed her further onto the desk. He wanted her beneath him. Not this time. She shifted their positions, pushing and pulling and guiding, until he lay on his back atop the desk and she straddled his waist.

There. Much better.

She gazed down at his strong, defined torso, running her hands over muscle and sinew, then tracing all the same paths with her fingernails, lightly scraping over his skin. His hips bucked, and his arousal pushed against her belly. Aggressive. Impatient.

Not yet. Not just yet.

She bent to kiss him, running tongue and teeth down his neck, over his nipples, relishing every hiss of breath and strangled groan she could draw from his body. His hands went to her hair, yanking pins from her upsweep and gathering fistfuls of the unbound locks. The sharp tug on her scalp sent a thrill racing down to her toes.

He'd taken back some control, and he used it, dragging her up for a clash of tongues and teeth. And then pushing her back down his body, down and down, until there was no mistaking his intent.

Fine. She would let him have his way. But she was going to take her time.

She teased open the buttons of his trouser falls.

One . . .

By one . . .

By one.

Then she slipped her fingers inside, curling them about his cock.

One . . .

By one . . .

By one.

Until she drew him out, thick and ruddy and straining. And dropped light kisses down the underside of his shaft.

One . . .

By one . . .

By one.

He growled like a beast. A beast who was hers for the taming. He tightened his grip on her hair. "Alex, you'll kill me."

Well, they couldn't have that.

Alex had never felt more powerful. To most of the world, she was small and slight and insignificant. Even invisible. But right here, right now, she had this man quivering at her slightest touch. Begging for her mouth.

She ran her tongue all the way from his root to the tip, and then took him into her mouth.

With a deep, yearning sigh, he released his grip on her hair. He arched his hips, pushing deeper. *Take more of me*, his body urged. *And yet more.*

She wanted more of him, too.

With a few last teasing licks, she raised her head. Hiking her skirts to her waist, she straddled his erection, trapping the rigid length between his belly and her cleft. She placed her hands flat on his chest and drew tall, rocking against him.

Yes. Yes. Yes.

His hands went to her hips, and he guided her into a faster rhythm. His hardness rubbed against her just where she needed it, pushing wave after wave of pleasure through her veins.

She locked eyes with him, riding his body with emboldened desire. Faster now. Her lips fell apart, and her breath rose and fell in her chest. The haze of pleasure descended on her, growing thicker and thicker until that one perfect, shimmering ray of light pierced the fog, pushing her over the edge.

She rode the climax to its sweet, sweet end, and then kept rolling her hips in pursuit of his pleasure.

His thighs went rigid. He was close.

"Chase," she whispered. "Stay with me."

There was no reply, spoken or otherwise. His head had fallen back. The tendons of his neck were strained. His eyes were closed tight. He clutched her hips and set his own tempo, dragging her over his length at a brisk pace until he shuddered with release.

All was quiet, save for his harsh breaths.

He pulled her down to him, clasping her to his chest. His spilled seed glued their bellies together. She laid her ear to his heartbeat.

"Where are you?" she asked.

He sounded befuddled. "Here. On the desk. Under you."

"At the end, I mean. Every time we're together, at the end you go somewhere else. I don't know where you are, but it's not with me."

He stroked her hair. "I'm not sure what you mean."

"I'm not, either."

She slipped from his embrace and climbed off the desk in an ungainly fashion. Why was it that in the prelude to lovemaking she was made of breasts and hips and confident hands, and once the pleasure was over, everything was elbows and knees?

She pulled the sleeves of her frock up over her shoulders, anxious to make her escape. If he could go somewhere else, she could, too. "This has to be the last time. I can't be your mistress, or whatever else you wish to call it."

"And I can't offer you anything more."

"I never dreamed you would."

Such a lie. She'd dreamed of it before she'd even known his name, and she'd dreamed of it as recently as five minutes ago. Foolishly, every time.

Because he was going to be a duke. And girls like Alex—part American, part Spanish, part island native, entirely orphaned, christened Catholic, and working class—did not become duchesses. Girls like Alex didn't even get invited to schoolmates' homes for the holidays. They were paid too little, worked too hard. Pinched in the corridor or overlooked entirely.

And they were forgotten, as soon as they left the room.

Chapter Twenty-Nine

Chase sat at his desk with a tumbler of brandy, sorting through letters he'd received from the headmasters of England's finest boarding schools for girls.

All acceptances, of course. The promise of a generous donation to the school worked wonders that way.

He was at a loss for the best criterion. Academic philosophy? Popularity with upper-crust families? Proximity to London or Belvoir?

By the time he'd sorted and re-sorted the letters four different ways, his quandary became clear. The question wasn't how to choose where to send them.

The question was whether he could bear to send them at all.

He was drawn from his deliberation by footsteps pounding down the stairs. As he watched from his desk, a figure in white flew past, dark hair streaming behind it. The front door opened, and then banged shut. Either Alexandra had just bolted from the house, or a ghost was playing tricks.

Chase didn't believe in ghosts.

He rose and followed her, walking out the door and into the brisk night air. "Alex?" He turned in every direction. No sight of her. He lifted his voice. "Alexandra."

"I'm over here."

The voice came from the green in the center of the square. It was only once he'd crossed the lane and run a fruitless scan of the garden that he pinpointed her location.

He found her by nearly tripping over her.

"Alex, what the hell are you doing lying in the grass in your night rail in the middle of the night?"

"The comet. This could be it." She kicked at his boot. "Now kindly go back in the house. You're blocking the sky."

Instead, Chase lay down on his back beside her.

"I told you, go back in the house."

"I'm not going to just leave you here."

She shivered beside him. "As you like, then."

"If this could be a comet, don't you need the telescope?"

"Not for this part. It's a definite smudge. It's not among Messier's objects, nor could I find it in my lists of identified comets. Now I need to watch it and see whether it moves in pace with the stars."

"Which bit of sky are we watching?"

"Follow the line of my finger." She leaned close and pointed her arm at the sky. "Do you see the three stars in a triangle? It's that tiny blur just above the bottommost point. Do you see it?"

"I think so."

In truth, Chase didn't see anything other than the usual flurries of stars, but he didn't want to disappoint her. He wanted to be part of this.

"How much time will it take for you to be certain?" he asked.

"A quarter hour, at least. Perhaps more."

"I'll make note of the time." He opened the glass cover of his watch, gently skimming with his fingertips to take note of the hands' positions.

They lay side by side in silence for what felt like an hour.

"How much time has elapsed?" she asked.

Chase consulted his timepiece, feeling around with his fingers. "I'm not certain. If I had to guess, I'd say . . . about three minutes."

She moaned. "This is so nerve-racking."

"You know what they say. A watched comet never moves."

Another eternity passed. Perhaps they were up to five minutes now. He couldn't bear the quiet tension.

"I have this nightmare," he said. "It comes back again and again. It's morning, and I'm standing in the nursery. All of us, looking down at the bed as usual. And I'm preparing to say something about the tragedy of pinworms, when I realize the hand in mine isn't flesh and blood. It's wood. Then I turn, and I realize I'm holding Millicent's hand, and the body on the bed is Daisy's."

Alexandra's hand slid into his, and he squeezed her fingers tight.

"She's just lying there. Pale, unmoving. And there are buttons on her eyes. I start shouting at her. Shaking her little body. But I can't move the buttons from her eyes to wake her, and then . . . Then the bed starts to change. Suddenly it's gray and uneven. The paving stones of an alleyway. There's blood pooling beneath her. I'm frantic to find the source, press my hand over the wound, but I can't. It just keeps spreading. And then . . ."

"And then?"

"And then I wake up. Drenched in cold sweat."

"Oh, Chase. I'm so sorry. That sounds terrifying."

"It *is* terrifying. And even when I've awoken from it, and I know it's only a dream, it doesn't stop being terrifying. The fear only grows, and I know it's because—" He paused to swallow hard. "I know it's because I love them."

She clasped his hand tight.

He swore. "I love those girls so damned much, Alex."

"I know you do. I've known it for ages."

"Yes, yes. You know everything." He gave her a nudge. "The least you could do is wait until I've finished spilling the *entirety* of my heart on the grass. Then you can gloat over it."

"I am duly chastened. Please continue."

"Between the fear and the fondness, it keeps getting worse. One feeds the other. The very idea of seeing them hurt—not being able to help—scares the shite out of me."

"I'm fairly certain that's natural."

"And it's not only the accidents and illnesses. It's everything. Rosamund's ten. What do I do if she tells me she fancies a boy?

Worse, what if a boy takes a fancy to her?" A fresh possibility struck him, and it was the most horrifying by far. "Good God, what the hell will I do the first time she gets her courses?"

Alex laughed.

"Don't laugh. I'm being serious here. I don't trust myself to be a competent guardian. How can I? If I were someone else, I wouldn't trust me, either."

"Well, *I* trust you to be an excellent guardian. That's the honest truth. Because I love Rosamund and Daisy, too, and I couldn't bear to leave them at summer's end if I didn't trust you completely. Does that help?"

"A bit."

It would help a great deal more if she wasn't going to leave at summer's end. Or if she wasn't going to leave at all.

"Chase." She clutched his arm, as if she'd suddenly recalled the reason they were lying in the grass in the middle of the square at midnight. "Has it been a quarter hour, do you think?"

He felt for his timepiece. "More than that."

"Oh, no. I've lost track of the smudge."

"The sky's only so big. It can't have gone far."

"Shush." She held her breath, studying the darkness overhead. "Oh. There it is. Chasing Altair now." She rose to her feet, leaving him sitting befuddled and alone in the grass.

"Wait," he called after her. She was halfway back to the house already. "Is that good or bad? What does Altair mean?"

"In Arabic, it means 'flying eagle.'" She reached the front door, and turned to answer him. "In practical terms at the moment? It means I must go to the Royal Observatory, at once."

FROM THERE, THE race was on.

Chase scrambled to his feet and followed her into the house.

She turned to him. "Where do you think I could find a hackney at this time of night?"

"A hackney? Don't be ridiculous. I'll order the carriage. Go and change into something warmer, and I'll meet you in front."

"You're coming with me?"

"I'm sure as hell not letting you go alone. All the way to Greenwich in the middle of the night?"

"What about the girls?"

"I'll let Mrs. Greeley know we've gone out. She'll watch them. We'll be home before they wake tomorrow morning." He took her by the shoulders. "Go upstairs. Fetch your boots and your wrap. Leave the rest to me."

She nodded. "All right."

"I'll go down and tell the coachman we're for Greenwich."

"Wait," she said decisively. The fog around her mind appeared to have lifted. "Tell him we're going to Billingsgate docks."

"Billingsgate docks?"

"Yes." She drew a breath. "We must take a boat."

"Are you mad? I'm not putting you on a boat. Not after what you told me about the shipwreck, and losing your father, and drifting about the ocean alone with no food and water for days."

"I know what I told you, Chase. This is not the time to rattle through the horrid details. The roads are too dark at night to travel swiftly by carriage. Taking a boat is the fastest way. If we don't arrive in Greenwich before the comet dips below the horizon, we'll have to wait until tomorrow night to have it verified. If we wait, it might be raining or foggy. Some other observer might claim it first. I don't want to take the risk."

"Very well. If you're certain."

She nodded. "I think I can do it." Her eyes briefly closed, and her hands clenched in fists. "No, I *know* I can do it. So long as you're with me."

Oh, I'll be with you. Just you try to get away. "You'll be safe, Alex. I'd say you have my word on it, but as little as that's worth, it scarcely feels worth offering." He stared solemnly into her eyes. "I'd part with my life before I let you go."

I CAN DO this, Alex told herself. *I can, I can, I can.*

It had been easier to believe that at the house. Now that she stood on the dock, it was proving more difficult to actually go through with the decision. The last time she'd stood on these docks, she'd fallen into the Thames, and her livelihood had slipped from her grasp.

But if that hadn't happened, she wouldn't be here with Chase tonight.

Chase joined her, having finished making arrangements with whichever boatman he'd roused from his sleep. "We'll be under way in a trice. He's just readying the skiff."

"You hired a skiff?" She'd been expecting a wherry.

"There's a breeze tonight. Sails are faster than oars."

Yes, but oars felt a great deal safer.

She looked down at the river. The Thames flowed like a river of ink beneath them, dark and silent. Ominous.

"You can still change your mind," he said.

She shook her head. "You sent the carriage on without us."

"So I can hire another."

"No. We'll take the skiff."

This night, this journey—it was what she'd been working toward all this time. She wasn't going to allow irrational fears to stand between her and that goal.

Chase boarded the craft first, then extended a hand to help her do the same. The closer she inched toward the edge of the dock, the more furiously her heart thrashed about her chest. Her tongue felt coated in sand.

"Don't look at the water, Alex. Look at me."

She obeyed. What with the darkness, the black of his pupils had swallowed up all of the dazzling green. There was no charm in his gaze; only sincerity.

"Take my hand," he said, "and I promise I won't let go."

She reached out to him. His hand took hers, and the clasp felt natural, easy. After all, they'd been holding hands every morning for weeks.

His other hand gripped her forearm, and he helped her into the boat. She made an ungainly landing in the craft, and the skiff rocked to and fro. Panic fluttered in her chest, but it didn't have the chance to grow proper wings. Chase caught her by the waist and tugged her down onto the bench. His arm slid around her back, drawing her close.

The boatman pushed away from the pier.

And then they were drifting. Bobbing on the waves, unmoored.

"I have you," Chase murmured in her ear.

"I know." Her dry throat worked to swallow. "I know." She twisted her hands together in her lap. "I shouldn't get my hopes up. There are so many observers not only in England, but on the Continent. Really, what are the chances I spotted it first?"

"Slim, I'd imagine."

"And that's *if* it's a comet at all. I could be wrong."

"Wouldn't be the first time."

"Exactly. So this will probably come to nothing anyway."

He nodded. "You're probably right."

She looked askance at him. He wasn't supposed to be agreeing with her.

"I mean, what kind of career plan is comet hunting?" he scoffed. "Not a very realistic one."

She stiffened. "It is a realistic one, even if it's uncommon."

"Oh, truly. Name one woman who actually makes her living as an astronomer."

"Miss Caroline Herschel."

"Fine. Name *two* women who make their living as astronomers."

"Miss Caroline Herschel and Mrs. Margaret Bryan. And if you require three, Mrs. Mary Somerville, by way of mathematics," she replied hotly. "That's only in Britain. Gottfried Kirch in Germany had three sisters and a wife, all of whom were astronomers. In France, you have Marie-Jeanne de Lalande, and Louise du Pierry taught astronomy at the Sorbonne. Shall I continue?"

"Please do," he said. "Twenty more, and perhaps I'll be convinced."

Alex bit off her reply. The amused gleam in his eyes gave him away. "You're doing this on purpose. Starting an argument to distract me."

He didn't deny it. "It seems to be working."

A wave lifted the boat, and then dropped it just as suddenly.

Alex's stomach pitched and rolled. She turned to bury her face in his chest, but her forehead plunked against something solid.

"Sorry. I'd forgotten that was there." He reached into his coat and withdrew a flask—a significantly larger one than he usually carried. He offered it to her. "Here, it's for you."

"That's kind of you, but I don't think I could stomach any brandy right now."

"No, no. It's water. Thought you might need it." He pressed the flask into her hands. Keeping one arm lashed about her waist, he used his free hand to unscrew the silver cap before tucking it away in his pocket. "There. Take a good draught."

She stared at the glimmering silver, too overwhelmed to speak.

For thirteen years, she'd avoided boats. She'd taken the long way around so many times, spending countless hours and precious shillings to quiet her fears. She'd confined herself to England, making her home in an unfamiliar country rather than returning to the homeland of her father or her mother. Insurmountable terror had made her its captive.

Now, at long last, she'd faced the fear and embarked on this most terrifying of journeys . . . only to find the purest, most perfect safety she'd ever known.

Oh, how she loved this man.

Alex wasn't thirsty any longer, but she held on to his flask for the remainder of their short voyage, keeping both hands wrapped about the cool silver. She traced the monogram with her fingertip over and over, following the dips and loops of the engraved scrollwork *R*.

When they reached Greenwich, she handed it back. "Thank you."

He capped the flask and tucked it away. "You're even braver than you are beautiful." He kissed her on the forehead. "And though I've no right to be, I'm excessively proud."

Then he picked her up by the waist, sweeping her off her feet and lifting her onto solid ground.

Alex was dizzied, in many, many ways.

"Now," he said, turning away from the river. "Where is it?"

"Where's what?"

"The observatory, of course."

Oh. Oh, yes. That was the reason they'd come, wasn't it?

"Up," she replied. "It's up."

"WHEN YOU SAID 'up,'" Chase said between panting breaths, "you truly meant up."

Good God. From the riverbank, there were stairs leading up to a green. The green became a gentle, grassy slope. Which turned into a miserably steep grassy slope. And then there were yet more stairs.

"It's an astronomical observatory." She held her skirts gathered as she trudged uphill, to avoid tripping on the hem. "Naturally it's on the highest ground."

When at last they reached the observatory doors, however, Alexandra hesitated.

"What is it?" he asked.

"I'm afraid to knock. What if they're sleeping?"

"I should think an astronomical observatory is one place where you can arrive at midnight and not be concerned about waking the occupants."

"Then what if they're busy?"

Chase could have reached out and knocked on the door himself, but he held off. "You belong here, Alex. Discoveries like yours are precisely why a Royal Observatory exists, and a passion for those discoveries is why the royal astronomer does his work." He swept a lock of hair behind her ear. "There is no place you belong more than right here, right now."

She nodded, then knocked at the door.

Chapter Thirty

*C*hase didn't understand much of what passed between Alexandra and the astronomer's assistant. But that didn't matter. What
captivated him was the excitement on her face and the passion in
her voice as she spoke with someone who fully understood her
discovery. He felt a bit jealous that he couldn't be, would never be
that person—but then, he'd helped her make it here tonight, and
that was important, too.

Though he was dying of curiosity, he tried not to interrupt with
questions. Only as they walked away a few hours later did he finally break down. "So . . . ? What's happened?"

"He's almost certain it's a comet."

"That's good."

"And it's not one he'd personally observed before."

"That's even better."

"But it will take time to see if anyone else has observed and
named it already. Corresponding with other observatories, scanning for notices in the journals."

"How long will that take?"

"Weeks, at least. Perhaps months."

"Months?" He grimaced.

"It's a good thing," she said. "It gives me time. Will you help me
find a patron who'll pay to name it?"

He pulled to a halt. "Hell, no."

"Chase, I don't have your connections. If I'm going to find a
buyer for it, I need help."

"You shouldn't sell it."

"I need to sell it."

"Fine. Then I'm going to buy it and give it straight back to you." She turned to him. "I never wanted that. I don't need it."

"Well, I need you to have it. Because you *found* it. Because your name *should* be on it. Because it's damned tiresome being the one person alive who understands how truly remarkable you are." He cupped her face in his hands, and not tenderly. "I won't help you hide that from yourself, or from the world. Not anymore."

ALEX COULD NOT believe what she was hearing.

"You," she said, falling back from his touch, "are the most shameless hypocrite. You would accuse *me* of hiding from myself? I'd thank you to go make that speech into a mirror, Chase Reynaud, because you've been hiding so long you've forgotten how it feels to breathe fresh air. You deserve things, too. Things like closeness and family and the forgiveness you've foolishly denied yourself, and it's downright *exasperating* to be the only one who understands it. Plus, I've been doing it far longer."

"You have not," he said. "I understood you first."

"Oh, no." She shook her head. "I knew your true nature the first time I held your hand and watched you eulogize a consumptive doll. That's ten whole weeks."

"Ten weeks is nothing. It's been ten months for me."

Alex was stunned. "What?"

"We collided in Hatchard's bookshop in November of last year," he said. "But perhaps you don't recall."

"Of course I recall." Not only did Alex recall, but she'd thought about it every day since. "You're the one who'd forgotten it."

He shook his head. "The memory's clear as day."

"Then why did you pretend you didn't know me?"

He shrugged. "You made an utter cake of yourself when it happened. It didn't seem kind to bring it up."

Oh, this man.

"But I recalled our meeting," he went on. "How could I forget?

It's not every day a man collides with a woman who prefers sky smudges to fairy stories." Smiling a bit, he caught a stray wisp of her hair and wound it about his finger. "Miss Alexandra Mountbatten, with midnight-black hair and a fetching figure, and who responded to flirtation with an immensely gratifying blush."

He gave her cheek a teasing caress, and Alex felt the pink rising on her face all over again.

"Miss Alexandra Mountbatten, who possessed the most captivating, terrifying eyes I'd ever beheld. Or more to the point, that had ever beheld me. Eyes that were not only beautiful—but bold, clever, fearless. Unafraid to search the darkness, trusting that something, somewhere will glimmer back." His voice deepened, weighted down with emotion. "I couldn't forget you, Alex. And I won't allow anyone else to forget you, either. Not the Royal Observatory, not the world. Not the universe, for that matter."

Curse him, he was so good at this. He had her toes melting into the evening dew. Her knees felt close to dissolving, too. Soon she'd be reduced to ten thousand drops of Alexandra scattered across the green, desperately clinging to ten thousand blades of grass.

Now she'd completely lost her edge in their argument. It wasn't fair. How could she compete with his years upon years of transforming women into quivering shimmers of condensation?

By being herself, she supposed. Straightforward, honest, practical.

"I love you," she said. "Take that."

Chapter Thirty-One

o.

No, Chase would not take that.

He *couldn't* take that. Not the impossible words, or the expectant look in her eyes. Not the sharp blade of joy she'd thrust into his heart, or the way it twisted with his every breath.

He couldn't take any of it. In his desperation, his mind seized on what seemed his only recourse.

He would take *her*.

Take her into his embrace.

Take her lips with his.

And, by God, take her breath away. Leave her dizzy and gasping, and completely unable to speak another devastating word.

That endless grassy slope he'd cursed on their way up to the observatory? He blessed it now. He shook off his coat and spread it on the grass, then laid her down atop it. The world was a darkened, private room with a ceiling of stars.

And somewhere between the kissing and caressing and unbuttoning, a sense of inevitability descended on them both.

They both knew what was going to happen. What *must* happen.

"Alex . . . You know I don't do this with everyone. In fact, I've not done this particular act with anyone in quite some time. Much as it pains my pride to say it, this might not be a virtuoso performance."

"I wouldn't know the difference."

"A fair point. That is some comfort." He settled himself between her thighs. "You don't want me to stop so you can count out sugar lumps or something?"

She laughed a little. "No sugar lumps required."

"Alexandra." He set aside teasing and spoke in an earnest tone. "If I take you this way, I mean to keep you always. Do you understand, love?"

She nodded.

"When I ask a question, I need an answer." He stared into her eyes. "Tell me you want this."

"I want this." Her hands slid to his neck. "I want you."

Chase hoped to hell she meant it, because he'd emptied his reserve of gentlemanly restraint. Nothing remained to him but fierce, mindless wanting. Blood-searing desire. The single-minded need to be in her, and of her. To face down anything that held them apart and shatter it with crude, primal thrusts.

He reached between them, taking his cock in hand and positioning himself at her entrance. The head of his cock slipped into her wet cleft, and that single inch of possession had him shuddering with pleasure.

He braced himself on his arms, gritted his teeth, and pushed into the hot, tight silk of her body. *"God."*

Her fingers clutched his shoulders. He heard her sharp intake of breath.

"Are you hurting?" Even as he asked, he dug his hips to steal another inch. *Bastard.* "Can you bear it?"

She nodded. "I . . . I'm fine."

Thank heaven.

He kissed her in gratitude. With each advance, he sensed her wince beneath him and felt like a monster for causing her pain.

All his rakish technique had been forgotten. He wanted to be gentle, patient. But it had been forever since he'd been inside a woman this way, and this wasn't just any woman.

This was Alexandra.

His Alexandra. His always. His only.

Just a bit more, he promised himself. He wasn't a selfish lover. He could be patient. He'd take this at a leisurely pace, allow her plenty of time to adjust.

But first, just a bit more.

A bit more. And a bit more. And oh, God, more. Until he'd taken everything she had to give. Sheathed to the hilt, his hips welded to her thighs, her body surrounding his.

He'd never known such bliss.

ON HER PART, Alex had never known such pain.

Good heavens. She knew virgins often found the first time uncomfortable, but she hadn't known it might be like *this*. Pleasure wasn't even a mirage in the distance. She would count herself lucky if she made it through the act without shrieking.

She bit her lip until she tasted blood, determined not to give herself away. She didn't want to hurt Chase's feelings.

"Alex." He rocked against her. "You feel so good."

She growled in pain through sealed lips, hoping it sounded like a moan of pleasure.

"Tell me what pleases you," he said.

"That's perfect. Just . . . keep doing what you're doing."

"At the moment, I'm not doing anything."

"Yes, I know." She let her head roll back against the grass and flung a hand over her eyes. "It hurts like the devil. I'm sorry, but you're either unusually large or unusually bad at this. I suspect it's the former."

Laughter rumbled through his chest. It rumbled through that painful part of him, too. Alex whimpered.

"You should have said something." He pushed up on his hands, kneeling between her thighs. "We'll stop at once."

He began to withdraw. She squeezed her thighs together, locking his hips in place. "I don't want to stop."

"But—"

"If it's going to hurt the first time, I'd rather have the first time over with."

"Yes, love. But I'd rather our first time not be something you grimly endure. Unusually large men have their pride, too."

"I don't see the way around it. There must be some solution."

"That's my girl," he said fondly. "Always sensible, never deterred."

Alex's mind began spinning. "I mean, there are a dozen positions for intercourse, aren't there?"

"Hundreds. If a well-worn, illustrated volume in my library can be believed."

"Perhaps we can find one that isn't quite so painful," she said. "If it's not an inconvenience."

"An inconvenience?" he echoed. "Alexandra, you are asking me to make love to you in a dozen different positions. If that's an inconvenience, I beg you. Impose upon me nightly."

Alex smiled. She loved him so.

Oddly enough, the pain had already begun to lessen. Their time spent talking had given her body time to adjust, and now that she wasn't trying to hide her discomfort, she wasn't holding every muscle tensed.

"Let's try this, then." He rolled onto his side, taking her with him. He grabbed her bottom, holding her close and hooking her leg over his hip. "Any better?"

"I think so."

Without the force of his body weight added to every thrust, the sensations were gentler. More within her control.

He still felt impossibly big within her—but Alex was gaining faith in her ability to conquer the impossible.

As a test, she cautiously rolled her hips, slowly moving up and down his length. The dull ache was still there, but it had a new, sweeter edge. A low moan eased from her throat.

He studied her face. "Still that bad?"

"No." She repeated the same subtle movement. "No, it wasn't bad. It was rather good."

"That's encouraging."

"Yes," she breathed, moving her hips again. "*Yes.*"

She didn't know how long they remained that way. Moving together in a slow rhythm, perspiration building between their bodies.

Alex felt as though she were climbing a mountain slope, one step at a time. Each movement taking her higher and higher. The nearer she came to the peak, the thinner the air became. Her lungs worked for breath. She was dizzy.

"Chase."

"I'm here." His reply was shaky. "Still good?"

"Very, very good. And how are you?"

"Dying by a thousand blissful cuts, thank you for asking."

Alex smiled to herself. He'd been so patient with her. So gentle. She thanked him by trailing light kisses along his neck and chest. She scraped her fingernails lightly down his arm.

His grip tightened on her backside. "For God's sake, Alexandra. You'll ruin my display of heroic restraint."

She looked up at him. "Perhaps that's what I'm hoping for."

He pressed his forehead to the crown of her head and gripped her tight. Then he thrust hard and deep, wrenching a gasp from her.

"Yes," she managed, worried he'd mistake her reaction for pain. "Don't stop."

She needn't have worried. He didn't even slow down.

If pleasure was a mountain slope, Chase was scaling its rocky face in determined strides. And Alex was slung over his shoulder, carried along for the ride.

He took her in strong, fierce strokes with an intensity that thrilled her. Even the gruff, desperate sounds he made were deliciously arousing. When he growled crude profanity in her ear, a naughty sense of excitement shot through her veins.

Yet the wilder he grew, the safer she felt. His need for her was so palpable, so raw. As though he would die before he let her go. She felt, for the first time in ages, truly, entirely protected. All the uncertainty she carried inside her—the constant fear she shrugged off as practicality or logic or common sense—it drained from her body.

The climax sent her soaring, weightless and free.

"God." His rhythm faltered. But he never buried his head in her neck, or her hair, or the crook of his arm. He never went away.

He was here. With her. With her. With her.

"Alexandra."

"I'm here."

"Talk to me."

"It's me." She stroked her hands down his back. "You're here, with me. I love you. There's no place you belong more."

"Alex. God, I—"

As the pleasure racked his body, she held him tight. He clasped her to him afterward, pressing kisses to every part of her face. When he kissed her nose, she laughed.

He rolled aside, and they lay as they'd begun, holding hands and staring up at the stars. Could it have been only five or six hours ago?

Chase drew her closer, tucking her head against his chest. His fingers toyed with her hair. "I think the world is spinning."

"The world is always spinning."

He exhaled in a soft groan.

"Well, that's the truth. It's spinning all the time."

"How about this. What if I say that you're my world. *You're* not spinning."

"But I am. We all are. We're on the earth, and it's spinning, so we're spinning, too."

"You are ruining all my sweet nothings."

"That's just it." She put her hand atop his chest, covering his fiercely beating heart. "To me, the truth doesn't ruin anything. Why should understanding the universe diminish our sense of wonder at it? We are spinning around and around, at hundreds of miles an hour, on a rock in the midst of a fathomless universe. Isn't that awe-inspiring enough?"

"If we're spinning at hundreds of miles an hour, it seems a miracle that we stay on this rock at all."

"That's not a miracle. That's gravity."

He kissed the top of her head. "I love you. There. Have you some astronomical way to ruin that?"

"No." She was grateful he couldn't see her face contorting with elation. "That's a miracle."

"See, to me it's the most logical thing in the world." He gently eased her aside and rolled over to face her. His fingertips traced the features on her face and the contours of her body. "Listen, I could make some excuse about there being no coaches or boats at this hour, or say there's a bridge that's been washed out. We could find an inn where there's only one room left and pretend we're forced to share. But the God's honest truth is this. I want to spend the rest of the night holding you, and I don't care what anyone has to say about it."

She smiled. "Then let's do that."

THEY MADE LOVE twice more at the inn, with a scant hour or two of sleep between bouts of passion. After all that exertion, nourishment was a necessity.

"Do you want a long engagement?" Chase mumbled the question around a mouthful of fried egg.

Alex set down her cup of tea. Suddenly, she didn't trust her fingers to grip it properly. "Wh . . . What was that you just asked?"

He buttered a point of toast, folded it in two, and downed it in one bite. "Waiting might spare you the worst of the gossip. You could return to your house, we'd allow some time to pass. Perhaps a wedding next spring." He set down his knife and fork, then looked at her across the table. "Damn it, I don't want to wait until spring."

"Chase, what are you talking about?"

"Our wedding. What else should I be talking about?"

"I don't know. Something that might actually happen?"

He pushed his plate aside, propped a forearm on the table, and leaned forward to speak in a low voice. "I told you last night, this means always. You said you wanted that, too."

"Of course I want that," she whispered back. "But *marriage*?"

"You said you wouldn't be my mistress."

"You said you couldn't offer me anything more."

"I changed my mind," he said.

"So did I," she replied.

He tapped one finger on the table. "I'm confused."

"Consider this. If the comet is *my* comet, I can find someone who'll pay to name it. Perhaps enough that I can be an independent woman with a home of my own. Your lover, not your mistress."

"I've had my share of lovers, and several other men's shares, as well. I don't need one more."

Alex sighed. "You can't marry me. My father was an American who made his living in trade. My mother was an illegitimate mestiza. I was christened Catholic. I've no money, no relations. For heaven's sake, you're going to be a duke. I'm the governess."

His eyes flashed with emotion. "After months of needling me about commitment, you're refusing my proposal. You've spent all summer telling Rosamund and Daisy that a woman can do anything. Now you're going to tell them you can't be a duchess. Were you lying to us all this time, or are you deceiving yourself now?"

"I don't know." A lump thickened in her throat.

He reached across the table and took her hand in his, tenderly stroking the back of her fingers with his thumb. "I'm sorry. We needn't sort it all out this morning. I just want to be with you."

"I want to be with you, too."

He kissed her hand. "Then let's go be together at home. I miss our mattress."

She loved that he called it their mattress.

She loved *him*.

Maybe . . . just maybe . . . this time, her hoping wouldn't end in disappointment. Perhaps dreams *could* come true. She wasn't wishing on a star. She had a comet now.

Adding in the coach journey, by the time they returned to Mayfair it was mid-morning. Alex planned to do nothing with the day, save for dragging herself into the house for a bath and a nice long sleep—in Chase's arms, if it could possibly be managed.

Upon arriving at Reynaud House, however, their plans for a rest were immediately abandoned. Mrs. Greeley rushed from the house before the carriage had even come to a halt.

"Oh, Mr. Reynaud. Thank the Lord you've returned."

"Good God, what is it?"

"Rosamund and Daisy, sir. They're gone. They've run away."

Chapter Thirty-Two

*R*un away?" Alex echoed, hoping that she might have misheard the housekeeper.

Mrs. Greeley broke down in tears.

Chase didn't wait for further confirmation. He bolted into the house, and Alex followed him.

Together they rushed up to the nursery and across the room to the open window. A knotted rope ladder dangled from the windowsill down to the street.

Oh, no. Oh, Lord.

Alex flew to the girls' trunk and dug through it frantically, all the way to the bottom. Just as she'd feared. "It's gone."

"What's gone?"

"Rosamund's bundle. I came upon it by accident once, weeks ago. She had money squirreled away. All those pennies and shillings added up to a significant amount. There were other things, too. Like maps and coaching timetables."

"And you didn't do anything about it? Christ, Alex."

She wilted under his stare. "I didn't want her to know I'd found it."

"You should have told me. You should have taken it away."

"She would have only packed a new one. The best way to keep her from running was to make her feel she had a home. And I thought she *was* feeling that way lately. I can't imagine what might have changed her mind."

Chase shook his head. "The letters. It has to have been the letters."

"What letters?"

"Letters from every decent boarding school in England, offering the girls admission. I left them on the desk last night."

"Oh, no."

"She probably came down hoping to pocket a shilling or two and saw them." He pushed a hand through his hair. "Where will they have gone?"

"I don't know. Perhaps toward a port city."

"A port city?"

She briefly closed her eyes, feeling sick. "They may be planning to pose as boys and find work aboard a ship."

Chase swore with a viciousness to rival even the most black-hearted pirate.

Alex cursed herself. She ought to have *known.* Rosamund hadn't joined the piracy game to indulge her whims. She'd been paying attention. Not only gaining the skills required of a ship's boy, but learning how and where to find work. All this time, Alex had been striving to make the girls feel they had a home. Instead, she'd given Rosamund lessons in how to run away, so fast and fearlessly that no one could catch them.

Chase left the nursery as decisively as he'd entered it, bounding down the stairs. And once again, Alex followed.

"I'm so sorry," she said weakly. "This is my fault. It's all my fault."

He didn't slow down to apportion blame. "I'll have the groom ready a fresh horse. I'll begin with the southerly coaching inns, ask if anyone fitting the girls' description has purchased tickets, and if so to what destination. If that turns up nothing . . . Well, let's hope it doesn't come to that."

"I'll go with you."

"No. You'd only slow me down, and one of us should remain here in case they return."

"But I—"

"Stay." Chase went to her and held her face in his hands. "I'll find them. No matter where they've gone. I'll find them, and I will bring them home."

NIGHT WAS FALLING when Chase finally returned to the house. He wasted no words on pleasantries. "Tell me they're here."

Alex dearly, fervently, with every fiber of her being, wished she could tell him just that.

Instead, she had to shake her head in the negative. "I sent notes to Penny and Nicola. Neither has seen them, but they've promised to send word first thing if they do. I wrote to your brother, as well. John's gone out searching."

"But no word yet."

"No."

The pale, bleak cast of his face was like no expression she'd ever seen him wear. He staggered to a chair, fell into it, and dropped his head in his hands.

"Oh, Chase." She hurried to him, kneeling on the carpet and wrapping her arms around his shoulders. "We'll find them. We will."

"I'll go back out." He braced his hands on the chair's arms and pushed himself to a standing position. "I can't just sit here."

"You're exhausted. Let me go instead."

"I told you—"

She laid her hand on his chest, firmly pushing him back. "It should be me. I have the best chance of finding them. I all but drew them their escape plan."

Alex would hire a ship of her own and sail off in pursuit, if that's what it took. The thought of sailing the ocean still terrified her, but that terror paled in comparison with her fear of losing the girls. And losing Chase, too.

The doorbell sounded.

They rushed to the entrance hall.

When the door was flung open, there she stood—the mulish, pilfering, ten-year-old answer to a prayer.

"Rosamund." Chase pulled her into his arms, clasping her head close to his chest. "Thank God. Thank God."

Alex scanned the steps and pavement. "Daisy. Where's Daisy?"

"She's in the hackney. She's been hurt."

"PETERSFIELD." CHASE TIPPED back a swallow of brandy. The amber liquid burned its way down his hoarse, weary throat. "They made it all the way to Petersfield. That's nearly to Portsmouth."

Alex nodded and sniffed. "I know."

The hours since Rosamund had appeared on the doorstep had been divided between three activities.

First, calling for doctors.

Next, teasing out the details of their adventure.

Last, sitting in the corner of the nursery, watching the both of them sleep.

"Petersfield," he repeated numbly.

Apparently, Rosamund's grand plan had been to travel to Portsmouth via stagecoach—only nine hours' journey, she made a note of mentioning. Upon arrival, just as Alex had surmised, the girls planned to cut their hair, put on homespun trousers, and search for work as ship's boys.

The plan had been executed flawlessly, except for one hitch. On her way down the rope ladder, Daisy had fallen and landed on her arm. Rosamund ignored her sister's complaints of pain for much of the journey. After all, Daisy was expert at inventing maladies. However, once the swelling and bruising set in, there was no ignoring that she needed a doctor. They'd exited the coach at Petersfield and caught the next coach going north.

"You must admit, it's rather remarkable how well they handled it. Rosamund knew to return home, and she and Daisy made it safely back. That shows a great deal of courage and ingen—"

"Don't," he clipped. "Don't look for the bright side of this. If Daisy hadn't fallen at all, they'd be a full day's sail from England by now. And if Daisy had taken that fall any harder, or from a slightly greater height . . ."

He shuddered, pushing aside the nightmarish image of Daisy's blood pooling on cobblestones.

"Their return journey took money, cleverness, and courage," she said. "They could have used that same money, cleverness, and courage to go anywhere else. But they came here. They came home."

Chase's jaw tightened. How dare she. How dare she praise their remarkable achievement of not quite dying, and try to spin this all into a moralistic fable designed to puff him up.

This time, she was the one who needed to face facts.

He would show them to her.

Chase stood and quietly motioned for Alex to follow. After leaving the nursery, he went to her bedchamber.

"This is what will happen." He yanked one of her cottage-for-let notices from where Alex had tacked it to the wall. "I'm going to buy you this cottage, or one like it." He took a closer look at the advertisement. "Actually, I'm going to buy you a cottage that's much better. One with enough room for you and the girls."

"Me and the girls?"

"Yes. I'm offering to extend your employment as their governess. Indefinitely."

"Their governess? I don't understand."

"You're right. What am I thinking? You won't be their governess any longer. I'll hire another governess to live with you and teach the girls. You'll be an astronomer, of course." He looked through the other advertisements tacked on her wall. None of the properties appeared remotely satisfactory. "You're going to need a larger property for that. One with a hill. Barrow can find something." He left her room, heading for the stairs.

Her footsteps pattered behind him. "Chase, stop. You are not making any sense."

This time Alex had it wrong. He was returning to his senses. Accepting what he'd known from the beginning, but had stupidly tried to ignore.

"You seem to be saying that you're sending me, the girls, and some other governess to live in a country cottage."

"A large cottage. Near a hill."

"And where are you in this plan, may I ask?"

Chase set his jaw. "Far away."

"Oh, no." She put her hand to her temple. "Yesterday, you were ready to embark on a life together. The four of us, as a family. One thing goes wrong, and the whole plan is off? Everyone goes back to living miserably?"

"At least living miserably means being *alive*. This wasn't a tiny mishap, Alex. She fell from the window. She could have died in the street. And once again, I was nowhere to be found. I was off in an inn with some woman."

Her chin jerked. "'Some *woman*'?"

"You know what I mean."

"Yes, I do." She reached out and took his hand in both of hers. Her voice was calm, rational. "I know exactly what you mean, and I understand precisely why this terrified you. But it isn't the same. Daisy's going to be fine."

He gestured wildly. "Her arm is broken!"

"Her arm is broken. But she is going to be fine."

He shook his head and went to the study, fishing the key from his waistcoat fob to open the money box. He counted out banknotes. "Five per week. Two hundred at the end of the summer." He squared the stack. "There. That's two hundred and fifty. Your wages."

"Chase, don't do this to them. Don't do this to me."

He flung the keys down with a clatter. "I *have* to do this. My mistake was believing, for even one moment, that I could do otherwise."

Alexandra claimed to be sensible. Practical. Straightforward. Chase had wanted to believe that, too. He'd almost been convinced that she saw him. Truly *saw* him, for everything he was and everything he wasn't, and that her mirror-finish eyes reflected everything he could become.

But that had been an illusion. Today was the proof he needed.

She would keep fooling herself that he was a better man, and she would persist in telling him the same. No amount of argument or evidence on his part had convinced her otherwise. She wouldn't see reason, and that left him only one way to get the message across.

He had to wound her. Deeply.

Even if it left him gutted and bleeding, too.

"I should never have suggested we marry. It was my mistake."

"Why are you doing this?" Her voice was shaky now. "I know what we shared last night. I know you love me. Perhaps you're too frightened to face it right now, but that doesn't change the truth."

"Even if I do love you, it doesn't matter. I'm Rosamund and Daisy's guardian, and I'm going to be Duke of Belvoir. I need to be heeding those responsibilities. As it is, I'm barely skating the boundaries of good society. Think of how it would damage the girls' prospects if I married so far beneath me."

"Beneath you? You're being absurd, Chase. I know you, of all people, don't believe that."

"Everyone else will. And the Sir Winston Harveys of London will make sure no one forgets that you were once 'just' a governess."

"I'm not 'just' a governess. I'm not 'just' anything."

He pushed the banknotes toward her. "As of this moment, you're not a governess at all."

A tear formed in the corner of her eye. It clung to her eyelashes, wobbling there. She didn't do him the mercy of dashing it away. She let it fall, and he watched it trail down her face.

Chase wanted to rip his own heart from his chest and hurl it into the fireplace. For all the good the thing did him, he might as well be rid of it.

She ignored the heap of banknotes. "I don't believe for a moment that you meant anything you just said. I know you better than that. You're a good man with a loving nature. But even if I can dismiss your words, that doesn't mean they don't hurt."

"Take the money, Alexandra. The telescope, as well. I've no need of it."

"I don't want your money. As if it's some even trade for your heart?"

"To be honest, I think you're coming out better in the bargain."

She shook her head. "Tomorrow, or the day after, or maybe next week, you're going to wake up and realize what an idiot you were, and you're going to want to make things right with me. I'm telling you now, it will be too late. This will be the last time I raise my hopes, Chase. The last time I dare to dream of a future with you, only to watch those dreams dashed."

He looked her square in the eye and nodded. "Good."

Chapter Thirty-Three

*A*s it happened, it didn't take even an hour for Chase to realize he'd been an idiot. There was no excising these girls from his life.

When the time came to set Daisy's arm, Chase had to pin her down with his body so the doctor could do his work. She screamed with the pain and struggled to get away. He would have gladly broken his arm and both legs if it meant he could suffer the pain instead. It was the most wrenching thing he'd ever done, but he would not have allowed anyone else to do it in his place.

At last, it was over. Daisy fell asleep, exhausted from the struggle. Chase was equally spent. He showed the doctor to the door, peppering the man with so many questions, he turned and looked to Chase as if to say, *Don't you know anything?*

No. When it came to this guardian business, he truly did not. But he was going to have to learn.

What came next? Supper, baths, stories? Some other loving ritual absent from his own youth, and therefore completely foreign to him? He didn't suppose wine was on the list, unfortunately. Not yet, anyway.

He heard the sound of sniffling coming from the dining hall. He bent to peer under the table. "Rosamund?"

She turned away from him, swiping her nose with her sleeve in an effort to hide her tears.

Chase went down on his hands and knees to join her under the table.

Steady, he told himself. *Don't frighten her.*

She needed assurance, and he had to provide it—even though he'd never felt less sure of himself in his life.

"Daisy's fine," he said. "She's fine."

"She was screaming. I heard it."

"The physician had to set her arm back in place, but it's done now. All splinted and bound. Now it only needs time to mend. In a few months she'll be good as new." He put a hand on her back. "It wasn't your fault. Do you hear me? It was an accident. You aren't to blame."

"You can't expect me to believe that. Of course it's my fault. I told her to climb out the window. She wouldn't have fallen if not for me."

"Very well, then. Perhaps it is partly your fault. But it's partly mine, too. I should have made you feel safer to stay." Chase made himself as comfortable as possible in the cramped space, bending his legs until his knees touched his chest. "I'm going to tell you a story."

"One of those improving tales with morals? No, thank you."

"It's a sad story, actually. No happy ending."

In clear, simple terms he told her about Anthony's death. He left out the more scandalous details, naturally. But the gist of the story remained the same.

"I promised to take care of him," he finished at length. "And I wasn't there when he needed me."

She didn't reply, and he didn't want her to feel she ought to. She was ten years old, and he was here to console her, not the reverse.

"When you and Daisy came into my care," he went on, "I didn't believe that I could be a good guardian. I'd failed my cousin already. What if I failed you, too? That's why I planned to send you to school at the first opportunity. We'd all be better off that way, I told myself."

She rearranged her legs within the cramped space. "Are you sure you weren't right?"

"I'm not right very often, so the chances are against it." He exhaled, releasing all the air in his lungs. "To be honest, Rosamund, I was terrified. It wasn't only that I'd failed Anthony. I missed him, terribly. I was afraid of losing someone else. I didn't want to care about you."

She sniffed. "I didn't want to care about you, either."

"Much as I tried to avoid it, however, it seems I've come to love you and Daisy both. Very much. When you were missing, I was frantic. All I could think about was how empty the house would be with you gone. How empty my life would be."

"I was thinking about how empty our stomachs were, and that I should have brought more sandwiches." Her chin met her knee. "Or that we should never have left at all."

He smiled a bit. "We are quite the pair. What are we going to do with ourselves?"

She shrugged.

"Here's what I think. There's no going back to change the past. If we allow our mistakes to consume us, we're stuck in one place—and it's not a good place to be. Believe me, I spent years there. I know. The only choice is to move forward. Try to do better. I may not be a perfect guardian. You may not be the perfect wards. But if we love each other and keep trying our best, perhaps we'll manage." He added, "Mind you, we'll all need to make a greater attempt at acceptable behavior—in public, at any rate. But I'll try if you will. What do you say?"

She was silent. He could sense her struggling. She didn't want to admit she needed him, or anyone.

"Blink once for yes, twice for no."

Instead, she leaned into his shoulder.

"I'll take that as a yes." He wrapped his arm around her and kissed the top of her head. "That's it, I hope you realize. No taking it back now."

She lifted her head. "Where's Miss Mountbatten gone? She took her things. Did you sack her because we ran away?"

"She was hired to teach you and Daisy for the summer, and the summer's come to an end. That's all. But you and Daisy are invited for tea at Lady Penny's house every Thursday. You'll see her there."

Rosamund leveled a doubtful gaze at him. There were hours of interrogation in those eyes. The girl could break hardened spies.

"Very well, that's not all. We had a falling-out."

"Can't you go apologize to her?"

"Not this time, I'm afraid." Not yet.

It will be too late, she'd told him. It would be too early, as well. If he had any hope of ever regaining Alex's trust—and her love—he had to prove he deserved it. Not only to her, but to himself.

"You must have done something truly horrid, then."

He nodded. "That's the sum of it, yes."

"So that would mean . . . the only choice is to move forward and try to do better?" Her voice was smug.

"Don't make me regret this guardian business already."

She lowered her voice in imitation of his. "No taking it back now."

He sighed, exasperated. "Are you going to keep throwing my words back at me?"

"That's the sum of it, yes."

"Then I promise to be a perfect young lady."

"Brilliant." She scrambled out from under the table. "I have some half-embroidered serviettes you can finish."

EVEN NICOLA'S BISCUITS weren't enough to soothe a broken heart.

Which was why Alexandra was currently sitting in the breakfast room of Ashbury House, with an entire toffee cake on a plate before her, and one solitary fork.

She dejectedly poked holes in the cake and took the occasional lick of icing. Emma paced the floor nearby, making cooing noises at the fussy babe in her arms. Breeches, the feline terror, was having one of his good-natured days. He rubbed against her ankle, purring.

Alex was surrounded by her dearest friend, a baby, a cat, and a cake. "Really," she declared, "who needs men at all?"

"It seems we'll have a new one in the neighborhood any day. Someone's finally let the house on the corner."

"The one next to Penny's?"

"Yes." Emma stood and walked to the window. "Workmen have been coming and going all week. The rumors passed through the servants say he's a gentleman of some sort, but no one knows anything else. Whoever he is, I'd wager the poor fellow has no idea what he's in for. I hope he doesn't mind goats in the back garden and otters in the rain barrel."

"Well, right now I only have eyes for one gentleman, and that's the young Marquess of Richmond." Alex scooped the crying baby from Emma's arms. "I'll take a turn. Have some cake."

"I've been meaning to ask you something," Emma said. "Ash and I would love it if you'd be Richmond's godmother."

Alex was stunned. "Really?"

Emma nodded.

"I'd love nothing more, but I was christened Catholic, and I don't practice anything lately."

"Khan will be godfather, and he's Muslim. Considering that my father was a vicar and the worst sort of hypocrite, and that Ash is Ash, we aren't ones to stand on ceremony."

"Will the clergyman allow it?"

"The Ashbury estate provides his living. He'll be persuaded."

"Then I'd be honored."

Transferring the baby to one arm, she used the other to hug Emma in joy. And then, as she clung tight, the embrace became one of despair. At last, the tears she'd been holding in began to flow.

"I'm sorry." Alex sniffled as she pulled away from the hug. "You already have one crying soul to soothe. I don't mean to be another."

"Don't be absurd. Cry all you like." Emma took the baby back and settled in a chair, unbuttoning the front of her morning gown. "I only wish I could mend it by feeding you, or changing your clout."

"I just feel so foolish. I let myself believe he loved me, and that we'd be together forever. One day later, it all fell apart."

"Perhaps it can be pieced back together. You know he loves you."

"That's not the problem. He's bollocks at letting anyone love him in return."

As she watched Emma nurse her baby at her breast, a tiny fist squeezed at her heart. She'd never expected to marry, never truly dreamed of having children at all. But now a longing had been opened in her. Those hopes of children had hollowed out a bit of her heart and made a home there. Now the hopes had vanished, but the space remained, empty and aching. Right next to two empty niches labeled Daisy and Rosamund, and the small cavern she'd blasted out to make room for Chase.

They heard the ring of the doorbell.

"Khan will answer it," Emma said. Then she added in a low voice, "Maybe it's him."

"It's not him," Alex said aloud.

Inside, of course, her thoughts were a riot. What if it *was* him? It could be him. Did she want it to be him? Maybe he'd beg her to come back. Maybe he'd have a diamond ring in his pocket, and he'd go down on one knee and ask her to marry him.

And then take her up on his unicorn and ride into the sunset, she supposed. *Really, Alex.*

Khan, the butler, appeared in the doorway. "Your Grace, there's a woman at the door collecting subscriptions for a charity fund."

Alex took up the fork and dug into her cake.

See? Her mind had betrayed her again. She simply didn't trust herself any longer, not where Chase was concerned. She had to fight her way through the pain and emerge stronger on the other side. Otherwise her longing for him would chip away at her heart, bit by bit.

Until there was nothing left.

Chapter Thirty-Four

Three weeks later

*T*he left side needs to be higher," Daisy said.

Chase put down his hammer and stepped back. Damn it, she was right. The shelf still didn't look straight.

He fished out a key and opened the locked drawer where he kept his tools—at least a few things had to be kept safe from Rosamund—but instead of a measuring stick, his hand fell on something that crinkled beneath his fingertips. A small, flat package wrapped with ivory tissue and tied off with a lavender ribbon.

He'd forgotten the thing entirely.

Chase couldn't help but laugh at the irony. It had been meant as a surprise gift for Alexandra, but it had ended up being a gift to himself. A gift he'd given himself weeks in advance, without even realizing it.

An excuse to go to her.

Finally.

"How long will you be?" Rosamund perched on the stepladder, holding one edge of the shelf in place. "My arms are growing tired."

"Be glad your arms aren't broken," Daisy said smugly. "Lift up a bit. Your side is slipping." The girl was enjoying her supervisory role a bit too much.

"You may let the shelf be," Chase said. "I'm leaving directly."

"Leaving for where?" Rosamund asked.

"To speak with Miss Mountbatten."

"Finally."

"Can we come along?" Daisy asked.

"Not this time, darling."

Chase had to do this alone, and he had to do it today, before he talked himself out of it somehow. The gift wasn't much. Nowhere near what she deserved. But he wanted Alex to have it, even if she refused to accept him.

With a bit of luck and a barge-load of apologies, was it too much to hope she might take both? Probably, but he had to try.

He bounded up to the entrance hall, where Barrow was just putting on his hat.

"We'll have to postpone our appointment at the bank. I'm going after Alexandra."

Barrow replaced his hat on the hook. *"Finally."*

"She won't want to see me." Chase wrestled into his topcoat. "How can I convince her to hear me out? What do I say?"

"You're the one with the silver tongue. I'm not certain what you want from me here."

"You're right. I don't know why I'm asking advice from a man who proposed to his wife in a haberdashery."

"At least *my* proposal was accepted."

"That's cold, Barrow."

"But true."

Chase yanked the lapels of his topcoat straight. Whatever powers of persuasion he'd amassed in his lifetime, this was the day to use them. "Christ, this is pointless. I treated her so shamefully. You have no idea."

His brother shrugged. "So you made a mistake."

"A mistake?"

"Very well, multiple mistakes."

"Try dozens."

"Never mind the number," Barrow said. "If you love her—"

"What do you mean, 'if'? You knew that before I did."

"If you love her," Barrow repeated with strained patience, "Alexandra just might forgive you. Think of how many of your flaws *I* overlook daily."

"You don't overlook my flaws. You like them. They make you feel superior, attached as you are to all those smug principles."

"I'm attached to you, you idiot. You're my best friend, and my brother by blood. No one who loves you expects you to be perfect. If by some miracle you managed it, we wouldn't recognize you."

Chase started to protest, but then he realized he didn't really want to.

"All you need to promise her is yourself. That's enough." Barrow put his hand on Chase's shoulder. "You're enough."

Over his adult life, Chase had built an unparalleled reputation for suave, spontaneous gestures of intimacy. Apparently, he'd fallen out of practice. The hug he gave his brother was the most awkward, embarrassing embrace he'd ever attempted in his life.

Barrow released him with a merciful thump on the back. "Now leave, so I can draw up some marriage contracts."

"What about the embezzling? Don't forget the embezzling."

"Chase, stop stalling and go."

For once, Chase took his brother's suggestion. Without argument.

He headed to Lady Penelope Campion's house first, but the housekeeper said she'd gone to Miss Teague's. On to Miss Teague's it was.

Miss Teague's door was ajar, seemingly to clear out a haze of smoke from within. The house smelled of charred chocolate and cinnamon.

"Chase!" Penny waved him in. "Just in time for tea. Do sit down and have a biscuit."

"He's not getting biscuits," Nicola said, incensed. She whipped the plate from the table, guarding it. "After what he did to Alex? Not even the burnt ones."

"But he's sorry now. He's clearly here to make amends. The poor man looks wretched."

Chase wasn't certain how to feel about that. "I don't have time for tea and biscuits, thank you. I've something for Alex. She'll want to have it at once."

"Leave it, then," Nicola said. "We'll give it to her."

That was an entirely reasonable suggestion. One he didn't have a ready excuse to work around. He decided to try the truth. "Please. I need to see her. Speak with her."

"See, Nic?" Penny said. "He's miserable."

"I'm miserable," Chase agreed. "So, so miserable. Also ashamed, regretful, desperate, ready to grovel on hands and knees."

"Don't forget 'in love,'" Penny said, smiling.

Lord bless Lady Penelope Campion for her indefatigable faith in romance. She had the most open, generous nature imaginable. Chase recognized the quality, because she was the sort of woman he'd always kept at a distance. A heart so completely unguarded was more easily bruised than a ripe summer peach. Someday, he would sit her down and give her a word of caution about being too trusting with devilish gentlemen.

But not today.

Nicola finally answered his question. "Alexandra isn't here."

"When will she be back?"

"She won't be. Not for some time," Nicola said.

"She's gone to—"

Lady Penelope's reply was cut short. From throughout the house, what seemed like hundreds of clocks began to chime the hour. And naturally, the hour would be noon.

Within that minute of bonging and clanging, Chase imagined a hundred dire endings to Penny's sentence.

She's gone to the docks to catch a ship.

She's gone to the Philippine Islands, to find her mother's family.

She's gone to grab the tail of her comet and soar away to a planet that deserves her.

She's gone to someplace, anyplace where you aren't, you contemptible bastard.

She's gone to Malta.

It didn't matter, he vowed. Wherever she'd gone, Chase would follow her, find her, pledge his love, and beg her to come home. Nothing would deter him. There was no journey too far. No obstacle too great.

"She's gone to stay at Ashbury House," Penny finished. "Across the square. Ash and Emma leave for the country tomorrow. They're taking Alexandra with them."

Ashbury House. Brilliant.

He would have rather gone to Malta.

CHASE'S RECEPTION AT Ashbury House was as he expected. And, quite honestly, no worse than he deserved.

The duke grabbed Chase by the lapels and slammed him against the wall.

"Listen, Ashbury. I know she's furious with me, and for good reason. But I'm trying to make it right. Just—"

"I warned you," the duke said in a fiendish whisper. "I told you what would happen if you hurt her."

"Yes, I recall," Chase choked out. "Something about my ballocks, a closet, and a demonic cat."

"Oh, that's only to start," the duke growled low. "You clod of wayward marl."

"I don't have to stand for this." Chase shrugged off Ashbury's grip. "And I don't need your permission to speak with Alexandra. You're not her keeper."

"I'm her friend. And you are not her anything."

The words gutted him. Ashbury might be correct, but Chase had to see this through to the bitter end.

"That's for Alex to decide." Chase sidestepped him and lifted his voice. "Alexandr—*ack.*"

Ashbury tackled him from behind, wrestling him down to the carpet and clapping a hand over Chase's mouth. "Shut *up*, you blackguard," he snarled quietly. "Not another word. Or a set of shredded ballocks will be the least of your problems."

Good Lord. Could there be anything *worse* than shredded ballocks? His stones retracted into his abdomen at the very mention.

Chase could imagine only one sort of pain that could possibly eclipse that prospect.

Losing the love of his life.

Chase planted his boot on the floor, levered for the advantage, and flipped them both. He straddled Ashbury's chest and stared down at his scarred face. "I've given you the benefit of the doubt on Alex's account, but now I'm angry. I may not have a blood-thirsty cat, but I know a girl who can make a small bowel obstruction look like an accident, and I have a great deal of experience giving eulogies."

"If you so much as—"

Chase planted his hand on Ashbury's face. By pushing the duke's head into the carpet pile, he lifted himself just enough to call out. "Alex!" he shouted. "I need to speak with y—"

A set of duke-ish, entitled teeth sank into the heel of his hand. *"Fuck."*

Chase jerked his hand away, and Ashbury made use of the momentary confusion to reverse the power once more. Scrabbling with knees and elbows, they rolled across the carpet no fewer than three times before colliding with a table.

Unhappily, Chase ended on the bottom of the tussle. Ashbury's knee sank into his gut. "God Almighty, man," Chase said. "What the devil's wrong with you? Besides all the obvious things."

"You veriest varlet." Ashbury lowered his mangled face to within an inch of Chase's nose. *"This. Is. Nap. Time."*

Chase was nonplussed. "What?"

The duke rolled aside, resting on his elbow as he worked for breath. "My infant son is currently upstairs, sleeping for the first time in nineteen hours. The only thing keeping me from disem-boweling you here in the entrance hall, you cream-faced rooting hog, is that you'd probably wake him with all your sniveling and sobbing for mercy."

"Oh."

Somewhere upstairs, a thin wail pierced the silence.

Ashbury closed his eyes. "I hate you."

"Just let me speak to Alexandra." Chase stood and straightened his coat.

"She's not here."

"You bastard. Why didn't you say so? You could have spared us all of this nonsense."

Ashbury struggled to a standing position. "I needed the exercise."

Chase glared at him. "The papers had it right. You *are* a monster."

Ashbury shrugged in admission.

"So if Alexandra's not here, where's she gone?"

"She went out to the shops." A woman who was presumably the Duchess of Ashbury stood at the top of the stairs, bouncing a baby in her arms.

"Don't *tell* him," Ashbury complained. "He doesn't deserve to know."

She shrugged. "He ate the sham. And the tuna-ish. He's at least earned the chance to talk to her." To Chase, she said, "Alex said she had a few things to purchase before we made the journey."

"What sort of things?"

"I don't know the full list." The duchess hesitated. "But she mentioned books."

Books. Of course. He should have known it would be books.

"Do you know which shop?"

She shook her head. "I'm afraid I don't."

Well, then. He'd done too much dashing about London to stop now.

Chase would simply have to check them all.

Chapter Thirty-Five

The bookshop had been a mistake, Alex now realized.

After weeks of shedding tears in her cake, a bit of shopping ought to have been a pleasant change. The prospect of escaping to the country gave her something to look forward to. Away from London, she hoped her heart might mend a bit faster. But simply being in this bookshop was opening the wound all over again.

It wasn't even Hatchard's this time. She'd known that would be too painful. Instead, she'd chosen the Temple of Muses. The shop's rotunda design had always delighted her. A set of stairs led to a balcony lining the interior dome. The shelves there were crammed with books as high as a person—a person significantly taller than Alex—could reach. This was where she always browsed first. Balcony books were better than ground-floor books. They just were. Really, anything put on a balcony was instantly improved.

The exception today was Alex's mood. The balcony had not lifted her spirits.

She couldn't help but see Chase's eyes connecting with hers, or feel the way his charming, rakish grin had made her heart and hands flutter. It was as though she could see him before her. Breathe in his scent.

She could almost imagine that she heard his voice.

"Alexandra! Alexandra Mountbatten!"

She opened her eyes and looked down over the railing.

Chase.

He was there. Bellowing her name through a quiet bookshop and dashing through the aisles like a madman.

Alex had the momentary impulse to hide, but something in her wouldn't allow it. She stood riveted in place.

Eventually, he spotted her.

"Alex. Thank God." He doubled over, hands on his knees. "Just give me a moment. I'm winded. Been running all over London."

"Why? So you could bump into me and make me drop my books again?" She put one forearm on the railing and allowed a slender volume to slip from her fingers. It bounced off Chase's shoulder. "Oh, dear."

He was unfazed by the blow. "Stay where you are. I'm coming to you."

"No," she said. "You are the last person I want to see."

"Well, you are the last person I want to see, too."

She gestured in exasperation. "Then why are you—"

"You are the last person I want to see before I fall asleep at night. Every night. The last woman I want to kiss for the remainder of my life. And your lovely face is the very last thing I want to see before I die. Because I love you, Alexandra."

Her eyes stung at the corners. "Why are you so good at these charming, romantic speeches? From practice, I suppose."

"Perhaps. But if I have practiced, it feels as though it was all for the sole purpose of winning you over right now." He gazed up at her. "Tell me it's working."

It seemed it might be working, and that was what terrified her.

"Please don't put me through this. Every time you're near me, I build up these silly hopes. It doesn't make any sense, but I can't help it. Then I get hurt all over again."

"So I'll speak to you from here. This should be a safe distance."

Alexandra wasn't so certain. His handsomeness had a greater range than a six-pounder cannon.

"You were so right," he said. "I regretted everything I'd said within hours of you walking out the door. I wanted to go after you at once, but I knew it would be pointless. You'd have no reason to trust me. To be honest, I didn't trust myself. But now I can stand here and tell you, sincerely, that I've changed."

She didn't know what to say.

"You should see us. Daisy's speeding through books faster than I can acquire them, and I've started Rosamund on geometry. Barrow helped me find a tutor. I still believe school may be best for them eventually, but you were right. They need more time."

The pride and love in his voice was too much for her. She turned away from the railing, overwhelmed. Within moments, he was bounding up the stairs to join her on the balcony.

She held him off with an outstretched hand. She was almost afraid to ask it, but she had to know. "What about the Cave of Carnality?"

"Ah, yes. That. Sadly, the Libertine Lair is no more."

"Did you give the space back to Mrs. Greeley?"

"No, no. The girls helped me convert it. It's now the Pirate Palace. One that occasionally serves as a general surgery."

She laughed a little, picturing it.

"They miss you so much. But I miss you more."

Alex's eyes were stinging. She blinked furiously. She wanted so desperately to believe in him, believe in this. But she'd grown mistrustful of her heart.

"Here, let's do this your way." He took a few steps toward her and gathered an armful of books from a nearby shelf. "We'll make two piles. For and against marrying me. We'll start with 'against,' because those reasons are easy to name. Terrible reputation. History of rakishness. Poorly behaved in museums." He piled book after book on the stack, with an increasingly absurd list of supposed detractors. So many that he had to empty a second shelf.

"I might as well add a book for every time I let you down." With a heavy sigh, he topped the stack of books with a half dozen or so more. "There. Anything else you care to add?"

After consideration, she placed one more on the pile. "Antlers."

He nodded. "I don't know how I missed that. Now, the 'for' column."

Alex had already started that stack in her mind. His wicked sense of humor. His protective, caring nature. The way he took an interest in things just because they interested her. She didn't suppose he'd leave "astonishing in bed" off the list.

Instead of beginning a second pile on the floor, however, he reached into his pocket and pulled out a small package. He held it out to her. "I love you. That's the sum of it, really. Can it be enough?"

She took the package from him, unknotted the lavender ribbon, and pushed aside the tissue. Inside, she found a small book, bound in blue calfskin. She turned it over in her hands to read the embossed title on the spine.

Messier's *Catalogue of Star Clusters and Nebulae.*

Alex looked at him, stunned. Her mind ran wild with all those familiar fantasies. All her dreams of his keeping the book tucked next to his heart and looking for her around every corner. Until he found her again, declared his love, and begged her to become Mrs. Bookshop Rake.

"Have you been carrying it around all this time?" she asked.

"No, of course not."

"Oh."

"Why would I do that?"

"I . . . don't know."

"I took the first one back to Hatchard's last autumn, in case you looked for it again. Also because I'd no idea what to do with the thing. I ordered this copy a month or so ago, and I meant to give it to you then, but between you finding a comet and me making a first-rate ass of myself, it slipped my mind until today."

Well, that was a significantly less romantic story, but one that made her heart soar just the same. Because it was undoubtedly real, and entirely Chase.

She ran her hands over the binding and lifted it to her nose to breathe in the new-book smell. "It's beautiful."

"You're beautiful." He reached for her, laying a tentative caress to her cheek. "I wish I could promise to never, ever hurt you. But

I'm new to this whole love and commitment business. I'm bound to cock it up from time to time. What I can promise is that I won't give up. Not on you, not on myself. Not on us. You taught me that."

"I can't believe you listened."

With a lopsided, charming smile, he pulled her close, drawing her into his arms. He looked at her with warm green eyes—truly *looked* at her—the way people rarely did, because it meant allowing the other person to truly *look* at them, too.

This time she didn't feel like the only woman in the universe. Or the only woman in the world, or even the only woman in the bookshop.

She felt like the woman in his arms, and that was enough.

"Alexandra. My friend, my lover, my love. Come home."

Epilogue

Oh, Alex." Penny lifted her head from the telescope. "It's so beautiful."

Alexandra laughed. "It's a tiny sky smudge."

"But it's *your* sky smudge," Chase said.

Alex corrected him. "Ours."

Her friends were trying so very hard to seem impressed with her speck of light, bless them. To Alex, it didn't truly matter if they understood. It mattered that they were there.

Everyone was there. The little sky-gazing picnic in Bloom Square had grown into a proper garden party. Even better, a *family* party.

Alexandra had never dreamed of having this many people to call her own. She had not only Chase, Rosamund, and Daisy—John, Elinor, and little Charles were her family now, too. As godmother to Richmond, she would always be connected to Emma and Ash. Nicola and Penny couldn't be rid of her if they tried.

And then there was Marigold the goat, who had more than justified her attendance at the event by "accidentally" consuming a hamper's worth of Penny's sandwiches. And half of the hamper itself.

"Even if it is just a smudge in the sky, at least it has a grandiose name," Nicola said. "Though I must admit, it doesn't quite trip off the tongue. 'Mountbatten-Reynaud comet' is rather a mouthful."

"'Rather a mouthful,'" Chase repeated, musing. "People are always saying that like it's a bad thing. What's so terrible about mouthfuls? I like mouthfuls."

"I enjoy a good mouthful myself," Ash declared. "Emma does, as well. Don't you, darling?"

Alexandra and Emma exchanged a look. It was lovely that their husbands were becoming a grudging sort of friends, but the two men were difficult enough to manage separately. Together, they could be exponentially incorrigible.

"You can blame my husband for the name." Alex had insisted they share the naming of it. After all, he'd been with her that night in the garden, and then when they confirmed the discovery. "I wanted to call it Reynaud's comet, since I'm a Reynaud now, too."

"Yes, but you weren't when you discovered it," Chase pointed out. "We discussed this. You can insist on sharing the credit, but you are not allowed to hide your accomplishment behind my name."

The irony of a husband dictating how his wife expressed her independence seemed utterly lost on him. Nevertheless, Alex let it pass without comment. There would be a more important naming conversation in the coming months, and she had to choose her battles.

She put her hand on her belly, and the tiny smudge growing within her. She'd kept her suspicions to herself thus far. She hadn't wanted to tell Chase until she could be absolutely certain. What if she raised his hopes—and her own—only to be disappointed?

Now she found herself reconsidering. Any hopes or disappointments belonged to Chase, too.

Perhaps she'd tell him tonight.

Emma handed off the baby to Ash. "I want another turn at the telescope. It's not every day one has a chance to view her friend's very own comet."

"No, indeed," Alex said. "Take a good look now. According to Mrs. Somerville's calculations, after this summer it won't be visible again for a hundred and forty-seven years."

"You had better leave a detailed note for the great-great-grandchildren," Ash said.

"That would require them to have children first," Emma pointed out.